HOUSE OF DECAY

BORIS BACIC

© 2025 by Boris Bacic

All rights reserved. No portion of this book may be reproduced mechanically, electronically, or by any other means, including photocopying, without permission of the publisher or author except in the case of brief quotations embodied in critical articles and reviews. It is illegal to copy this book, post it to a website, or distribute it by any other means without permission from the publisher or author.

Contents

Prologue	11
One	19
Two	24
Three	28
Four	34
Five	45
Six	54
Seven	58
Eight	66
Nine	71
Ten	80
Eleven	86
Twelve	96
Thirteen	104
Fourteen	113
Fifteen	118
Sixteen	129
Seventeen	138
Eighteen	143
Nineteen	154
Twenty	158
Twenty-One	161
Twenty-Two	169
Twenty-Three	175

Twenty-Four	178
Twenty-Five	183
Twenty-Six	186
Twenty-Seven	191
Twenty-Eight	200
Twenty-Nine	211
Thirty	222
Thirty-One	229
Thirty-Two	234
Thirty-Three	244
Final Notes	251
More from the author	252

Warning: This book contains scenes of explicit violence, gore, and sexual content. Reader discretion is advised.

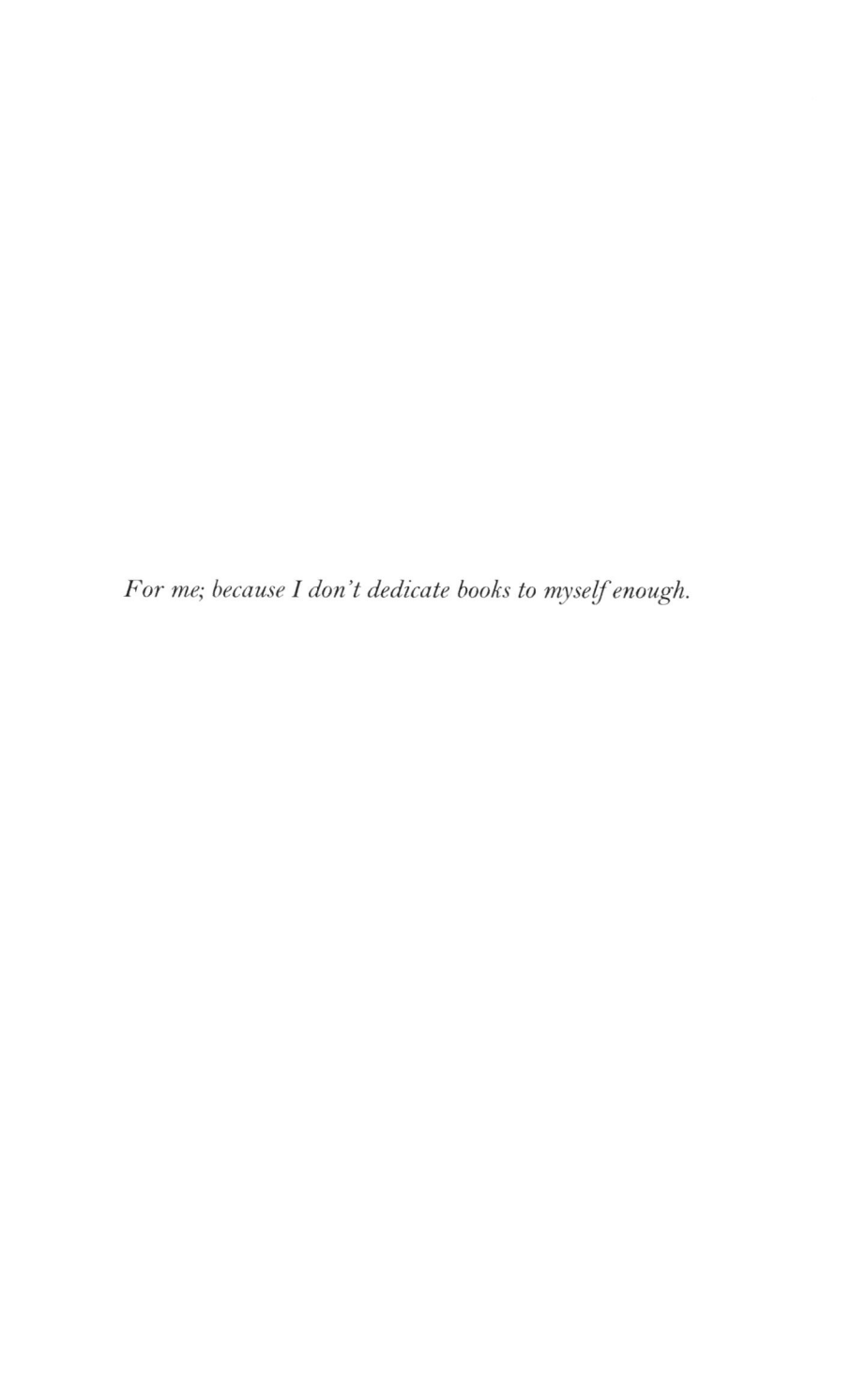

For me; because I don't dedicate books to myself enough.

Author's Note

Years ago, when I was just starting my writing career, I wrote *The Grayson Legacy*. The story is still dear to me: Two journalists with a passion for justice sneak into a corrupt politician's mansion nestled deep inside the woods. They find more than they bargained for when their hunt for a scoop becomes a fight for survival.

I got the idea when I went to climb Fruška Gora, a mountain in Serbia. There, I found a hidden lake that had been bought and made private by a powerful politician to exploit for resources. The area had been fenced-off, and offering to bribe the guard did nothing to offer access.

The book follows a stuck-in-a-house and chased-by-a-psychopath trope similar to the movie *Don't Breathe*. It combines elements of suspense with gore and psychological horror.

The book failed miserably, and I'm not ashamed to admit I did way more than it deserved to try to bring it into the spotlight. I changed the cover, I re-edited the book front to back, I ran promos and ads on it... After everything failed, I figured *The Grayson Legacy* could still serve a purpose, so I began giving it for free to increase my mailing list. People who read it say they loved it, so the story itself is not at fault, I'd like to believe.

Looking back now, I think *The Grayson Legacy* was probably released at a bad time and then lost momentum on Amazon, which makes it impossible to come back to the world of the living. Or maybe it's too bland: Neither bad nor good, just sitting in limbo, unnoticed by the readers whose attention is snagged by the polar opposites.

Why am I writing all of this? Why mention *The Grayson Legacy* in a book not related to it?

Don't worry, I'm not going to try to pitch the book to you. I've long since given up on that pipe dream. *The Grayson Legacy* will forever stay my passion project and a permanent reminder of the failure that shaped my career in some ways.

The reason why I'm mentioning *The Grayson Legacy* is because *House of Decay* was originally going to be titled *The Grayson Legacy 2*. Due to marketing reasons, however, that's not possible. In a way, *House of Decay* is a spiritual successor to *The Grayson Legacy*, and an excellent testing field for this sort of sub-genre.

And perhaps, it's also a testament to me not being ready to let *The Grayson Legacy* go just yet.

Even though the book is by no means special in my opinion, I do hope the story leaves a lasting impact on you (positive or negative), or at the very least helps you pass time.

Thank you for your continued support.

Prologue

The old house loomed above them. It was even uglier up close. Once upon a time, it might have stood proud and vibrant in the middle of a neatly trimmed lawn, a statue ridiculously reminiscent of the Renaissance era or a fountain in front because why not?

That was the whole thing about this house. Its architecture exhaled a fume of hubris, an *envy me, you peasants* kind of shallow egoism that spoke volumes about the owner.

Its days of glory were long gone, though. The decaying corpse of a structure that stood in front of them, nestled in the middle of the tall grass field murmured only an echo of its past grandiosity. A fitting end, Gretchen thought. One that awaited everyone, no matter what lavish lives they lived.

"You coming?" Ethan asked.

He was at the front steps leading to the door.

Standing in front of the behemoth building, staring at the panes of glass clad in layers of thick dust that concealed the secrets within, Gretchen wasn't sure she wanted to go anymore. She'd promised Ethan, and breaking a promise would make her a hypocrite, but there were situations that warranted a broken word.

Was this one of them?

Gretchen searched her mind hard for that convincing excuse that would allow her and her boyfriend to go back to the car.

A wash of movement in one of the upstairs windows caught Gretchen's attention. Her eyes snapped up, scanning the house, but there was nothing there.

"Gretchen?"

Had it been her imagination just now, or had she really seen a silhouette of a person in one of the windows? A convenient occurrence to keep them away from the house.

"I don't like it, Ethan," she said. "What if someone lives here?"

"Nah," Ethan said. "Look at it. It's old."

Gretchen looked up again, and it suddenly became so much easier to dismiss the movement she'd seen as her imagination.

"What if it's under surveillance?" Gretchen shot back. A weak attempt, but she had to keep trying.

"This old place?" Ethan hooked a thumb behind himself at the house. "No way. Hey, if you don't want to go, it's fine, babe. You can wait for me in the car."

He was giving her an easy way out, and he wouldn't even hold it against her later because that's what Ethan was like. But this wasn't about *her* not going into the house. It was about neither of them going inside. Letting Ethan go into that old thing while she waited in front would be even worse in many ways.

What if a squatter stabs him with a needle?

What if he collapses through the floor and breaks his legs?

What if he inhales some noxious gas or mold in the house and passes out?

No, between staying outside alone or heading in with him, Gretchen preferred to keep an eye on Ethan.

"No, it's fine. I'm going with you," she said as she stalked through the grass.

Ethan cocked an eyebrow. "You sure? I won't be mad if you stay."

Last chance to bail.

"I'm sure," Gretchen said because there was no way she'd be able to convince Ethan not to go inside.

As they climbed the steps and Ethan twisted the doorknob, Gretchen found herself hoping that the door wouldn't budge.

Oh well. We tried. Time to head back.

When the door creaked open, revealing the dark, musty interior, she cursed herself for ever agreeing to a compromise with Ethan about this. Urban exploration should be illegal. It was stupid, childish, and outright dangerous, and while she understood the appeal behind exploring abandoned places, the risk far outweighed any merit.

Ten minutes. That's how long she would give Ethan before asking him to get back on the road. Enough to satiate his hunger for urban exploration without holding it against her how she was being like a parent too much.

He took her by the hand before crossing the threshold, a gesture that meant the world to her because it said, "I'm here. I'm with you. We're doing this together."

Even with it being broad daylight, the house was too dark on the inside. Not so much that they had to use their flashlights but dark enough to leave the ends of the branching corridors veiled in a fog of black. The place was too big, Gretchen realized. As if the house itself had somehow expanded from the inside.

"Fucking badass," Ethan said. "This must have cost a fortune."

The peeling wallpapers and the framed black and white photographs on the walls gave Gretchen an idea. "Back when this was built? Probably around ten dollars."

"Imagine the amount of upkeep required here."

"Well, whoever was responsible for it was obviously slacking."

Ethan entered the room ahead. Gretchen followed, wary of her surroundings. Something crunched under the risen linoleum. The old smell in the air was thick. Even breathing through her nose felt wrong, like the stench would coalesce in a thin film inside her nostrils.

Gretchen had expected the house's interior to be stripped of most, if not all, of its mementos speaking about its past. Places like these were usually left bare-boned, littered with trash thrown by inconsiderate squatters neglectful of the shelter the property provided.

The living room Gretchen and Ethan stood in resembled a museum more than an abandoned house. Despite the look of uninhabitance betrayed by the thick layers of dust, the room itself seemed intact. An old TV, an antique coffee table, a carpet tattered at the edges, a wall clock that stopped at 2:19 all caught Gretchen's attention.

"Wow." She couldn't help but utter in amazement.

She took her phone out and snapped a few photos. This was going to be an amazing post on Instagram once she edited the pictures a little bit. No, she didn't feel guilty about it. Everything on social media was a lie, even the colors. It was a dick-measuring contest, but that's what algorithms favored nowadays. Gretchen could post her pictures raw and get a couple of likes from friends and family, or she could touch them up and join the rat race to get the most likes.

"See?" Ethan said. "Most of the time, you find shit while exploring. But sometimes…" He gestured to the room. "It's worth it."

"I wonder who lived here," Gretchen said absent-mindedly.

"Maybe a big family. With a maid and a butler," Ethan said.

"A butler?" Gretchen raised the corners of her eyebrows.

"Yeah, what's wrong with having a butler? If you can afford a place like this, you can afford a butler. And a maid."

"Please, we're not in England, and this isn't a royal family. Here, we exploit immigrants from third world countries."

Ethan brushed his fingers across the top of the TV and rubbed them together to get the dust off. "I'm gonna look around the house."

The state of the living room made Gretchen a little more comfortable. She herself was eager to see what other wonders she'd find here. Still, a healthy dose of skepticism never hurt anyone.

"Okay, but let's meet up here in a few minutes. A *few minutes*, Ethan. Don't keep me waiting," she said.

"Okay," he conceded.

"And no funny business!"

They split up. Gretchen ventured into the hallway. She walked past each room, peering inside but not entering. The house was way too big for every room to be explored, so she settled for a peek where the doors weren't locked or stuck by the wood flooring that had swelled.

Toys lay scattered on the floor next to child-sized beds. Books forgotten on shelves collected dust. Unwashed dishes sat in the sink, an indication that the house was abandoned without prior preparation.

Each room sang a symphony of the life that had occupied the house. Free from her worry about squatters, dangerous animals, and diseases, Gretchen could finally understand the fascination behind Ethan's need to set foot in every dilapidated place they ran across. It was like watching history unfold through a carefully curated narration.

Still dangerous and a hassle, but the appeal was apparently worth it to some people.

She raised her phone and took a picture of the corridor. She went through the photos she took, deleting the redundant ones. She stopped at the last one she took. Something about it was... unsettling, though Gretchen couldn't tell what just yet.

Her eyes lingered on the doorway, on the darkness that wasn't just darkness. She zoomed in, squinted, and gulped. A shape began to emerge—not clear but undeniable, no matter how hard she tried to convince herself otherwise.

The more she stared at it, the more the shape took on almost-recognizable features. *Almost.* Like trying to recall a word at the tip of the tongue. Was that a head peeking around the corner? Fingers curling around the door frame?

Or maybe, just maybe, a trick of the light.

Gretchen looked up, but the brightness of the screen had blinded her, making the darkness thicker. Turning on her torch, she timidly raised it to illuminate the corridor. The cone of light washed over the doorway, revealing...

There was a thud somewhere in the house behind her. In Ethan's direction.

Gretchen spun, holding the torch of her phone ahead of herself.

"Ethan? Is that you?" she asked, casting a cautious glance over her shoulder just to make sure that shape wouldn't reappear. The house was silent. "Ethan?"

The ancient beauty within these walls evaporated in an instant, turning grotesque and claustrophobic.

Okay, that's enough of this.

She went back to the living room where she and Ethan had split up. He wasn't there.

"Ethan?" Gretchen called out.

Now frustrated as well as afraid, she dialed his number. To her dismay, there was no service.

Just freaking great.

Another dull thud snapped her attention to the door. This one was closer. He must have been fucking with her. She'd asked him not to do it, and he'd refrained from it a few times, but today the opportunity must have been irresistible. Despite that, there was a reserved part of her that refused to let go—a part that said her boyfriend was not up to any shenanigans.

She poked her head through the door. "Ethan?"

It was too quiet. No one in sight. Gretchen gulped. "Eth—"

A figure jumped out in front of her. The scream already left her mouth by the time she realized it was Ethan. She was about to scold him, but that's when she noticed how wrong everything about him was.

"Gretchen..." he half-uttered, half-coughed.

A trickle of blood was running down his forehead. His eyes bulged with unforeseen terror. His hand was on his side, blood trickling between his fingers.

"Oh my God!" Gretchen shouted. "Ethan, what happened?!"

"You have to—" He groaned and collapsed to one knee.

One hand gripped Gretchen's forearm hard.

"Ethan!"

Ethan looked like he was going to pass out. He took a few shallow breaths. A looming shadow appeared behind him. Tall, slender.

Menacing.

"Run," Ethan said.

She didn't want to, but the way Ethan shoved her kickstarted her legs into a dash in the opposite direction. Just before rounding the corner, she saw her boyfriend on all fours, head slumped, and the silhouette behind him floating closer.

A scream—Ethan's scream—tore through the house, interrupted by a hollow *thunk* like a baseball bat slamming against a head. In her panic, Gretchen was running blindly through the house, a voice inside her head screaming at her on full blast.

Run! Get out of here!

But the exit eluded her memory, and the corridors seemed to stretch forever and change directions, drawing her deeper into the house. She couldn't tell how long she had been running for. When her lungs started burning, she hid behind the corner, and the horror of everything that had happened started to weigh on her.

Oh my God. Ethan.

She'd left him there with that… thing. To die. She had to go back for him. To save him.

But she couldn't. She was too scared. If the monster was able to overpower Ethan, then what chance did Gretchen have?

Not thinking, she got her phone out and fumbled to unlock it. It slipped from her trembling fingers and fell loudly on the floor. Gretchen froze, expecting the patter of footsteps to come running at her.

When it didn't happen, she sighed in relief. She bent down, picked up her phone, and—

She froze at the distinct feeling of a presence in the vicinity.

The footsteps didn't come because they didn't need to come.

It was already here.

Gretchen turned her head to see the tall figure watching her with patience. She let out another scream and threw herself into a run. Before she could get around the corner, something tethered itself to her ankle, hard. The momentum with which Gretchen had bolted was enough to cause her to crash to the floor headfirst. Her forehead slammed against the wood, and for a moment, she was dazed, unaware of her surroundings.

Then, she let out another scream as her nails and feet clawed the floor in an attempt to run.

Her screams only increased as she was dragged into the darkness.

ONE

CITY

"What did Caleb say?" Quinn asked.

Tyler picked up the phone from the dashboard, intermittently casting glances between the screen and the road before putting it back down again. "Says to pick him up in five minutes."

"Nice. Hey, you don't need to rush. You know Caleb. When he says he'll be ready in five minutes…" Quinn rolled down the window and flicked the cigarette out.

"Quinn, noooo. You're polluting the city," Tyler quipped with a grin.

She knew Tyler was joking, but she couldn't resist replying. "This shithole of a city can't get any more polluted than this," she said, rolling the window back up.

"That's not very eco-friendly of you. What if those climate activists saw you?"

Quinn scoffed. "Those guys are morons."

"Oh, you think so?" Tyler asked.

Quinn hadn't intended on elaborating, but since the opportunity presented itself…

"Don't you think so?" she asked. "Wasting their days screaming about nonsense in front of companies that don't give a shit. They're never gonna change the world by glueing themselves to the asphalt and creating roadblocks and getting flights canceled. They're just making people hate them more." She put one foot up on the dashboard. "If I'm eating a steak at a restaurant, and a vegan comes up to me and calls me a murderer for eating an already-dead cow, I'm not gonna go vegan. I'm gonna eat double the amount of meat just to spite them."

Tyler stopped the car in front of an apartment building and turned on the hazard lights. "You mean if someone is a nuisance in your life, you won't actually listen to their opinion? Who would have thought?"

He was referring to his dad, Quinn figured, who always had plenty of unwanted advice to dole out to his son, apparently. Quinn knew the man as this hulking but polite figure that would throw corny remarks in the presence of Tyler's friends, but parents were known to shapeshift into different creatures when guests arrived.

Quinn liked him, though. He was always polite to her, tried to make small talk with her, and she liked the eye-rolling jokes that caused the room to boom with his laughter.

Tyler killed the engine and fished his phone out of his pocket; then he looked at the entrance of the building. For a street as tight and as devoid of pretty much anything other than apartments as this one, there sure was a lot of traffic.

Every couple of minutes that a car rolled by, Tyler would follow it with an unblinking gaze just in case they came even an inch within scratching his precious Chevy. The less patient drivers would honk in passing to let him know he couldn't park here, and Tyler would shout something back at them or flip them off from the safety of the car.

Quinn never saw a problem with it—just park, turn on your lights, and fuck what the other drivers think. If they want to get through, they go around. She understood Tyler's stress, though. God forbid someone scratch his car.

Then there were the ones who outright refused to risk driving past the Chevy. They were the drivers who held up traffic, Quinn thought. She could see it in the way they white-knuckled the steering wheel with both hands, the way their seat was set so that their back was ramrod straight, the way they compulsively glanced from one rearview mirror to the other, checking their surroundings. Mostly old people and female drivers, Quinn had to note.

Tyler pressed his palm on the horn twice. "Come on, Caleb. Every fucking time."

"Relax. We got the whole night ahead of us," Quinn said. "Nowhere to be. Nowhere to rush."

She raised her arms in an expressive gesture of freedom.

"You don't work tomorrow?" Tyler asked.

"Second shift."

"How's work, by the way?"

"How can work be?"

"Guess your side hustle is still your go-to method for extra cash, huh?"

Quinn gave him a look that was supposed to confirm his question without actually verbalizing it.

"You got anything on you right now?" Tyler asked.

"Of course. I never go on these rides without some. What would we do all night long? Talk?"

Tyler chuckled. "I can't remember the last time we had a sober conversation. Imagine how awkward that would be."

Quinn knew it was a joke, but a jab of something unpleasant nestled inside her chest nonetheless. The significance of tonight's rendezvous that had lain dormant this entire time hit her like a truckload of bricks.

Their lives were changing. They were growing up and, as much as she hated to admit it, drifting apart. Life no longer allowed them to spend as much time together as they used to when they were younger. There was work; there were occasional relationships, and with each passing year, they were drawing closer to the crossroads at which they would be forced to decide how their futures would unfold.

After tonight, they would probably never be able to hop into Tyler's Chevy and drive out of the city for a whole night of getting high and drunk. Some would have work in the morning; some would be off to college; some would have a partner, maybe even children.

House of Decay

And in all those scenarios, one thing bothered Quinn. She saw lives of her friends changing, but not her own. In her mind, ten years from now, she still saw herself working as a waitress at a knockoff restaurant of Olive Garden, dealing and smoking weed, sharing a cheap two-bedroom apartment in Lents with a promiscuous roommate, and finding flaws in every partner that showed interest in her.

Left behind—the words popped into her mind because that's how she felt. Because that's what it was.

Caleb got into a reputable college. Sure, Tyler's job was as dead-end as Quinn's, but he was also in college, and it didn't matter that it was a community college no one had heard about, because while you're studying, you're absolved of making decisions for your future.

It also didn't matter that Tyler was going to college just to get his old man off his back, and that he wouldn't put the diploma to any good use, because he was clever, and his laziness incentivized him to look for shortcuts in life. He was constantly applying to new job positions because he heard 'there's money without work there.' Sometimes he got lucky. It was only a matter of time before he struck gold, or whatever the closest thing to gold in Portland was.

They're doing something with their lives, and you're just sitting in one spot, exactly where the three of you met years ago.

Another long honk of the Chevy's horn snapped Quinn out of her despondent thoughts. Except, when she looked at Tyler, she realized it wasn't the Chevy's horn.

"Go around!" Tyler waved to the car behind.

In that moment, the door of the building opened, and Caleb stepped outside.

"Alleluia, the prince decides to show himself," Tyler said, voice dripping with impatience.

Caleb opened the door and hopped inside just as the driver behind let out another toot. The moment Caleb closed the door,

Tyler turned the engine on, and the car lurched forward, almost spastically.

"Hey, guys. Sorry I'm late," Caleb said.

"No worries." Quinn smiled because she needed to shove those imposing doubts out of her mind.

Because tonight they were going to have fun one final time before they each left their own way.

Two

The Road

They left the city behind and ventured into the Oregonian wilderness. No one spoke for the past ten minutes. After the initial pleasantries were shared, the car's interior had descended into an almost funeral-like silence. That quiet was a part of their road trip ritual. The moment they left the road leading out of Gresham, all conversations would stop. If music played on the radio, the volume would be decreased so that the roar of the car's engine was the only audible noise.

They hadn't agreed on that tradition. It just sort of happened enough times for the ride to become awkward otherwise.

The sun had dipped below the pointy treetops, bathing the sky crimson. This stretch of road was empty most of the time. No other drivers, no speed traps, no cops. Nothing except fear of crashing to stop a person from going way over the allowed speed limit.

That's why Tyler loved this road. It was one of the rare occasions when he felt like he was free—from rules, from society, from everything. Just him, the Chevy, and the infinite road winding between trees.

"So. UC Berkeley, huh?" he asked when he noticed how sleepy the atmosphere in the car had become.

"Yeah," Caleb replied.

His impassive tone suggested that such a huge achievement was nothing notable, but that was Caleb. Humble, although Tyler liked to tease him from time to time that he was fake humble.

Quinn must have noticed Caleb's lack of enthusiasm as well because she shifted in her seat to face him and said, "Come on, dude. This is a big thing. It's okay to brag."

"It… it's impressive I got in, I'll admit," Caleb said reluctantly.

"It's all right," Tyler joked.

"Dude, you're the only kid from the neighborhood who's made it big," Quinn said.

"I haven't made it big. I just got into college." Caleb continued to downplay his success.

"Yeah, but it's UC Berkeley! And you got a scholarship. A fucking scholarship!" Quinn said.

"True, but you know how many people do that and never amount to anything?" Caleb asked.

"Because they don't play their cards right. But you will." Quinn faced upfront again. "And one day, when Forbes interviews you, you can thank your buddies Quinn and Tyler, and everyone from the neighborhood will read that and be like, 'Damn, that's one of us. Someone from our shitty block actually made it!'"

"Someone from our block already *has* made it," Tyler added.

"Oh yeah? Who?" Quinn asked.

"Marco McCormick."

"Wait, really?" Caleb leaned forward. "Sweaty Marco?"

Quinn shook her head. "Sweaty Marco didn't make it."

"Yes, he did," Tyler interjected. "He moved to LA."

"Yeah, and he's making ends meet there doing freelancing gigs as a producer and sharing a one-bedroom studio apartment with two other guys. Everyone can pack up and move to LA if they have a little bit of Mom and Dad's savings because everybody wants to be part of the elite, but actually making a name for yourself is an entirely different story." She craned her neck toward Caleb. "So, no. No one from our neighborhood has amounted to anything before you."

"But no pressure, buddy," Tyler said.

They drove past an abandoned gas station.

"We really should stop here sometime." Quinn rubbernecked the place. "It might be a cool hangout spot."

"What if it's haunted?" Tyler asked and let go of the steering wheel just long enough to imitate ghost sounds.

"It's not haunted," Quinn said, but she sounded like she was trying to reassure herself. "Why isn't anyone doing anything about it? It's been sitting like that since before we started driving."

"I read rumors online about the place," Caleb said. "There's this legend that says, if you follow certain rules when you drive past the station, you're going to end up in a town that supposedly doesn't exist."

"How do you end up in it if it doesn't exist?" Tyler asked.

"And that's not all," Caleb continued. "Once you enter the town, you can supposedly never leave."

"Why?"

"I don't know. You just can't." Caleb shrugged.

"Well, what's stopping you?"

"I obviously haven't been there."

They kept quiet for a moment, after which Tyler mouth-farted. "Bullshit. What do you think, Quinn?"

When Tyler looked at Quinn's side, she was staring out the window, not paying attention to the conversation. She didn't care that much for the paranormal, the occult, and the unexplained.

It was paradoxical really. Tyler had seen her pick fights with guys who would have no trouble crushing her with one hand, had trespassed, and risked getting arrested, and she had done all that with such confidence that it put Caleb and Tyler to shame. But tell her there's a ghost in the house, and she'd be miles away from it before the sentence was finished.

"I think I'm ready to light one up," she said.

"We'll find a spot," Tyler said.

The sky was growing ever-darker, and with it, the world itself was changing. Just like in the city, the wilderness became a completely different dimension with the fall of the night. Familiar places could shapeshift into something both comforting and repulsive. Animals and insects relieved each other of duties for the third shift. As the hours drew on, that transmogrification intensified until it was completely alien to day dwellers.

There was something vastly comforting in being awake in the hours when most of the world slept. A feeling similar to that of the freedom experienced on the road.

On the left side of the road, an opening in the trees caught Tyler's attention. He eased his foot off the gas, and when he noticed the dirt road, he gently stepped on the brake.

"What's up?" Quinn asked.

"We never went down that road." Tyler pointed.

Caleb leaned closer to his window.

"How about we take the scenic route for a change?" Tyler suggested.

"We don't know if it leads to a private property," Caleb said.

"If it does, we'll turn around."

Tyler was already rotating the steering wheel in the direction of the road. Neither Quinn nor Caleb objected. Venturing down different roads—especially those forgotten by time and shrouded in mystery—was another one of their rituals. Would the adventurous exploration reward them with breathtaking scenery or extra repairs for the Chevy? It was a lottery.

And that's why they loved it so much.

THREE

ABANDONED ROAD

It was Tyler's car, sure, but both Quinn and Caleb took care of it like it was their own. If something broke, it didn't fall on just Tyler to cover the costs of the repairs. All three pitched in—voluntarily. The Chevrolet was their only means of going on road trips, after all.

Tyler drove slow at first, probably testing the uneven ground to see if the car would protest it. Gravel crunched under the tires. Quinn stared at the infinite rows of trees and the darkness settled among them.

"Well, this is exciting, isn't it?" Tyler asked.

Both Quinn and Caleb remained stoically quiet. For a moment, at least.

"It looks narrow. I think it leads to a private property," Caleb said.

Quinn couldn't tell if that was a subtle suggestion to turn around. Tyler looked as indifferent as he had a few minutes ago.

Slowly, the road expanded, and the trees retreated, giving more room for the car to speed up. Once Tyler was sure he could step on the gas without hurting the Chevy, he did so.

Empty plots of land occasionally popped up on either side, lessening the claustrophobic feeling the firs and pines had naturally instilled with their presence.

"Can't believe we never drove past here," Tyler said.

"Yeah, it's nice," Quinn replied. "Listen, how about we find a place to stop? I gotta pee."

Translation: *I really want to light one up.*

They parked on the side of the road and stepped out of the car. Tyler stretched with an exaggerated groan.

"There's a cooler with beers in the back," he said.

Caleb popped open the trunk, pulled out a can of beer, and tossed one to Quinn then one to Tyler. They leaned on the car and stared at the big house nestled in the middle of the tall grass across the road. The chirping of the insects around them was momentarily interrupted by the cracking and fizzing of their beer cans.

Quinn didn't even like beer. She drank it just to get a little buzzed. She did enjoy the first few cold sips that refreshed her mouth. Afterward, it tasted like piss, and she couldn't understand the people who drank beer for the flavor.

"Can you imagine living out here in the middle of nowhere?" Quinn jutted her chin at the house in the distance. "What a fucking hermit you have to be to move here."

"Maybe it's a family." Tyler shrugged.

"It looks abandoned, though," Caleb said before taking a sip of his beer.

"Yeah, but it's here. Which means someone built it with the intention of living all the way out here."

"What? Can't imagine not living right next door to a Starbucks?" Tyler flashed her a shit-eating grin.

"Oh, fuck you. Like you'd be okay driving half an hour to the closest liquor store," Quinn retorted.

Tyler brought the beer to his mouth and made an expression that confirmed Quinn was right.

A few minutes later, Quinn rolled a joint on the car's hoodie, lit it up, and inhaled the first whiff of it. She made an O with her mouth and exhaled the smoke into the air before passing the blunt to Tyler. When it was Caleb's turn, he shook his head and said, "No thanks."

Both Quinn and Tyler looked at him incredulously.

"What? You get accepted into college and suddenly you're too good for this shit?" Tyler asked.

"It's not that. I just don't feel like it," Caleb said.

"Come on, dude," Tyler said. "This is the last time in a while we'll get to do something like this. Hell, it might be *the* last time we do this. No more driving and getting high every week. Once you start college, the fun is over."

That same unease from earlier hit Quinn. The weight of the finality of this road trip. Tyler was right. This was the last ride they'd go on together as adolescents. Sure, Quinn and Tyler wouldn't change, but that didn't matter. Caleb was about to go to college, and that meant he would change, and that meant the whole group would never be the same again.

Caleb still hesitated, so Quinn chimed in, "Come on, dude. Don't be a pussy."

Because she knew nothing hurt a man's ego more than alluding to him not being masculine.

Reluctantly, Caleb accepted the joint. The tip glowed brighter when he inhaled. For a moment, everything was okay again. They were in a timeless limbo, three friends unrestrained by responsibilities and rules and worries of the future. It was the weed helping Quinn relax. Those effects would wear off soon, and the dread would return, maybe even intensified, but she didn't worry about it right now.

Right now, she just wanted to enjoy the night.

"The fun isn't over when college starts," Caleb said, more to himself than to his friends, it seemed.

"Not for me. But I go to a local community college. UC Berkeley, though? You'll have your nose stuck in books on party nights," Tyler said. When Caleb didn't respond to the remark, Tyler gently punched him in the shoulder and said, "I'm just messing with you, man. Your life won't change. You'll still be boring and not get laid."

Caleb shook his head but gave no reply to that.

Quinn's gaze was fixated on the house. She tried to study its details, but she was having trouble focusing. She imagined a family living there. Not a typical, suburban couple with a son and a daughter but an overweight group of hillbillies with too many loud children and a bad sense of fashion. If that were the case, the house would smell like dead rats and booze, and walls would be crumbling because the house hadn't undergone renovations for about ten presidential terms.

"Hey. Hey, Quinn." Tyler nudged Quinn's arm.

He and Caleb had been saying something for the past few minutes (had it been minutes?), but she hadn't caught any of it. She focused her gaze on the sky above the house. It had gone from amber to a shade of indigo, so she must have been musing about the house for a little longer than a few minutes.

That was the part she liked about smoking marijuana. It allowed her to appreciate the things she never would while sober. Maybe that's what people needed in an age where the internet and digitalization created hectic workloads that made people blaze through life without even glancing up from their screens.

Tyler tried saying something to Quinn again, but she ignored him. Her focus had drifted back to the house. It was definitely abandoned. She could tell from the boards on the windows, the decrepit look, and the fact that all the lights were off.

"Truth or dare," she said.

Tyler blew smoke out and asked, "What?"

"Truth or dare." Quinn emphasized each word.

"Truth."

"Okay." But her mind was drawing a blank.

The weed had somehow made her start a game she didn't even like, and now she had no idea what to even ask Tyler. And she couldn't just go for a kindergarten question like, "Who do you like? or "When was the first time you kissed someone?" It had to be something more challenging. Something that would make Tyler sweat, like, "What's the most fucked-up sexual thing you did?" or "When's the last time you cried?"

Quinn thought, and the question that came out of her mouth surprised her. "Ever wonder what your future wife's gonna be like?"

Tyler looked at her with a frown. Caleb was staring into empty space, seemingly unaware of the conversation.

"Damn. Starting off strong," Tyler said. "You sure you don't wanna take it easy? We're not even high yet."

"I'm sticking to my guns. Go on, tough guy," Quinn said because it was not like her to admit she had made a mistake, that the question would awake more of those insecurities from before.

Tyler passed the joint to her and looked at the sky. Some of the brighter stars were already appearing up there.

"Blonde. Short. Big tits," he said.

Quinn rolled her eyes. Of course Tyler would focus on the physical descriptions.

"That's not what I was asking," she said.

"What do you want to know then?"

"What she'll be like. Her personality. That kind of thing."

Tyler assumed a pensive gaze. "Soft-spoken. Sarcastic as hell. Selfless. The kind of selfless that would influence others without having to be overbearing about it."

"Damn, So you want someone to neuter you?" Quinn asked. "Isn't that like a fetish or something?"

In the background, Caleb let out a small chuckle.

When Quinn noticed that Tyler didn't appreciate the joke, she said, "I'm kidding. Go on."

"Just kind and shy. That's all," he said softly, but there was clear reservation behind his words. A moment that could have turned into Tyler opening up about something important was ruined.

Quinn didn't push further. Since Tyler wasn't doing anything to continue the game, she craned her neck to Caleb. "Caleb. Truth or dare?"

Sometimes, people needed kickstarting with truth or dare like an old generator.

Caleb looked at her and puffed up his cheeks.

"Oh, come on. You don't even need to ask him," Tyler said, his inflection back to its jovial self. "You know what he's going to choose. He's afraid of a little challenge."

"You think you know me that well?" Caleb asked.

Both Tyler and Quinn laughed.

Of course he was going to choose truth because that was Caleb. The safe, boring guy who never risked because—

"Dare," Caleb cut her off.

For the longest moment, silence permeated the air. Then came the *oooh*s from Tyler and Quinn.

"Shut up," Caleb said. "You think I can't handle a challenge? Bring it on. Throw your toughest challenge at me."

"Careful, you might hurt yourself," Tyler joked, which caused another eruption of laughter between him and Quinn.

Quinn could see Caleb was getting worked up, so she quickly defused the situation by saying, "Okay, you want to go with dare? Fine, let's do it."

"Give him something easy for starters," Tyler said.

"No, screw that." Caleb shook his head. "I can both attend a prestigious college *and* be a fun guy."

"Okay." Quinn smiled. "I dare you to go into that house."

Four

In Front of the House

Caleb was staring at the house, mouth open. Tyler could almost imagine the thoughts that were running through his mind. He was trying to think of a convincing excuse to not go inside the house.

"Well?" Quinn urged, then elbowed Tyler and the two of them silently giggled.

This was a typical dynamic. One person would often be the butt of the joke while the other two laughed about it.

"I can't do that. That's trespassing," Caleb said.

Tyler rolled his eyes at the lame excuse. "It's not trespassing if it's abandoned."

"It is if it belongs to someone."

"Who's gonna know?"

"I think I saw some lights turn on there a while ago."

He was trying really hard to wiggle his way out of this. Tyler looked at Quinn for support. It was her dare; she was the one who could bend the rules of the game.

"Fine, let me rephrase that," Quinn said. "I dare you to check if the house is abandoned."

"Okay. I can do that," Caleb said.

"But you can't ring the doorbell. You have to go inside," Quinn added.

Caleb's shoulders drooped in disappointment. "Now you're just changing rules."

Quinn shrugged and took a sip of her beer. "A dare is a dare. No backsies."

"Sorry, bud. Rules are rules," Tyler said because nothing was more fun than adding fuel to an already raging fire.

There was no way for Caleb to wimp out of this one.

And still, he was staring at the house across the road, his Adam's apple bobbing as he swallowed compulsively, the beer can in his hand rotating between his fingers.

"You know, you could just refuse to do it. No one's forcing you," Quinn said.

But he had already accepted the dare, so he knew what the consequences were. No matter how embarrassing a dare was, it was less painful than bearing the repercussions of the penalty for refusing to do it. Other people would probably be chill about it. Tease Caleb a little bit and that was it. Not Quinn and Tyler.

The truth was, Caleb didn't need to stand and take the punishment. He could outright refuse the dare and there would be nothing Quinn and Tyler could do about it. Most likely, Caleb had either forgotten he was under no blood oath to follow the rules because it had been such an integral part of their game for so long, or he was simply respecting tradition.

Which made the game all the more fun.

"No. I'll do it," Caleb said.

He brought the beer to his lips and tilted his head back, chugging down the rest of it, crushed the can, and tossed it in the grass.

As he started toward the road, Quinn suppressed a chuckle, but a snort slipped out.

Caleb turned around and said, "You guys coming?"

"You want us to hold your hand?" Tyler asked.

"How else are you gonna be able to tell I actually did the dare?"

Oh, he's getting serious, Tyler thought to himself with a complacent grin.

He was already thinking of ways he could scare Caleb while he was inside the house. Watching someone perform a dare successfully was fun, but sabotaging it was way better—as long as the dare itself wasn't already risky. A little harmless fun to bruise someone's ego from time to time was okay. Tyler had been the laughing stock many times, so he knew how it was.

"Okay, we'll come with you," Quinn said.

Only after Tyler closed everything on the car and made sure it was locked did they cross the road and venture into the tall grass.

"I hope there are no ticks here," Quinn said, parting the blades with both her feet and hands.

"Nope. No ticks this time of the year. Only snakes probably," Tyler said.

His attempt at eliciting a reaction out of her failed. Caleb was the leading man, trampling grass and marching toward the house with an unrelenting determination.

As they got closer, Tyler had to notice how impressive the structure looked up close despite its ramshackle state. Most of the windows were intact, albeit covered by a patina of dust so thick it might as well have been the wall. Paint was flaking off, exposing layers of bricks underneath. The roof tiles that weren't covered in moss were either cracked or missing. Vines crept along one side of the house, its tendrils reaching toward the roof and window. Given enough time, they would engulf most of the house. By then, the building would most likely be unrecognizable from its present state, perhaps even concealed entirely by nature reclaiming its territory.

The question Quinn had asked earlier resounded in Tyler's head: *Who would live here?*

Buying a house in a place like this might be cheap, sure, and living in the countryside had its perks, but this place didn't fit that description. The surroundings were too feral and untamed and the house itself too isolated from the rest of the world. Not even a nearby neighbor to discover your dead body if you passed away.

When they neared the front door, Caleb hesitated. His gait wound down to a shuffle then to a halt. Tyler and Quinn stopped near him.

"Something wrong, cowboy?" Tyler asked.

Caleb stared at the door. His mouth opened and closed.

"Nothing," he said finally as he braved the porch steps.

His shoes dully thudded with each step he took. Tyler and Quinn held their breaths in anticipation as Caleb raised his hand, hovered it inches from the doorknob, and...

Finally, he twisted the old thing, which produced a loud rattle but refused to budge.

Caleb turned to the group. "It's locked."

The way he spread his arms and let them fall to his sides suggested he was hoping that was it; he was getting off the hook easy with the dare. The courage he'd displayed earlier was all but gone, and he was back to his timid self.

"A lot of these windows are broken. Might be one in the back you can go through." Tyler was quick to suggest because he didn't want the fun to end so fast.

Caleb looked disappointed at that, but instead of saying anything, he nodded and climbed down the porch. They walked alongside the house, glancing up at the ancient walls and barricaded windows. The grass rustled and swooshed as they plodded through it.

"Damn, this place is huge," Tyler said.

"Yeah. Imagine having to clean this many rooms," Quinn said.

"Maybe they had a maid that did it for them."

The opulence of the house somehow felt misplaced here. The architecture alluded to a rich owner, but the location and the lack of surrounding fences and gates didn't fit with the personality of someone who valued their privacy. The mystery it was shrouded by made Tyler wonder all the more.

"But seriously, who would live here?" Tyler asked.

"Someone who's had enough of people," Quinn said.

"Yeah, but if you've had enough of people, you move farther out into nature. And you build a small house with sustainable sources, not... this." Caleb waved his hand at the house.

"That's not people who are looking for some alone time. That's Ted Kaczynski," Quinn said.

Tyler didn't know who that was.

On the side of the house, the undergrowth wasn't as bad. Bald patches of the ground sprouted here and there, along with remnants of cobblestones and flowers that somehow managed to bloom in this chaotic environment.

Behind it...

"Whoa..." Tyler said.

A bevy of rusted cars stretched in the grass in front of them. Tyler recognized both cheap models and old-timers. Jesus, was that a Cadillac Eldorado? The car was gone beyond repair. Must have been sitting here for decades, just like the other vehicles.

"Fuck me," Quinn said. "Is this a junkyard?"

But it wasn't. Junkyards were usually barren, surrounded by mountains of scraps and tires and other car parts. This was... a cemetery for cars.

"Who the fuck would do this?" Tyler asked with such disgust that one might think he was speaking about murder.

Neither Caleb nor Quinn gave an answer because they were too busy meandering between the vehicles, peering at each one. Some were relatively fresh, Tyler noted. Abandoned for no longer than a few years, he deduced from the progress of corrosion and decay.

"Maybe the owner was a mechanic or something," Quinn said.

"Then he was fucking terrible at his job," Tyler replied, staring at torn leather seats stained with something brown.

A shed stood in the back, its state as forlorn as the rest of the property. Boards were falling apart and rotting away. One side of the wall slanted steeply, somehow without toppling the entire structure. A gnarled branch twisted in front of the entrance with the missing door, which opened up into a black maw. A rusted rake was leaning on the side of the shed.

"This place gives me the creeps," Quinn said. Tyler saw her wiping the tips of her fingers on her jeans after touching the hood of one of the cars.

"I don't know. I think it's kinda cool." Caleb shrugged. "How often do we get to see something like this while driving?"

"I'm okay seeing this while driving. From inside the safety of the car. Up close like this, it's dirty. And it smells bad."

The Chevy popped into Tyler's mind. He instinctively looked toward it, but the house was blocking the view. Hopefully still there, not towed away, which was a constant fear of his when he left it parked. Sometimes, he even dreamed about not being able to find his car where he parked it.

Like anyone would give a shit over here. He could park right in front of the house entrance, and no one would bat an eye.

"Look over there." Tyler pointed.

Walking around the back, they finally ran into a window that was neither barred nor closed.

"There's your entry point, Solid Snake," Tyler said.

Caleb's face stiffened. Clearly, the side expedition to the car yard made him hopeful they'd forget about the dare.

The three stopped in front of the windowless pane and stared at the inky blackness enveloping the interior. No one spoke for some time. Tyler, ever the impatient one of the group, broke the silence.

"So, you gonna go in or what?" he asked.

"Yeah, yeah." Caleb nodded. "I just…"

"Just what?"

But Caleb didn't answer. He was focused on the window with an unblinking stare, perhaps weighing his options if this dare was worth the hassle. Tyler could see the struggle in his head: You're about to be a UC Berkeley freshman, this shit is below you. Who cares if they make fun of you? Who cares if you're penalized? Not like you'll be here long enough to suffer the consequences.

"Before we grow old, Caleb," Quinn said.

Caleb licked his lips, approached the window, and placed one hand on the frame. Right away, he pulled it away, looked at it, and scanned the frame from all sides.

"There's sharp glass here," he said.

That was the first time that night that an inkling of doubt materialized in Tyler's mind. Maybe they were going too far with this dare. Caleb was a klutz. What if he got seriously injured inside? They weren't exactly close to any hospitals or places where they could call for help.

When he saw the amused look on Quinn's face, his doubts ebbed away.

"Then you better be careful," he said to Caleb.

Caleb pulled out his cell phone, turned on the torch, and illuminated the window frame. He plucked a shard of jutting glass and tossed it into the grass. He proceeded to do this for almost a minute before he finally hoisted himself up.

He got one leg onto the sill, propelled himself forward, and hopped inside. The beam of his torch pivoted here and there for a moment before he turned to face the group.

"There. Happy?" he asked, and it wasn't just sarcasm lacing his voice. It was annoyance, too. Annoyance with his friends for making him do this and annoyance with himself for allowing himself to get worked up enough to go for a dare.

"You hardly even dipped your toes, dude," Quinn said. "We're not in elementary school. Come on, go on a tour around the house or something."

Caleb's lips pressed into a thin line. "You fucking assholes."

With that, he turned around and walked deeper into the house. Tyler and Quinn could hardly wait for him to be gone before they erupted into a muffled laughter.

"I wish we did this to him more often, it's so goddamn fun," Tyler said.

Quinn's smile dropped. "Yeah."

She pulled out a cigarette, lit it up, and blew smoke out. They couldn't see Caleb's torch anymore. Couldn't hear his footsteps, either.

"Do you think we'll still be friends in the future?" Quinn asked.

"What?" The question caught Tyler off guard.

"When we're older. Say, in ten years. Do you think the three of us will still be friends then?"

The weed imposing on Tyler's current mental capacity didn't allow room for such thoughts. He usually didn't think past the next Friday, let alone the next ten years. It was an important question, one that had been drilled into their minds since early childhood. Think about the future. What kind of a job you would like to have. The house you'd like to live in. The person you'd want to be.

And all those outcomes depended on the present, on the decisions of the current self. Fix your grades, don't do drugs, go to church—because school systems wanted them to believe those were the only things that mattered. In reality, a person's future hinged on so much more than being an exemplary student.

"I think so," Tyler said because he didn't know what else to say. He didn't know what Quinn expected him to say.

"Oh yeah?" The cigarette dangled between Quinn's fingers. "What makes you so sure?"

"I don't know. I just think we will." Tyler said. "I don't see it changing."

"Huh. I guess you're so used to this it's hard for you to imagine things being different."

"No, it's not that. It's just… It's us. We don't drift apart."

Quinn thought for a moment. "Okay. Let's say, ten years from now. No, fifteen. When we have full-time jobs that we do fifty hours a week because it puts food on the table, and we're all married, and we have little brats running around, screaming, and pissing, and shitting, and when my tits start to sag and you and Caleb start going bald, do you think the three of us will still be friends?"

Tyler ran a hand through his hair. "I'm not gonna go bald."

"Well?" Quinn raised her eyebrows.

Tyler opened his mouth with an attempt to ask where this was coming from, but he could tell by the concerned look on Quinn's face that this was important to her; that she needed some kind of reassurance.

He sucked in a sharp breath of air through his teeth. One of his back teeth hurt at the cold breath.

"A lot can change in fifteen years," he said. "But we've been friends since childhood. I don't see why life would get in the way if it didn't already."

"That was different. Our lives are changing now. Caleb is leaving for college. You and I are staying, sure, but we'll be seeing each other less and less. Hanging out every day will turn into a few times a week, then a few times a month, and before you know it, we'll remember we haven't given each other a call in almost a year. By then, our conversations aren't gonna be the same as they are now. We'll be talking like strangers. You know? Like, how is the wife? How are the kids? Congrats on buying the house. Sorry to hear your mom died. That kind of thing."

"Bro," Tyler said because Quinn's monologue left him feeling a mixture of unease and awe. "You sure can be a buzzkill, you know that?"

Quinn stomped the cigarette butt under her tennis shoe. "Forget I said anything."

And Tyler was happy to do that because he was presently not capable of having a conversation of such magnitudes. Fifteen years from now? A boring full-time job, which was an inevitability for all of them? Being tied down with a marriage? Kids?

Fuck, that last one made him depressed beyond words. Having a toddler that would disrupt his free time pretty much all day long made him want to throw up.

"Where the fuck is he?" Quinn asked, shifting weight from one foot to the other.

"I'm sure he'll be back soon," Tyler said.

When he looked at the sky, he realized it had become a lot darker since they arrived here. Crickets were chirping loudly around them, and although a fraction of the sky was still fighting against the tide of darkness, it was clear that graveyard shift had started.

"It's been almost ten minutes. I'm gonna try calling him." Quinn reached into her pocket and got her phone out. A few taps on the screen later, she said, "No service. Of fucking course."

"What'd you expect? We're in the middle of Nowheresville."

"We should go look for him."

"Yeah. Okay. Or—just hear me out—we go in to scare him."

Quinn didn't seem amused by this. "That's childish."

"No, I don't mean like jump out at him and scream 'boo.' I mean really mess with him. Like, make sounds that'll make him paranoid, think it's ghosts. You getting me?"

Quinn's lips curled into a lopsided smile. "I'm listening."

"We make small sounds, just enough for him to know he's not alone. And when he calls out to us, we stay quiet."

"Okay. Fuck it. Let's do it." Quinn threw her hands in the air.

Tyler was the first one to approach the window. He peered inside, but he couldn't see a thing from the blinding darkness.

"Caleb? You in there, buddy?" he asked, but not too loudly because he wanted to maintain the element of surprise. When he got no response, he looked at Quinn. "Okay, we're clear."

Quinn was already holding the light on her phone pointed at the window. Tyler jumped inside, got his own phone out, and turned on the light.

"Hey, give me a hand," Quinn said.

"What? You can't climb on your own?"

"There's something slimy here. I'm not touching that."

"Come on, you big baby." Tyler offered his hand.

Quinn wedged one foot on the bottom of the window, grabbed Tyler's hand, and he effortlessly pulled her in. She was small and weighed almost nothing, after all.

"All right," Tyler said. "This is where the fun begins."

Five

1F Reading Room

"Ew, what is that?" Quinn asked.

It wasn't the glass crunching under her shoes that convinced her going inside was a mistake, nor was it the peeling floral wallpaper, nor the sticky-looking stuff on the ground, nor the particles of dust that so heavily danced in the air they tickled her nostrils.

It was the faint whiff of piss she'd caught coming from somewhere nearby.

"Wow," Tyler said, illuminating the grimy furniture and the bookshelf in the corner that was only half-full of books. "Was this a study or something?"

"Maybe," Quinn said.

She was firstly shining the light on the floor to make sure she wasn't stepping on anything alive. Once she was sure the ground was safe, she scanned the rest of the room.

"People willingly make rooms for reading? Imagine the gaming setup that could have been here," Tyler said. "A huge TV mounted right up here. Instead of this shelf, we could have all sorts of consoles so you can play whatever you like."

Quinn stalked past him and out the door into the hallway. She could see multiple passages opening on both sides. And every door looked the same. How did the owners not get lost here? On top of that, taking into consideration that this was only one part of the house, the place was labyrinthine.

"Anything interesting out here?" Tyler followed her out.

"Shh." She raised a finger, listening.

She thought she'd heard something at the same time as the moment Tyler started speaking. Some kind of a whir or a hum or—

From somewhere in the house came two thuds. This was followed by a silence so deafening Quinn could hear her heartbeat.

"Is that him?" Tyler asked.

Quinn gave him a look, silently asking how she should know. Without uttering another word, she broke into a tip-toe down the hallway in the direction where she best thought the sound might have come from.

Framed pictures hung on the walls. Quinn stopped in front of a black-and-white picture of a handsome young man and a beautiful woman standing in front of a house. Not *a* house. *This* house. The blurry quality and the lack of color confirmed the picture had been taken decades ago. Was it common for couples to take pictures in front of their homes back then? Maybe this was after they first moved in, so they took it to commemorate the moment.

"Damn, she's hot," Tyler said over Quinn's shoulder. "What do you think this house cost back then?"

"I don't know," Quinn said. "Be quiet. He'll hear us."

"Right. Sorry."

The pictures were too unnerving for Quinn's taste. The people—who were most likely dead by then—seemed to stare at her a little too hard. A story brewed behind the photos. Something sad and forgotten.

This house may have been a dump, but it hadn't always been that. At some point in life, someone was able to call it their home. It was the place where they would return after a long day of work to be with their loved ones and relax. The place that was free of judgment, free of societal standards. A place of safety.

Quinn knew what a shelter was, but not home. She wondered if she would ever get to know that. What would home be for her, anyway? Certainly not a house like this one. A cozy apartment, maybe. One she would have to herself, not shared with a roommate. And it would be hers. She wouldn't be renting it.

She still had some of her things in boxes tucked away under her bed. She hadn't bothered to unpack them and find a place for them in her room because she didn't see the apartment as a place where she would stay long-term.

It happened in the past all the time. The landlord was either a douchebag who raised their rent, or the roommate would move back in with her parents or her boyfriend (which never ended well), and Quinn would be forced to find another apartment and another roommate.

Someday, maybe, her personal belongings would have a forever home.

They plodded on, and Quinn snuck a glance inside each room they walked past. Despite the initial objective being to scare Caleb, she was suddenly intrigued by the story of this house. Each room, each decoration, and each blemish gave her a piece of the puzzle, one she knew she would never fully complete, but if she could find enough pieces, she could have an overall picture.

On a whim, she flipped one of the light switches on. The click was audible, but the illumination didn't follow.

Another thud came from somewhere. The sound seemed to have migrated from down the hall to… To where? Quinn couldn't tell where it had come from.

"Did you hear that?" she whispered.

"Uh-huh," Tyler said.

It occurred to her that maybe the tables had turned. Maybe Caleb was the one who was trying to fuck with them. Oh, that clever motherfucker.

There was a grating noise, brief but jarring, as if something heavy was dragged across the ground—once, twice, then once more, each pause amplifying the anticipation for the next scrape.

What is that?

Quinn swallowed, the sound like a trumpet in the absence of all other noise. She suddenly wanted out of there. The house was too big, and yet the walls pressed in on her too much. It was dark. It smelled bad. If she could only see a sliver of daylight peering in through the windows, she'd feel a lot safer.

"It's gotta be him," Tyler whispered a little too loud.

He never did learn to whisper properly. That's why he and the person sitting next to him in class always got into trouble.

"Shh," Quinn said again. "Lower your voice."

"You won't be able to hear me then."

Quinn motioned up and down with her palm facing downward. "I'll hear you just fine. We gotta be quiet if we're gonna surprise him. Wait."

She grabbed Tyler by whatever the closest part of his body was. In this case, it was his arm.

Footsteps, soft but deliberate, came from nearby.

Tyler leaned into Quinn's ear and whispered, "What do you want to do?"

Still loud but better than before.

She motioned for him to follow her. She tip-toed across the hallway, her hand retracting from the dry wallpaper she had instinctively touched for support. She remarked in her head how much she hated wallpaper in houses because it reminded her of old homes. How anyone had gotten onboard with it being popular for home decoration in the past was beyond her.

Tyler walked past her and took the lead. He stopped in front of the door that stood slightly ajar, peeked through the crack, then turned to Quinn and raised a forefinger to his mouth, suppressing laughter.

Was he in there?

With his free hand, Tyler pushed the door. It let out a deafening creak as it opened wide. Quinn hadn't realized she was digging her heels into the ground at the loud noise until she understood that was probably exactly what Tyler wanted—to make a sound that would scare Caleb.

Tyler slunk inside. Quinn saw the pale light of his phone sweeping left and right before fading deeper into the room. She followed him inside and shone her light around. The stench of wet laundry present throughout the entire house intensified in this room, but at least the miasma of piss that made Quinn want to gag was gone.

A prehistoric TV sat in front of a coffee table cluttered with tattered and sticky newspaper. An overturned coffee mug sat on top of a 'FOUR DEAD IN MINING ACCIDENT' headline, the brown streak that snaked to the edge of the paper fused with it. A landline phone whose shine contrasted its surroundings was battling the newspaper for space on the coffee table.

Sponge leaked out the missing leather patches on the sofa and the couch. The carpet rose on one end under the swollen wood flooring. A fireplace filled with ashes and unburnt remains of wood sat by the wall. Framed pictures adorned this room, too, but they were landscape photos, not photos of loved ones.

Why put photos that meant something to you out in the hallway and not in the living room where you'd be spending most of your time anyway? If guests took notice of those pictures, then you'd be standing stupidly in the hallway, explaining who this or that person was. In the living room, you'd already be conversing so it wouldn't be weird.

Whatever.

Quinn approached the mirror suspended above the credenza. It was so smudged she couldn't see herself as anything more than a silhouette with a blinding light in her hand. Her gaze gravitated to one of the half-open drawers. The decorative carvings made it look antique. Even the drawer knob had an expensive look to it.

Curious, Quinn reached a hand to the drawer. She pinched the knob between her thumb and forefinger, and—

The loud crash behind her made blood drain from her face. She whirled around so quickly she thought she would lose her footing. Tyler was staring down at a vase at his feet that somehow, miraculously, hadn't shattered. The look on his face said he didn't mean to do it, but that didn't reduce Quinn's annoyance with his cavalier attitude.

Be careful, she mouthed. He didn't have to understand her words, just what she was trying to convey with her temper.

Not far from them, a door creaked open and clicked shut. Tyler and Quinn snapped in the direction of the noise. Then, that same silence from before followed—thick and ubiquitous.

"It's Caleb," Tyler said. "We—"

"Shh!"

"We should scare him."

Quinn nodded. "Okay."

She walked to the door, shone her phone through the crack at the dining room that looked even worse than the rest of the house, and motioned for Tyler to follow her.

God, this house stinks, she thought to herself as she entered the room.

The dining room didn't fit the grandeur of the rest of the house. No comically long tables with dozens of plates and silverware set in front of each ornamental seat. Just a small table with two chairs that looked like the weight of a feather could make them collapse.

There was a plate on one side of the table where a half-eaten... something was still inside. The sound of flies buzzing could be heard, probably swarming the leftovers, which Quinn refused to illuminate for her own sanity.

A loud bang behind startled her. Tyler had pushed the door hard enough for it to slam against the wall. It was intentional; she could tell from the complacent look on his face. In the distance came footsteps.

Tyler was already at the door leading out of the dining room, so Quinn broke into a light jog after him to catch up. She didn't think the house could smell any worse than it already did, but the kitchen took the crown. She couldn't even define the redolence. It was something putrid, ammoniacal, and that faint trace of wet laundry lingered, too.

She resisted the urge to sweep the torch across the countertops and fridge because the last thing she needed was to see mice or cockroaches scurrying away. Still, the thought had come, and with it, her skin had permuted the slight cold to an itchy sensation, simulating insects crawling all over her.

More footsteps. Right next door.

Caleb.

Quinn repeatedly tapped Tyler on the arm to do something to frighten Caleb. Tyler puffed up his cheeks as if he was trying to contain his laughter. He then cleared his throat in an exaggerated manner.

The house instantly went quiet. Quinn thought it would be funny, and to Tyler, it was. To her, though, the punchline fell short. After a brief moment of silence, the footsteps resumed, not rapid with panic but slow and calculated, as if the sound of another person clearing their throat in an abandoned house was a completely normal thing.

This was becoming boring. Tyler was only just starting, though.

He peeked through the door and then leaned in to Quinn.

"He's there. I just saw him go inside a room," he said.

Before Quinn could protest, Tyler snuck outside the kitchen in Caleb's direction. He stopped at the corner, peered, then pulled back. He pointed a finger at the doorway. Quinn shone the light just in time to see Caleb's figure disappearing out of view.

Finally.

His footsteps shuffled to a stop. When Quinn looked at Tyler, she saw him holding an object in his hand. Some kind of piece of plastic toy or something. She knew what he intended to do with it, and her lips curved into an amused smile.

Tyler tossed the toy in the room with Caleb. The surrounding walls made the clang much louder. In that instant, Caleb's feet shuffled again, this time with a suddenness that alluded to startlement. Quinn expected to hear his voice at any moment, for him to say something like *Haha you got me*, or to call their names, or to say this wasn't funny.

Tyler's hand was over his mouth, suppressing laughter. Quinn herself was amused, but it wasn't enough to assuage the discomfort of being inside the house. Not bothering to conceal the noise of her footsteps, she walked into the room where Caleb was, ignoring Tyler's hand tugging her sleeve.

She shone her light in Caleb's direction,

"Boo!" she said.

The grin on her face was frozen. For a moment. And then it dropped.

The uneasy feeling she had somehow managed to suppress until then rose to her frontal lobe. It was a feeling she couldn't explain in words but which manifested like a primordial, instinctive reaction of her body. She was suddenly colder; her muscles were tense, her mouth dry, and her breath shallow.

Quinn's mouth hung open with words ready to leave, but she couldn't give a response because her tongue refused to cooperate, although she didn't understand why.

The truth was she should have screamed, but something was stopping her. Crippling fear? No. She had developed an instinct to uphold a certain image, and that image was being the fearless female in their group. If she showed fear in front of Tyler and Caleb, she would lose that status, and he would never let her live it down. Every future drive past an abandoned-looking place would be riddled with jokes about how scared she got that one time Caleb was dared to go inside an old house.

That wasn't Quinn. Even when it was, she had to push it down because everyone had a role in a group of friends.

Her hand was shaking, which she hadn't even noticed until she saw her torch trembling. She heard Tyler's footsteps joining her, and a small gasp escaped his mouth.

Caleb turned around to face Quinn.

The scream she suppressed somehow traveled to her arm, which spasmed in startlement, shaking the entire light. Something in her mind, perhaps a part that wanted to believe it, vaguely told her it was Caleb, but that was when the scene in front of her actually unfolded, and she saw the person in front of her for who they really were.

The face that stared back at her was not Caleb's.

Six

1F Hallway

Tyler's body refused to cooperate. He couldn't move no matter how hard he tried. All he could do was stare at the stranger in the hallway, petrified.

The old man was gaunt, shriveled, his oil-stained clothes hanging loosely on him. The top of his scalp was smooth. The grizzled strands of hair that jutted over the side of his head and ears glistened under the cellphone torch. Where the cluster of deep ridges and orange-like wrinkles didn't crisscross his face, zits and moles dappled the skin. The eyes bulged inside their sockets above the accentuated circles and the flabby cheeks. The space between his nose and upper lip, marked by a pronounced philtrum, gave him a Neanderthal look. The lips were curled inside like a snarl, revealing pink gums and a row of white teeth that contrasted the rest of his face too much with their perfection to be real. Despite his face having been clean-shaven, patches of bristly hair remained on his cheek, under his chin, and on his neck.

No one moved for the longest moment. The old man's unfocused eyes, even with a light shining directly on his face, made Tyler suspect he might be suffering from dementia or a similar condition. He reached toward Quinn with one hand in an attempt to gain her attention, to tell her they could sneak past the old man before he became aware of their presence.

At the sight of even that small movement, the old man's eyes became alert. The previously lethargic gaze turned to an intermittent shift between Quinn and Tyler, and that's when Tyler knew—he saw them.

"W-we— We're sorry," Quinn blurted. "We didn't—"

"Who are you?" The old man's deep voice belied his frame.

Quinn looked at Tyler for support, but his tongue was just as tied up. Just moments ago, they were having fun. Funny how it could all ebb away so instantaneously.

Tyler cleared his throat in an attempt to restart his vocal cords, but he didn't even know what to say.

"We thought the house was abandoned." Given the shock of the situation, the complexity of the sentence that came out of his own mouth surprised him.

This, in turn, seemed to encourage Quinn.

"We'll leave, okay?" she said. "But our friend is inside. We lost him here."

The old man asked them a question, but Tyler couldn't make out the garble as more than that.

"What?" he asked.

The old man stared at Quinn for a perversely long moment before repeating the question. "How did you get in?"

Although the question was of an aggressive nature, the old man hadn't even budged yet, let alone done anything to kick them out, and that told Tyler that he was just as shocked as he and Quinn were.

"We're sorry," Quinn said, her voice taut and strained. "We're leaving, okay?"

"No," the old man said, but he still did nothing to act on it. "You're not supposed to be here."

There was a slur in his words, which Tyler hadn't noticed until then, like someone drunk or someone who had just woken up.

"Come on, Quinn." Tyler raised a palm at the old man in an attempt to let him know they weren't hostile and they had no bad intentions. "Just—"

He cut off his own sentence when his eyes fell on the old man's bony hand, on his fingers stained with something dark that gleamed under the torch. Tyler should have known right away what it was, but his brain refused to accept it because it just seemed so out of place.

"Is that…?" he asked, pointing aloofly to the old man's hand.

His initial thought was that the old man in his senile state had hurt himself without even realizing it. But there was too little blood for that. No injury in sight.

That's when Tyler's thoughts went in a different direction at the sight of the blood. A direction he himself couldn't quite determine but which, for some reason, made Caleb come to his mind. And with the fear sliding away, indignation plopped to the surface like a beach volleyball dipped under water. Anger at the adults who constantly pointed fingers at teens like Tyler, Quinn, and Caleb just because they were young enough to take the blame.

Anger at himself for even explaining anything to this old fool when, clearly, he and Quinn were not in the wrong.

"Whose blood is that?" he asked.

The old man didn't answer. He didn't even bother looking at his hand. Tyler shone the light over the stranger's shoulder in an attempt to see what was behind him. All this time, the old man hadn't budged. He was still standing in the doorway, one shoulder concealed behind the frame.

"Is Caleb there?" he asked. When he received no answer for a second time, he broke into a confident stride toward the man. "Where's our friend?"

That same confused stare that said the old man didn't know what century he was in, let alone anything else.

"Hey. Do you hear me?" Tyler asked as he brushed past Quinn. "I said—"

The air in the room went dead when the old man moved. Tyler vaguely registered the small gasp that came behind him from Quinn's mouth. He himself had stopped dead in his tracks, both his hands raised, not in a universal stop sign this time but way high up above his head in a sign of defense.

He was pointing a rifle at Tyler's chest.

"Whoa," Tyler said, but he barely even heard his own voice.

The old man's expression hadn't changed. Not even a flicker. It was the same as it had been this entire time. The only difference was that his eyes were no longer flitting from Quinn to Tyler. They were fixated on Tyler with undetered focus that hadn't been there previously.

"You think you can just walk in here? Huh?" he asked, jerking the rifle slightly upward.

The way his finger curled around the trigger made Tyler expect a loud bang to come at any moment, if not on purpose, then because of the erratic movement.

"Look, I'm sorry, man," Tyler said. "We'll leave, okay?"

He was backpedaling to put some distance to the firearm. He was waiting for Quinn to come to their rescue because she was the one who was good at de-escalating situations. But even Quinn was too stunned to talk, and if that was the case, then they were in huge trouble.

Tyler looked at the open door on the left between him and the old man. He recognized it as the room they had entered the house from.

"We're just gonna leave, okay?" he asked.

The old man blinked but said nothing. The rifle was still pointed at Tyler, but he was holding it with a languid grip. From here, Tyler could see that the top of the man's bald scalp was glistening with more than just sweat. A faint streak of blood traced a thin line over his head.

Tyler pointed to the room and slowly started toward it. "We're leaving, okay?"

His hands were still raised. The old man followed him with his gaze. Tyler was about to reach the door.

That's when the gunshot went off.

SEVEN

1F Hallway

Quinn screamed, but she only realized that much later when she noticed how raw her throat was. The only thing she was aware of moments after the gunshot was her running blindly through the maze-like rooms of the house, bursting through door after door, searching for a way out, only to see every window blocked by those damn boards.

Her mind replayed the image that had happened seconds ago, and all she could think was, *He shot at us. He fucking shot at us. He was gonna kill us.*

The loud gunshot. The way Tyler recoiled when the bullet ricocheted off the doorframe, spraying the air with tiny splinters of wood.

Quinn ran up to the closest door in the hallway and rattled the doorknob. Her distraught mind couldn't comprehend right away that the door was locked, so she continued jangling it even when she heard footsteps running toward her, even when she saw the light bobbing around the corner, drawing closer.

Oh God oh God oh God— He's coming he's coming—

"Run!" a voice shouted.

A familiar voice. A friendly voice. One she couldn't connect to a face right away. Tyler grabbed her by the arm and pulled her down the hallway. His expression was contorted into a rictus.

"Stop running!" the old man screamed.

The source of his voice was indeterminate, but his footsteps were stampeding closer. Quinn's legs weren't cooperating. Tyler was pulling her, and her feet were shuffling just enough to avoid tripping, but her eyes were fixated on the end of the corridor, which she knew was where the old man would come from. It was like standing in the middle of the tracks, staring at a speeding train, and not being able to step out of the way despite the action being simple.

Only when the footsteps grew so loud that they might as well have been in her ear did the invisible shackles unclasp from her ankles and allow her to run. She tore her hand free from Tyler because he was pulling too hard and she didn't want to risk falling.

She could hear the footsteps of the old man right at her heels.

He's gonna shoot me! He's gonna—

He was shouting something, but the distance of the voice didn't match the footsteps, so somewhere at the back of her mind, Quinn convinced herself she and Tyler would manage to lose him.

That's when the second gunshot tore through the air. Something next to Quinn exploded and crashed on the ground. She screamed, but it sounded muffled against the ringing in her ears.

Oh fuck fuck fuck fuck

Her legs forgot how to work, and she stumbled on her hands and knees. When she looked up, Tyler was rapidly distancing himself from her.

"Tyler!" she cried out, but the word came out as clipped, choked out by a sob.

"You come into my house!" the old man shouted, not too far away. "I'll show you!"

Behind, Quinn could hear the mechanical *click-clack* of what she assumed was the old man's gun being reloaded.

She was going to die here. Tyler was going to leave her, and the crazy old man was going to shoot her.

Would it hurt? How would dying feel? How slow would it be?

Please God no not like this please

Tyler's torch stopped, spun, and then he was running back toward her. She would have laughed out loud in relief had she not heard the *rack* of the gun behind her, and she knew the old man was presently aiming it at the intruders, ready to squeeze the trigger.

Quinn scrambled to her feet with Tyler's help. They barely resumed running when the third gunshot exploded. Up until then, the rational part of her kept telling her the old man had simply been firing off warning shots and that no person in their right mind would consider killing two harmless, unarmed teenagers. The third shot snapped something inside of her when she felt the gust of the bullet whizzing past her ear, and then a voice in her head said with stern finality, *He's trying to kill you.*

She ran through a door so hard she almost crashed into the table. The door slammed shut behind her. When she looked back, she saw Tyler fumbling with the lock. He stepped back, and the doorknob violently jangled.

"You dirty little rats! I'm going to skin you alive and fuck your corpses!"

There came a loud *thud* as he crashed into the door, but his small frame did nothing to it.

"Tyler. Tyler!" Quinn called, but he wouldn't stop staring at the door. She walked up to him and tugged his hand. "Tyler!"

At the gesture, he yanked his hand free and snapped at her, eyeing her up and down like *she* was the threat.

"Quinn..." he said, perhaps only just then recognizing her. "He almost shot me. He could have shot me in the head."

"We have to hide. Now," Quinn said between breaths.

Slam!

Both turned to the door.

"I'm going to catch you, and I'm going to kill you!" the old man threatened.

How the fuck did someone who looked so worn out have so much strength and stamina?!

"Tyler! Come on!" Quinn begged.

Each bang at the door seemed louder, growing to a crescendo it never reached. And then...

It stopped.

The banging at the door. The voice of the old man. Everything went quiet. The only thing Quinn could hear was the pulse throbbing in her throat. The silence was bad. Really bad. But she couldn't yet tell why. The cogs in her head turned and turned, but the panic was making it so difficult to think. Even the most basic functions had become a challenge.

And then it hit her. And her legs cut off.

"Oh God." She grabbed Tyler by the hand again. "He's gonna try to go around to get to us. We have to hide right now! Tyler!"

She kept pulling at his hand until she was sure she had his attention. He nodded and looked at the windows—too late because that was the first thing Quinn had looked at for a potential escape route upon entering, but they were nailed shut.

Her eyes fell on the dining table for a hiding spot, but she quickly dismissed it. That was the first place where the old man was going to look. That's where she would have looked if she were looking for intruders in her home.

Shit, they were going to die here! They were running out of time and—

She was relieved when she saw Tyler taking the initiative. He put one hand on her shoulder, raised a finger to his mouth, and crept to the other side of the dining room.

"What? Where are you going?" Quinn asked.

Tyler closed the other door almost all the way and leaned to peek through the crack.

"Tyler," Quinn whispered, her voice a squeak.

Tyler wasn't budging. When Quinn started toward him, he raised a finger at her. She froze and held her breath despite the irresistible urge to heave in deep gulps of air.

Then she heard it. Footsteps. Heavy and deliberate, not at all rapid and intense like when he was chasing them just moments ago. More like he was approaching a kid he was about to scold. He was drawing closer.

Quinn clamped a hand over her mouth to stop herself from screaming. Tears flowed down her face, and she let out a muffled squeal into her palm. A door nearby burst open so loudly she jumped.

A painfully long moment of silence full of anticipation ensued. Was he gone? Did he leave? Were they safe for the moment?

She heard a small gasp from Tyler just before he slammed the door shut—hard. That's when she knew they'd been spotted.

"Hold it right there!" the old man shouted from the kitchen.

He threw the weight of his entire body on the door. Tyler's eyes met with Quinn's. An expression washed over his face. Not fear. Something else. He was planning something.

"Run!" he shouted.

Quinn took two steps back, poised both to run and to help him brace the door. His mouth worked as he looked at Quinn, saying something she couldn't hear over the sound of the banging on the door and the old man's shouting. It was a simple word like 'go' uttered over and over.

The door slightly opened with each pound, but Tyler held it firm. When he saw Quinn still standing there, he looked like he was about to start yelling at her.

"Call help!" Tyler shouted in a single exhale, the two words strung together.

Quinn didn't need any more encouragement. She spun on her heel, ran up to the door, unlocked it, wrenched it open, and ran as fast as her burning legs would carry her.

She lost track of how many doors she ran through. Aside from the aching in her muscles warning her that her stamina was nearing its end, she was aware of the rooms repeating and, in despair, realized she had made at least one full circle back to where she had been.

Panicked, lost, and disoriented, she ran into the closest room. She put her phone on the ground, grabbed the planks covering the closest window, and began pulling. They didn't budge.

"Come on! Come on!" She tugged so hard her biceps felt like they would tear. "Please, please, please!"

A fourth gunshot rattled the walls of the house. Quinn froze, turning her head in the approximate direction of the sound.

Oh no. Tyler. Oh God.

She wished now she could hear the sounds of commotion, of footsteps, the voice of the old man because it would mean the struggle was still ongoing. It would mean Tyler was okay, still in the fight. This silence, however? It could only mean bad news.

She stood there for far too long because soon, she heard those damned footsteps again. And they were approaching her location. Quinn picked up her phone, slunk into the next closest room, and gently closed the door behind her. She looked in the hopes of recognizing the room. She didn't. She couldn't even tell what kind of room this was. There was a couch, a glass table with a chessboard on top, the pieces of which mingled mid-game, two chairs, an empty bookshelf... The room connected to another one.

The footsteps were too close now, and Quinn pressed her palm over the torch of her phone, engulfing the room in darkness. Under the crack of the door, she saw the source of a jaundiced light growing. A scream threatened to burst out of her, so she firmly pressed her palm to her mouth.

She watched as a shadow appeared under the door, lingering, the silence draped in viscous anticipation.

Don't come in here. Please, don't come in here. Please, please.

House of Decay

The moment seemed to last forever, but eventually, the footsteps moved away along with the shadow and the source of the light. She was alone once again.

She tip-toed to the other door, prayed to God it was unlocked, and closed her fingers around the doorknob. It was then that the door where the shadow had stood just moments prior clicked open. Time seemed to freeze as she waited for the creaking of the door to stop and the inevitability of her doomed situation to unfold.

For a second, she believed she would be unnoticed if she just stood perfectly still. Her hope for that was short-lived.

"Stop!" It was the old man's voice that kicked her into action.

She shoved the door open, thanking whoever was watching over her for leaving it unlocked, and ran down the hallway.

"Stop!" The old man was running after her.

Any moment, she would hear the gunshot again.

Run run run run run—

At the far end of the hallway, she saw a door. Reinvigorated, she sprinted toward it as fast as she could, praying it would be unlocked, still bracing herself for that gunshot to come.

"No! Don't go there!" the old man screamed, and this time, his tone had changed.

It wasn't the rabid, murderous voice of a man gone crazy. It was the timid voice of a man desperate to protect something precious to him.

Quinn skidded to a halt too late because she collided with the door. She fumbled with the knob, rattled it, tried to push the door open, but it wouldn't budge. Oh shit. She had nowhere to go. She was done for. And the old man was so close now.

On a whim, she pulled, and the door cooperated.

Yes!

"No!" the old man screamed.

Quinn ran inside. One step in, the ground beneath her foot was gone. The next thing she knew, she was tumbling down a set of stairs, each roll and fall painfully stabbing into a part of her body. All she could do was pray that it would be over soon.

Before she knew it, the stairs ended in a cold floor.

Silence took over once again.

Quinn's body was throbbing, and she was blinded by the darkness save for one thing. Somewhere above her, she saw a bright beam of light being pointed at her, and she heard the old man saying, "Now it's your turn."

Then the door closed, and the lock clicked, and Quinn was stuck in that abyssal blackness.

Eight

Basement

With the old man gone and the adrenaline ebbing away, Quinn's mind scrambled in various directions. She focused on the most immediate concern first: Did she injure herself seriously?

The throbbing in her body had subsided. Mostly. Her side still hurt, and so did her palm and the middle finger of her left hand. She touched the sore spots then rubbed her fingers against one another to see if there was anything wet and warm on them.

She raised herself into a sitting position on her elbows and let out a moan. She blinked over and over, darting her eyes to various corners, but all she could see was darkness. The floor was hard and painfully cold. That's when understanding set in, carrying with it a faint odor of panic that swelled her chest like a balloon.

Something was coming. Inside her, a rope was being stretched to its snapping limit. On the outside, this manifested as the closing of her throat and an ever-shrinking ability to inhale. What little air she did have tasted stale and smelled of urine and feces—and she was losing that, too.

Her breaths came as ragged and shallow, a drowning woman's final gasps of air. She righted herself into a sitting position in an instinctive attempt to help transport oxygen easier into her lungs. Her head snapped in various directions in search of... of what? What would she possibly find in this hellish place?

Anything. Anything other than the darkness. Anything she could hold onto. Please, just something.

Tears dripped from her eyes. A sobbing hiccup unfurled from her mouth, shaking her in her foundation, urging her to just let go and allow despair to take over.

So, that's what she did. She buried her face in her hands and sobbed, rocking back and forth, and the weight of the world seemed no lighter than moments ago. If anything, the burden had further solidified, crushing her under its existence. She was locked inside the crazy old man's basement. She had no way out. Her friends were dead, and she was a prisoner in this cold, damp place where she was probably going to die, too.

Every bad decision she'd made in her life flashed in her mind, magnifying the regret and guilt. One particular decision kept returning to her—the one that happened earlier tonight culminating in the old man hunting them like animals and her ending up trapped in the basement.

The dare. The fucking dare.

It was such a stupid thing, but wasn't that how most accidents happened? By ignoring the faraway consequences in order to have a little fun? No one thought the bad thing would happen to them while doing something innocuous that would evoke a few laughs and memorable moments—until they happened.

And, oh boy, did they happen to Quinn and her friends. This was quite possibly the worst kind of situation she could find herself in. The exact situation that adults and authorities had been warning them—especially girls—about.

This wasn't like taking a school test she didn't study for. Failing here wouldn't give her a chance to correct things. And the worst thing was she had already failed. Now she was merely suffering the consequences of her results.

Quinn opened her eyes. She tried breathing through her nose, but it was too stuffy from crying. She continued breathing through her mouth. It might have been her imagination, but she thought the action came a little easier than a minute ago. She managed to confirm that a moment later when she came to the conclusion that her thinking had cleared up somewhat, too.

She still couldn't see anything around herself. Not even outlines of her surroundings. She whipped her head to the right then to the left, and then she saw a little something that contrasted this congealed darkness. A sliver of light on the ground, not too far from her.

She crawled toward it a little too eagerly. She knew what it was even before reaching it, and it made her heart jump with a flicker of hope that meant the world in that moment.

"Yes! Yes!"

She reached for her cellphone. The torch was facing the ground, but she had seen the light framing the rim of the phone. She scooped it up, located the lock button with her trembling fingers, and squeezed it. The screen lit up, a constellation of spiderweb cracks worming along the wallpaper of a sunset above a treeline, distorting the clock in the sky. The screen had already been cracked, but even in her frazzled state, Quinn recognized an additional crevice that must have appeared when she fell down the stairs.

Her insides unspooled with relief at the sight of the electronic device that would save her life still functioning. She didn't care about the visual damage. The phone was working, and that was all that mattered because it was her lifeline.

She wasted no time dialing 911 and pressing the phone to her ear. It was too silent. No indication that the call was going through at all. She then remembered not being able to call Caleb while they were outside.

Shit.

If she couldn't get a signal outside, there was no way in hell she could get one in this basement. One glance at her battery showed she was at twenty percent.

Quinn squeezed her phone, biting her lower lip in a 'fuck' that never came out. Why the fuck didn't she charge it at work? And the ironic thing was she checked her battery while working, and it was at fifty percent, and she contemplated whether to plug it in or not, eventually deciding against it because she would not need her phone on the ride.

Fuck!

She took a deep breath, forced herself to ease the grip on her phone, and whispered to herself, "Okay. You're okay. You're going to get out of here. You're going to… let's see… You're going to look for a way out of the basement, and you're going to get out, and you're gonna call the police, and—"

Her voice trailed to a suppressed sob when she remembered Caleb and Tyler. She exhaled like a pregnant woman going through labor, composed herself, and continued, "And if you can't find a way out, you're going to find something to defend yourself. He's not going to keep you locked in here forever. He'll have to come check up on you, and that's when—"

A distant clang interrupted her self-pep talk. Quinn held her breath, trying to discern whether the sound came from the basement or elsewhere. Noise traveled in a weird way in this house, and the direction could be deceptive, she told herself.

She waited for whatever would follow the sound, and when nothing happened, she decided she had wasted enough time down here.

The first thing she did before even checking her surroundings was to locate the stairs using the light on her phone. From the bottom step, she shone the door above her. Gingerly, she climbed up. Parts of her body still ached from the fall. No broken bones luckily, but she would definitely have a bruise or two if she lived through the night.

At the top of the stairs, she reached for the doorknob, hesitating for a moment because she knew the futility that awaited her. She twisted, but it wouldn't budge. That's what she expected, and yet despite mentally bracing herself for the disappointment, a new wave of despair washed over her with something she didn't think was possible to manifest in a place like this one.

Rage.

Quinn jangled the doorknob harder. She slammed her palm on the door, multiple times, until her hand started to hurt. No one was coming to let her out. The old man might not have even heard her.

She had only one choice. Turning around, she looked at the stairwell descending into darkness.

Nine

1F Morning Room

Tyler's brain was screaming at him to breathe, breathe, just freaking breathe. But he couldn't. Holed up in the wardrobe, he couldn't see where the old man was. Minutes ago, he'd narrowly lost him in the house (Thank fuck for the size of it and the connecting doors between the rooms), but for all he knew, the psycho was still close by, searching for him.

Just outside his hiding spot, the steady *tick-tock* of the wall clock drilled into his skull, elevating his need to let loose a scream at the top of his lungs.

On top of that, he had a song stuck in his head. A song that had followed him from home to this house. No amount of music he'd played in the meantime was able to stifle the lyrics playing in his head on repeat.

The Kids Aren't Alright.

His dad played that song a lot. He'd played it earlier that day as well just before Tyler left, blasting it in the living room at full volume—despite the multiple complaints by other neighbors in the building—and drinking a beer.

That kind of music was commonplace around his dad, but this particular song by The Offspring could be heard more often than the others. It was strange, though. The frequency of it being played made it obvious Tyler's dad loved the song, and yet he only played it when he was in a dark mood.

When Tyler asked him once why that song, his dad had shrugged and said, *It speaks to me.*

Tyler didn't know what that meant then, and he didn't know what that meant now. His dad didn't talk about his childhood a lot, and it was that exact avoidance that made

Tyler learn early on that something had happened to his dad that he still hadn't gotten over even after all these years.

Despite that lack of understanding of the song's meaning, the title struck a chord with him. The kids aren't alright. Nope. No, they aren't. They're stuck in a house being chased by a crazy old man.

Tyler stayed in that wardrobe long enough to grow desensitized to the smell of musty clothes, for his breathing to become as normal as the situation allowed, and for his thoughts to simmer in his mind with all sorts of catastrophic conclusions.

The old man had had blood on his hand. *Blood.* He didn't want to face the obvious, but it was impossible not to do so. The blood had to have been Caleb's. Tyler wracked his mind, but he didn't see a scenario where Caleb was still okay.

And Quinn? He hadn't seen her since he told her to run, but he did hear a commotion somewhere in the house—footsteps and the old man shouting. Tyler would have helped her, but he had barely managed to escape himself without losing his life.

After Quinn had run away and he could no longer hold the door closed, he had propelled himself through the dining room and into the hallway. From there, everything was a blur. He had been running through rooms; there had been a gunshot behind him—one that hadn't come close to taking his head off this time—and when he had been so out of breath and his muscles burned so much that he thought he would puke, he had found the wardrobe inside this bedroom and waited.

His decision was either a divine intervention from the universe or some kind of subconscious instinct alerting him to danger because, not even ten seconds after he entered the wardrobe, he heard the old man approaching with the footsteps of someone who only could have known exactly where to look for the intruders. The door barged open violently enough for Tyler to consider jumping out and running for it, but he trusted his instinct instead.

The old man's footsteps were muffled on the carpet as he paced here and there, opening some doors, mumbling something under his breath. Tyler wasn't sure when he had left. His exit was muted by the carpet, and he didn't hear him out in the hallway either.

He was sure the old man had left, though. He could somehow sense it in the tension that had abated from the air in the room.

Tyler could stay in that wardrobe for an eternity, and he would still not be ready to brave what awaited him out there. In the end, he had no choice. He could stay here, eventually be discovered, and get killed, or he could try to leave and find help.

Finding his friends was not even an option anymore. Not when the psychopath was armed with a fucking firearm. Not just any firearm. It was a goddamn double rifle. One shot from that—especially at the proximity this house dictated—and the victim was a goner.

He peeked through the crack of the wardrobe but couldn't see a thing in the darkness. Earlier, he had turned off the flashlight on his phone to avoid being detected by the old man. He had tried calling the police, too, but there was no service in the area.

Tyler gently placed his hand on the wardrobe door and nudged it open just enough to be able to take a look at the room. His eyes were well-adjusted to the dark by then. The old man was not there. For now.

He started opening the wardrobe, but the door creaked, so he stopped. He sidled through the gap that was wide enough for him to exit through, closed the door, and tip-toed to the open door. Poking his head out into the hallway, he looked both ways before retreating, contemplating where to go.

Considering where the room with the open window was would be futile because he was hopelessly lost. He needed to look for the front door because that was most likely his ticket out of there.

No sooner had he finished that thought did the banging start. Not gunshots this time, even though it took Tyler a second to come to that conclusion. This was the sporadic, echoing *bang-bang-bang* of construction work coming from somewhere deep inside the house, a sound Tyler was well familiar with.

The old man? Was that him?

Either way, the distance of the sound encouraged Tyler to step out of the room and start looking for a way out. Both directions of the corridor ended in darkness, so Tyler picked the right side on a whim. He walked through, the sound of that banging muffling his footsteps. His, and hopefully not the old man's, if there was someone else in the house.

Now that he was relatively calm, he could see just how big the house was. Jesus, there were so many doors on either side it was not even funny. Who in the fuck would live in such a place unless they had a huge family?

Tyler also considered the obvious state of the house, which he and Quinn should have taken note of as soon as they entered. It was dilapidated, both inside and outside, but there had been subtle signs of habitation. Disturbed dust here and there, food recently left out that hadn't rotted yet, scuff marks on the floor where furniture might have been moved, and the general lack of destruction that time would wreak on an abandoned place.

Bang. Bang. Bang. Bang. Bang.

The sound faded behind Tyler, much to his relief. The corridor wound to the left around the corner and, after a few doors, did the same again. Finally, on his right side came an alcove that served as a foyer—and in it, the door leading outside. Before Tyler could allow his excitement to surge, he looked at the knob, and his heart dropped.

Chained. Fucking *chained*.

The links tightly snaked around the knob and the latch on the wall. A heavy padlock sagged in the center. Tyler could see the night air pressing into the opaque glass at the top of the door. Just on the other side lay freedom. So close and yet lightyears away.

Fuck!

The part of him that hoped for a miracle made him approach the door nonetheless. He tried to get the chains off, hoped that maybe they would simply slide off without resistance. Was that really so much to ask for?

Bang-bang.

The noise was unpredictable. Its volume vacillated, stopped abruptly for an indeterminate amount of time, only to resume on a whim without prior warning.

The links clinked, but only a little because that was how much room they had for moving. It was just as he thought. The chain was so tightly cinched that only the padlock key would be able to open it, but with the way rust had eaten away at it, even that was questionable.

Okay. Think. Fucking think.

He could still use the window to escape. If this was the front door, then the window…

Bang-bang-bang.

The fucking banging just wouldn't stop. He couldn't think because of it. If he could just have a goddamn moment of silence to…

Bang-bang. Bang. Bang.

When it stopped, Tyler hoped that was it, but his reprieve was short-lived when the noise resumed a moment later. He put his hands over his ears, closed his eyes, and thought.

They had stood in front of this door when Caleb tried to open it. Jesus, that felt like days ago. How had so much changed in such a short time? How had they gone from high and laughing to trapped in a house and scared for their lives?

Who the fuck did this old man think he was anyway? Shooting at a group of kids. And they had gotten so close to getting shot by him. It hadn't been a bluff. It had been too close for a warning shot.

Focus. We stood in front of the door, and we went around to the right. Which is here. He looked to his left to better visualize the direction because he didn't trust his mind not to get confused. *We went all the way to the back, and the window was... The window was there.*

Okay, he knew where to go. That was it.

He wasted no time ambling through the corridor. The room with the open window was there. Freedom was there. His beautiful Chevy was there. If he could hop into it, turn it on, and drive off...

Tyler slowed down when he realized he was approaching the construction noise. At the corner, he peeked where the hallway veered. The banging was a lot louder there. Oh, it was definitely coming from exactly where he was supposed to go. He would have raised his hands, looked at the sky, and ironically thanked Jesus had this been any other situation.

He stood there for a long time, mentally bracing himself, his mind jumping to reasons why he shouldn't go there and convincing him he had no other choice. He struggled with that decision for so long that the banging finally stopped.

Stopped. Not paused. Too much time had gone in that silence for a pause.

Had he been spotted?

Tyler didn't think the quiet could be more unnerving, but it was. At least while the banging was ongoing, he could pinpoint the epicenter of danger. Like this, not only was he deaf but also blind in this darkness. And the old man had a fucking rifle.

Come on, you pussy. Just go. Get to the window. You're close. Get out, run as fast as you fucking can to your car, and get the fuck out of there.

Even in this life-threatening scenario, he thought of his friends, and the selfless, caring part of him urged him to look for them, but the rational part shook its head, and he knew he had no choice but to listen to it. The house was way too big. Caleb and Quinn could be hiding somewhere. They could be *dead*. Every second Tyler spent in this house increased the likelihood of him joining them.

If he was the only survivor—*Jesus, what a weird thing to say*—then the old fuck had to get what was coming to him. He had to be arrested so that no one ever ended up like Tyler, Quinn, and Caleb. It was the only right thing to do.

With that, he stepped out from around the corner and snuck forward. He tried to remember how many windows they had walked past before running into the open one. Was it three? Or four? Shit, he wished he paid more attention to those kinds of things.

He walked past one door on his right. The second one, he tried to open. Locked. The third one, too. Still holding the doorknob, he craned his neck to see the fourth one wide open. He managed to take two steps before a figure silently emerged from the room.

Tyler instinctively retreated, pressing his back against the door he had just tried to open. It was the old man.

Shit shit shit shit.

Tyler's heart was pumping so violently he was sure the old man was going to hear him just based on that. And then the worst possible thing happened—footsteps began approaching him.

It wasn't just his back pressed against the door anymore. His head, his palms, his legs were all squeezing the door as if attempting to sink through it.

The old man walked past him without so much as turning his head. One second there and the other gone. Tyler waited for the footsteps to recede, his breath held in his throat.

Only when he was sure the old man would not be returning did he dare to lean forward to peek at him. He saw the silhouette of the stranger disappearing around the corner. He was still carrying his rifle in one hand. In the other, a toolbox.

Tyler pushed himself away from the door and just then remembered to breathe. Keeping his eyes on the corner where the old man had left and tracing his hand along the wall, he backpedaled toward the open room. He knew right away it was the right room because he recognized the layout of the furniture.

Yes!

As soon as he was inside, he gently closed the door behind himself. It didn't matter how slow and careful he was—the click of the door latching onto the frame might as well have been an alarm. It didn't matter now anyway because he was out of—

When he turned to look at the window, he was sure his eyes might be deceiving him. He blinked, but the illusion refused to dissipate.

"No," he said aloud. It was the first word he'd spoken in what felt like hours, and his voice cracked. "No, no. No. This isn't…"

He pulled out his phone, turned on the torch, and pointed it at the window. Even with the evidence clearly in front of him, his mind refused to wrap around the enigma. He approached the window, shone the light at it from various angles, and then slowly, the understanding sank in.

The window was boarded up.

Three thick planks were nailed over the pane, just unevenly enough for Tyler to be able to see the yard outside. He was standing at the precipice of freedom, and it was still beyond his reach.

But that wasn't going to stop Tyler. He placed his phone on the ground with the light pointed up, wedged the fingers of both hands under the lower board, and pulled. He expected to at least hear a crack that would indicate the nails were budging. He might as well have been trying to lift a five-hundred-pound rock because nothing happened.

He propped his heel on the wall, pulled again, but nothing happened. He tugged as hard as he could. Nothing. By then, he was panting and huffing, but the groan he so desperately wanted to unleash was swallowed down. After minutes of struggling, he finally gave up.

He was stuck in this house.

Ten

Basement

The plan was to get out of the house, not go deeper inside where Quinn couldn't see the sky and where she was forced to inhale this putrescent air. Maybe she could find a window in the basement she could sneak out through. Even as that thought entered her mind, a voice in her head sabotaged it.

Why would he lock you in a place you can escape from?

She didn't let that dissuade her. She wasn't going to roll over and die. That wasn't who she was.

At the bottom of the stairs, she illuminated her surroundings with what limited range the phone light had. She tried not to look at her battery too often because the rate at which it was draining was elevating her fear. Once her phone died, she would be blinded again. She had to find a way out before that happened.

This place was a lot more spacious than she initially thought. The ceiling was too tall, too. Everything about this house just seemed so damn off. Too many rooms that clearly weren't being used and now this oversized basement? What on earth did Quinn get herself into?

When she took three steps deeper into the basement, it seemed as though darkness expanded into infinity all around her, as if walking too far from the stairs could cause her to forever be lost in this abyss. She wasn't even sure anymore what was worse: Staying by the stairs where she knew she was trapped or traversing the darkness.

She took a slow step forward, then another, and slowly, her surroundings came into view. A workbench with a solitary hammer sitting on top of it sat to her left. To her right, some kind of a metallic wall. In front of her, something hung in the air.

A pull-cord. Quinn already knew nothing would happen when she pulled it, but that didn't stop her from doing so anyway. That's why, when a red lightbulb ahead of her turned on with an audible click, she was surprised.

What the...?

She didn't even question how there was power in the basement when there was none in the house. She was more discombobulated by the room she was in. The crimson light was faint, but it illuminated enough for her to see the most important things.

The spaciousness of the room hadn't been her imagination. The basement, although narrow, seemed to expand farther ahead than the lightbulb could illuminate. The metallic wall wasn't that at all but a large shipping container.

What the hell?

She stared at the open door flap, now even more questions running through her mind.

And that's when she heard it.

Quinn's ears registered the sound, but she was having trouble deciding what it was right away—the whir of a machine or the sound of something being dragged, she thought. When it finally clicked, she couldn't unhear it, and the heat drained from her face and limbs.

The basement rumbled with a low groan.

Quinn's eyes shot wide open. She once again found herself stunned, unable to do anything more than stand and listen to that noise.

Hrmmm, the sound came again, and this time she was able to pinpoint it. It was coming from the other side of the shipping container.

Something clinked at her feet. Her eyes fell on the heavy chains spooling on the ground and weaving through the open door.

They were moving.

And as the chain dragged itself across the ground, kicking dirt along with it, that groan came again, and this time, it had migrated to directly below the lightbulb. Quinn felt something inside her die when she looked at the source of the light. A distended, angular shadow appeared on the ground from the direction of the other side of the container. As a heavy footfall came, so too did the chains rattle, and so too did the shadow grow more elongated.

The thing was just around the corner, and Quinn was left with no doubt that her life was in grave danger. She bent at the knees, and that seemed to break the petrification spell. She slunk behind the closed door of the container, peeked through its hollow interior, and noticed the chains snaking through the open door on the other side out of sight.

Hrmm—

The groan was interrupted by a small snort. Silence ensued. The footsteps resumed. Faster. The chains pulled along the floor like an anchor dropped from a ship. Without thinking, Quinn stepped inside the container and made herself smaller.

All movement ceased. Silence veiled the basement.

The *thing* was just on the other side of the container. She could hear its ragged breathing. The flashlight of Quinn's phone illuminated an ancient red stain on the ground. She brought a hand to her mouth to silence a scream for what felt like the millionth time that night.

The chain moved a few inches again—scratching against the door of the container, producing a loud clang—just as a shuffling footstep came from the other side of where Quinn stood.

The phone!

Instead of turning off the light, she tried to put it into her pocket. The pocket of her jeans suddenly seemed too tight, too uncooperative. She gave up on trying to shove it inside and covered the torch with her hand instead. By then, the creature in the basement was at the spot in front of the container door where she had stood moments prior.

With a vengeance, the old man's words entered her head, mocking her.

Now it's your turn.

The chain budged again. Then again. And every time it did, the stench of something dead approached the container.

This isn't happening. This can't possibly be happening. I'm stuck in a fucking nightmare. When the monster reaches me, I'll wake up. I'll wake up. I'll wake up.

She kept chanting that last sentence over and over in her head like a mantra, but no matter how many times she said it, she couldn't make herself believe it. The effluvia of feces and rotten eggs was so deep inside her nostrils it was tickling her brain and giving her a massive headache.

She glanced at the illuminated area outside the container. Despite the crimson color, she could see dark splotches against it. The chain moved again, and the footsteps reverberated inside the container.

Oh, hell no.

Quinn broke into a run toward the red light. The moment she began running, a blood-curdling shriek tore behind her.

What the fuck!

Quinn's shoulder grazed the one closed door flap of the container, which knocked her off balance. She tottered forward but quickly regained her composure. Right beside her, the chain went *tok-tok-tok-tok-tok* as it scratched against the edge of the container door, its volume tenfold louder than before.

Oh fuck fuck fuck fuck—

She had no idea where she was going and whether she would be cornering herself in this basement. She just wanted out of this place. Out out out. Fuck this place. Just get the fuck out of here, away from the monster, away from the smell, away from this entire fucking house, hell, away from the entire state of Oregon.

House of Decay

As she passed under the red lightbulb, she was momentarily blinded. Then she merged with the darkness, the torch of her phone illuminating no more than a few feet of the ground in front of her. Any moment, she could slam hard into a wall, and then that thing behind would catch up to her and…

And what? Tear her to pieces? Eat her alive? Something worse? What could possibly be worse than those things?

The basement tapered into a dark passage. She didn't think where it could lead. She ran into it headfirst for her life. She was trying to run too fast, and she saw too late the bucket on the ground that she awkwardly stepped on. She was instantly thrown off balance so hard she stumbled and slammed her chin on the ground enough to cause ringing in her ears.

Her phone was no longer in her hands. Another shriek erupted behind her, and there was no doubt about the rage in the creature's voice this time. On top of that, it was right behind her. She would never have time to get up and outrun it.

Tap-tap-tap-tap, the footsteps sounded as they ran toward Quinn like a freight train.

She looked behind herself, raised a defensive hand, bracing herself for the inevitable collision. No more than two feet in front of her, the chain clinked loudly with the unmistakable sound of growing taut. Quinn screamed, and the thing in front of her screamed, and then she went quiet and realized what was going on.

The chain rattled on and on, and in the darkness, Quinn saw a pale hand with elongated, contorted fingers and broken and dirt-caked nails clawing at the air, desperately trying to reach her. The screams of the monster were replaced by strained groans of frustration.

On and on, it kept pulling itself forward, but the chain didn't let it get any closer. Quinn let out something between a sigh and a laugh. She couldn't get herself to move. She feared as though any microscopic motion could cause the defensive spell to break.

Finally, seeing the futility of its attempts, the monster stopped trying. It didn't leave, though. Quinn could sense its foul presence just in front of her—could smell its stench—standing stock still, watching her with a studious and hungry stare. An apex predator and its prey separated by a few feet, thanks to a flimsy chain holding the beast in place.

She searched the ground near her and found her phone just behind herself. She picked it up, stood, and pointed the torch at the monster. The light couldn't reach it, but in the darkness, two gleaming orbs came into view, only for a moment before blinking out of existence.

Then, they reappeared, sharper and wider than before.

Hrmmm, the thing went at the light pointed in its face.

Quinn's hand trembled, and she let out a suppressed scream.

Shuffling footsteps drew away, and the eyes merged with the darkness. The stench of death slowly ebbed but never fully ceased.

As Quinn stood there, the light still pointed at the passage, she couldn't get those eyes out of her head. There was a kind of intelligence concealed under the feral nature. Something that told Quinn it had been watching her as more than just a meal.

Something that said its intellect rivaled with that of humans.

Eleven

1F Hallway

When the light in the hallway above Tyler flickered, the sheer shock made him freeze in confusion at the phenomenon. Ahead of him, a patch of the hallway remained engulfed in the darkness, and even farther ahead, light blinked in and out of vague existence. One look at the room next to him proved that there was light there, too.

So there *was* electricity in the house after all. The old man might have flipped a breaker or turned on a generator. Tyler assumed it was a generator because he doubted this house was connected to anything run by the government.

With the dispersal of darkness, he no longer needed his phone for the moment. He turned off the torch, checked the battery, and, satisfied with it being over fifty percent, he slid it into his pocket and plodded on.

He couldn't help but notice how all the lights in the house were weak and yellowish as if the person living here couldn't stand brightness. The boarded-up windows would stop most of the sunlight from filtering in, which further confirmed that theory.

With the power restored, the house was an entirely different place. Each room he peeked into told a story of its own, and they all ended the same way—with a happy life shattered into a million pieces.

A child's room, impossibly tidy and free of clutter, felt too untouched to belong to a boy who surely would have left a mess behind as children usually do. The clean bed in the corner, the neatly sorted toys on the shelves, the sky-blue wallpaper with clouds, and the lack of anything else alluded to a future that never happened.

Perhaps the adult—in this case the old man—was still hoping for that future. A son he never had. Or maybe it was just a reminder.

Some of the other rooms, however, were left abandoned, or rather preserved exactly as they had been the last time they were occupied. Ancient mementos were strewn about. Dust settled on most of the room but not on photographs. Tattered books were open on pages, waiting for the reader to finish them.

Despite all that, Tyler felt no pity for the old man. He tried to kill him and Quinn. Probably already got Caleb. You don't become a murderer because of the way life treated you. Especially not a murderer of innocent teenagers.

Tyler wanted to believe the old man was just crazy. That made it easier to deal with this situation. If he was sane but malicious, though… That was the kind of evil a person only saw in documentaries. The kind of evil Tyler never thought he'd run into. At least, not in an isolated place like this one where it could violate him.

Also, how many freaking bullets did the old man have? If he was splurging ammo on the teens so willingly, then he must have had boxes of ammunition stockpiled somewhere. It was a double-barrel, which meant it could hold two bullets at once before he needed to reload. If things got really bad, Tyler could use that to his advantage. Attack the old man while he's reloading.

That was what he should have done right away, but panic had gotten the better of him. There were no guarantees that wouldn't happen again.

Those were all the thoughts running through his head as he tried out each doorknob, each room, hoping for that one window that the old man forgot to barricade, that would be his escape route. The more he explored the labyrinthine corridors, the more he sank into despair. An idea kept rising at the back of his mind that there was only one way out of this mess, but it was such a ludicrous thought that he kept shoving it down to the deepest recesses where it had spawned from.

At some point, his ears picked up the faintest trace of a conversation in the distance. Tyler listened, but he couldn't discern more than the muffled garble. Was it the old man? Or one of Tyler's friends? He decided to embrace the risk and follow the noise because, if there was even the slightest chance that Quinn or Caleb needed help, he needed to come to their rescue.

He walked past rooms he recognized. He thought he was starting to familiarize himself with the house. Mostly. He needed to know the layout to avoid running into a corner.

The closer he got to the conversation, the more he was able to make out. It was a calm conversation between a man and a woman. At the end of the hallway, a pale glow dripped from one of the rooms onto the floor, the colors intermittently pulsating.

Tyler meandered toward the room, enough to be able to tell what the conversation was about.

"Why Harold, how could you?" the woman asked in an overly dramatic tone.

"Don't you 'why Harold' me, Elizabeth. You know how the banks operate these days. It's like dealing with your mother," the man replied.

Laughter from an audience exploded.

A fucking TV. Not real people. Tyler didn't know how he hadn't been able to come to that conclusion earlier. The corny voice acting distorted by the bad audio typical for old TV cinematography should have been an indicator, but panic must have been doing a number on him to confuse him that badly.

Tyler stopped at the door just as another bout of laughter came. This time, the chortle on the TV was joined in by a raspy, wheezy laugh of someone in the room. The old man. It must have been him. Tyler peeked inside. The room was dark save for the bright glow of the black-and-white screen. Sitting in front of the TV on the battered sofa leaking sponges was the figure of the old man.

From here, Tyler could only see his bald top. From time to time, he would tilt his head back and slurp a can of something that he would then lower onto the armrest. On the coffee table next to him sat a landline phone—and the rifle.

At the sight of the weapon of salvation in front of him, that suppressed thought from earlier visited Tyler again, throbbing against the forefront of his consciousness, and this time, he didn't bother denying it. He embraced it with open arms.

The old fuck has to die.

In order for Tyler to save his friends and get out of the house, the threat had to be removed. He could just take the rifle from the old man, sure, but what if he had other firearms he could get? He struck Tyler as a Republican who stashed more than one firearm in this house—especially a house this size.

The words hadn't registered in Tyler's mind until then— he was contemplating *murdering* the old man. That wasn't a threshold that was ever meant for crossing. Tyler had committed his fair share of crimes, but it was mostly the things that would earn him tickets, not felonies. Murdering someone, however, was not something a person did when they were young and stupid to brag about the experience. Murder changed a person forever, ruined their viewpoint on life. The weight of such an action had to be carried for a lifetime. Tyler wasn't sure if he was capable of doing that.

In the end, though, if he didn't kill the old man, the old man would kill him.

No. No.

It didn't have to be that way. If he took the rifle, he could tie the old man up and get out of the house. Easy enough. The old man looked frail and weak. The firearm was really the only thing that gave him an advantage. Remove that from him, and he would be nothing.

Another raucous laughter came from the old man along with the audience. "You tell her!"

Okay. Rifle. Go grab it.

Tyler was tempted to simply run up to the gun and snatch it, but something told him the old man would be faster than that. No, best not to risk it. Play it safe until the gun was in his hands.

Slowly, Tyler moved to stand in the doorway and took the first step across the threshold. Thank God for the TV that muffled any noise he might have made. He crouched behind the couch and composed himself. He was too close to the old man to run, and not close enough to grab the gun.

You can still run before he shoots you, a voice in his head said.

He shut it up. No backing out now. He had to get the gun from the fucker. Peeking toward the sofa where the old man was sitting, he saw his vein-riddled arm holding a can of beer on the armrest. Tyler's eyes were fixed on the rifle.

He got down on all fours and crawled around the couch, trying to find a good way to approach the weapon. The annoying dialogue on the TV went on, interspersed with occasional laughter that belied the comedic sentences. The old man mostly laughed with them, too. Tyler also heard the occasional sound of a slurp and swallow.

Tyler was peeking at the coffee table, the butt of the gun facing him as if it was waiting for him to grab it. The problem was, if he were to run to grab it, he would be directly in the old man's peripheral vision, and there was no way he would not see Tyler.

"Does this dress make me look fat?" the woman on the TV asked.

The man replied, "Not at all. The lasagna does that perfectly fine."

The old man laughed along with the audience.

Tyler weighed his options between going for the gun from this side of the couch or simply walking up behind the old man and grabbing it, but he didn't like not having any cover. He went back and forth like that for way too long, taking time he could have been using multiple times over to grab the rifle, but he was too frozen with fear. He felt like he was in a minefield, unable to move in any direction without severe consequences.

Come on. Do it. Just do it. Grab the gun, and save your friends.

He tensed his body up. His palms and toes pressed into the floor, ready to propel him toward the firearm. He studied his surroundings once more. He would need to sidestep first to avoid bumping into the couch. Use his left leg to start running. Grab the shotgun as close to the trigger as possible with one hand and by the barrel with the other. That way, he would have better control of it in case it came to wrestling over it.

If push came to shove, he needed to keep the barrel pointed at the old man at all times or, at least, away from himself. Get his finger on the trigger, blast the bullets out, and it didn't matter if he would miss. As long as the gun was empty and he gave the old man no time to reload, he would be able to overpower him.

Okay. Ready. Let's—

A muffled scream erupted upstairs, loud enough to thwart Tyler's attempt to seize the weapon, despite the desperate voice in his head screaming at him to go, go, go, and just grab the shotgun. In the end, it was a good thing he didn't listen to it because if he had, he probably would have had a hole the size of a watermelon in his gut. In fact, the scene that unfolded before his eyes gave him a glimpse into how foolish this entire plan had been and how narrowly he'd dodged death—for the moment.

The moment the scream came, the old man's hand was no longer on the beer can. It was on the shotgun, and he was on his feet at such an explosive speed that Tyler knew he was so much more fucked that he initially thought. This old man wasn't a geriatric case that couldn't tell left from right. This was a man with cat-like reflexes and a blue-collar resilience that would give an average Gen Z-er a run for their money.

"What the fuck is that racket?!" the old man shouted, the cheerful mood replaced by instant frustration.

His head turned in Tyler's direction just as Tyler jumped behind the cover of the couch.

Oh shit. Shit, shit, shit, shit. He saw me. He saw me.

The TV went mute. The glow of the screen bathing the room was replaced by darkness.

"I'm trying to watch my show!" the old man exclaimed. "Don't make me come up there!"

Another scream ripped upstairs, accompanied by thumping and scraping this time like a chair upstairs being dragged.

The old man made his anger known by stamping past the couch—past Tyler—and out of the room without even glancing in the intruder's direction. He slammed the door shut behind himself, leaving Tyler alone in the darkness.

Holy shit. That was the only sentence Tyler's mind could conjure over and over while he sat with his back against the couch.

No time to rest. Whatever had grabbed the old man's attention wouldn't last too long before he returned. Tyler had to get out of there before he—

No. The landline phone. He had to call the police. But did he have enough time to dial them? He had to. He wouldn't get another chance.

He rushed over to the coffee table so fast he almost knocked the phone off of it. He picked up the receiver, reached for the dial pad, and his hopes plummeted. The rotary numbers might as well have been Egyptian Hieroglyphics.

Shit!

He'd only once seen a rotary phone, and it was in an escape room he went to with Caleb and Quinn. Although he had messed with the phone back then, Quinn had been the one who figured out how to use it. Fuck, what was it that she said? You have to… have to what?

Ohh, I get it now. You rotate the thing along the numbers, she had said.

What? How? What did it mean? Dammit, why hadn't Tyler paid more attention back then?

He heard heavy footsteps upstairs. He still had time, but would it be enough to figure out how the phone worked?

He poked his finger into the hole with the number 9—it took him a few tries because he was shaking badly—and pulled it in a circle all the way as far as it would go. The dial returned to its original position with a mechanical whir.

Wait, was that how it was supposed to be done? Or was he supposed to rotate it a certain length? Or was he supposed to rotate it to number 9 instead of going all the way?

Shit.

He put his finger on number one and traced it the short length. He did it once more. He waited, the receiver pressed against his ear, eyes plastered to the door. The footsteps came directly above him this time, followed by a muffled grumble that undoubtedly belonged to the old man.

"Come on, come on," Tyler said, fingers tapping on the coffee table. "Hurry it up."

A click came from the receiver. That was something. It had to be. Right? A light scratch that followed confirmed it wasn't a dead line.

"Hello?" Tyler said. "Can anyone hear me?"

"Calls don't go out here," a feminine voice spoke into the receiver.

Tyler was too dumbstruck to give any kind of response. He wasn't sure if he should be scared or intrigued. A part of him wanted to slam the receiver back on top of the phone because he'd been discovered.

"You shouldn't have come here," the woman said, and perhaps the sentence was a mere warning, but Tyler didn't see it as anything other than a threat.

"You don't have much time," she said, watering down the previous sentence. "If he finds you, you're dead."

"I can't get out of here, and I can't find my friends. Can you help me?" Tyler asked.

There were a million other things he wanted to say, but his mind was working faster than his tongue, and he knew there wouldn't be enough time to answer all of those questions.

"Forget about your friends," the mysterious woman said.

"What? What do you mean forget about them?" Tyler asked.

"Listen to me—"

"I can't just leave them here—"

"Your friends are already—"

"—with that fucking psycho!"

He realized he had raised his voice too much, and his eyes instinctively went back to the door, expecting it to burst open. The line on the receiver was silent, and a pang of panic splashed Tyler at the thought that he might have just lost his only ticket out of there.

"Hello? Are you still there?" he asked.

"Listen to me," the woman said. Her voice was strained like she was talking at the edge of breathlessness. "You and your friends have no idea what you got yourselves into. Rufus is not an amateur."

Rufus? The old man?

"Then help me," Tyler said. "What should I do?"

"You have to find me," the woman said after a moment of pause.

"Where... where are you?"

"Upstairs. Bedroom."

Upstairs. In his panic, Tyler had completely forgotten there *was* an upstairs in this house.

"Bedroom?" he asked. "There's a million fucking bedrooms in this house. Which one?"

He heard the sound of the receiver being scratched against fabric, silence, then a rustle before the woman said, "He's coming. Find me!"

The line clicked, and no matter how many times Tyler called out to her, the woman no longer responded.

Twelve

Unidentified Room

Caleb awoke with a start. He raised his head, and pain flared through the back of his skull. He groaned, brought his fingers to the spot, and felt his hair matted with something sticky. He looked at his fingers, and they were red.

Wha—

His throat and chest tightened at the sight of it, his breaths becoming shallow and ragged. A rattle behind him made him snap. His ankle was shackled to a chain attached to the wall.

What the fucking fuck—

He looked around at the small and dimly illuminated room. It was empty—just a cold, hard concrete floor and cracked walls. A solitary lightbulb hung from the ceiling. Splotches and streaks of faded red and brown dotted the floor and the wall like a messy canvas.

"Oh my God. Oh my God. What's going on here? What's…?"

He couldn't speak because of the shortage of breath. He grabbed the shackle and frantically ran his fingers across the surface, looking for a way to open it, but there was none. He tried to pull his foot free. Not even close. By then, his breathing had turned into gasping, and any rational thoughts he had possessed metamorphosed into pure fear.

The corners of his vision darkened, his body was itchy all over, he heard nothing around himself, and despite there not being any possible way for him to brute force his way out of this situation, he stood and yanked the chain in an attempt to pull it free from the wall until his hands were raw.

He needed to get out of this room because the walls were closing in on him, crushing him, and the air had been sucked out leaving only a stench-filled vacuum, and he needed to go home, please God, just let him go home to his normal life and he swears he will never again smoke weed or drink alcohol or trespass.

"What the fuck what the fuck what the fuck—"

He grabbed his head with both hands, took two steps back—because that's how much the chain allowed him to move before growing taut—and forced himself to think.

The first thing he did was tell himself this wasn't real. He was high and drunk. This was some kind of a side effect of the weed. Maybe Tyler spiked Caleb's drink. Yes. Yes, that would explain this because there was absolutely no freaking way in hell someone like Caleb—an exemplary teenager about to attend UC Berkeley—would ever find himself in a horror movie situation like this one. That just didn't happen. Not to people like him. They were things seen in documentaries and heard about on the news, not real life.

Just the thought of all of this being a product of his imagination took the load off his panic-wracked brain. But it didn't help get him out of the predicament. As he stood there, trying to convince himself that he was merely dreaming, reality started to dawn on him. The burning in his shackled ankle. The throbbing and the blood on the back of his head.

This isn't a nightmare. This is fucking real.

Caleb bent at the waist and retched. Nothing came out. He leaned on his knees, gagged twice more, and felt acidic bile shooting from his stomach into his throat. He swallowed it down and blinked the tears out of his eyes.

"How…? How did this…?"

He couldn't remember how this had happened. What was the last thing he remembered? He thought hard, but he couldn't focus. This room was pressing in on his eyeballs, giving him a headache.

He had been with Tyler and Quinn. Quinn had dared him to go into the house. He went inside, walked around, and…

Yes, it was coming back to him. He was starting to remember. The house. Something had happened inside the house.

He had thought he heard a sound. Something like a shuffle. That's when he decided to leave. He remembered having thought how he had spent long enough in the house to win Quinn's dare. He had been on his way out, and then...

Blank.

He couldn't remember anything past that point. He searched his pockets, but his phone wasn't there. His wallet neither. Whoever put him in this room had taken his possessions, too.

"Oh God." Caleb put his hands on his head and paced what little distance he could in the room, tears welling up in his eyes. "Help! Somebody help! Please!"

The screaming voice felt like it belonged to someone else, not him. He kept shouting for a long time before his throat stopped cooperating. He alternated between being overpowered by panic and trying to free himself from the chains. When he realized the action was useless, he looked at the door. It was right there, seemingly within arm's reach. Except when he tried to reach the doorknob, he didn't even come close. His fingers grazed the air, and the tendons in his arm and shoulder strained and screamed, but no matter how much he tried to stretch himself or force the door with his mind to come closer, he couldn't reach it.

Eventually, he fell into a sitting position and rocked back and forth while sobbing. Why was this happening to him? He was so confused and scared, and he just wanted some answers.

He couldn't tell how much time passed before he heard the heavy footsteps approaching the door. Caleb was instantly on his feet, his eyes unblinking at the door in anticipation of who would appear at the entrance.

To add insult to injury, the door wasn't even locked. There was no *click* of the lock. The door swung open without a warning, causing Caleb to recoil to the back wall. In the doorway stood a decrepit old man. The first thing Caleb noticed about him was the rifle—or was it a shotgun?—in his hand. The second thing he noticed was the heavy-looking toolbox in the other hand.

"What did I tell you about shutting the fuck up?" he asked with a no-bullshit tone.

Caleb had so many questions. How did he get here? Why was he here? Why was he chained up? Who was the old man? What was he doing with the shotgun in his hand? Where were Quinn and Tyler?

But none of the questions percolating his mind made it out of his mouth because all Caleb could do was stare at the old man with an unblinking gaze, eyes shifting from his face to the firearm to the toolbox.

After a painfully long moment of silence, the old man approached the corner of the room and placed the toolbox down. The momentary lack of eye contact encouraged Caleb's tongue to untwist.

"Who— Who are you?" Caleb asked. The old man silently rummaged through the toolbox. "Why am I chained up?"

The man pulled out something metallic that rattled. It took Caleb a second to understand it was a pair of handcuffs.

"Turn around," he commanded.

Caleb couldn't stand his gaze for more than a few seconds. He felt as though maintaining eye contact for too long would make the old man lose his shit.

"Please, man…" Caleb started.

His pleas came to a full halt when the old man leaned the stock of the shotgun on his hip and pointed the barrel at Caleb.

"The next time I have to ask, I'm blowing a hole through your kneecap," he said.

Jesus. He's not screwing around. He's serious.

"Okay. Okay." Caleb raised his hands defensively and immediately faced the wall.

"Get on the ground," the old man said.

Although he sounded calm, his voice exhibited a hint of strain, like he was merely bottling up anger that was seeping out nonetheless.

Caleb did as he was told. He got down on his knees, and when the man commanded him to put his hands behind his back, he did that, too. He knew what was coming next, but the shock was still there when the handcuffs clicked around his wrists.

Next, he heard the old man taking a step back and rummaging through the toolbox again. Caleb dared to sneak a look to see what was going on. He caught sight of pliers being pulled out.

"What— what are you going to do with that?" he asked.

The old man tossed the pliers on the ground next to the toolbox and continued searching. He got a hammer out, a wrench, a screwdriver… After the handsaw, Caleb looked away, shut his eyes, and tried to force himself to block out the sound of clatter, to stave off the mounting panic, unsuccessfully.

"Stop it! Please!" he screamed when he could no longer take it.

The old man went quiet, and Caleb knew right away he'd messed up. The old man dropped something that clanged loudly on the floor, and before Caleb knew what was going on, a fistful of his hair was being grabbed and his face was being shoved to the floor. For a brief moment, pain that exploded in his cheek when he hit the cold concrete made him forget about his predicament.

When he tried to lift his head, the old man pinned him down hard. A screwdriver was in front of his face, too close to his eye.

"You and I are going to talk now," the old man said. "And you're going to tell me everything I want to know, or I'm going to hurt you, bit by bit. Do you understand?"

"Y—yes."

"Do you understand?" The old man pressed the screwdriver into Caleb's cheek.

"Yes!" Caleb cried out, his eyes closed.

This could not be happening. No way in hell. This wasn't real. It wasn't real. It wasn't real. Caleb just wanted to go home.

"Now then," the old man said, tentatively putting away the screwdriver. "Who sent you here?"

What did that even mean? Jesus, what was wrong with this old man? Why would anyone *send* a person to this house? Was the old man on the run from the law or simply delusional?

"What? N—n—no one! I came here alone with my friends!" Caleb said.

The old man was silent, possibly waiting for Caleb to elaborate. A second later, he realized he was wrong when a hot, sharp jolt shot through the back of his leg. Caleb caterwauled. At first, that scream was from the shock, not the pain. His body instinctively bucked, but the old man held him down in place firmly with a strength that didn't fit his skinny stature.

Only a few seconds later did the pain arrive, and it was a searing scream of his nerves unlike any he'd felt before. He felt the spot going wet with something warm, but he refused to believe that it was his blood.

"Take it easy," the old man cooed, too calm given that he'd just stabbed a screwdriver into Caleb's leg. "Relax, or it's going to be worse."

Sure enough, the more he resisted, the more the knife-like tip of the screwdriver dug inside his flesh. Once he relaxed, the initial surge of pain was replaced by a persistent burn. Tears were running down Caleb's face, and that feeling of disbelief at being stuck in this situation hit him once more with a potency of all the emotions he'd ever suppressed.

"See, that's not the answer I was looking for," the old man said.

Caleb needed a very long moment to remember what the last thing was they spoke about. When he did, he said, "I'm telling you the truth, I swear! We thought this house was abandoned, and we were just drinking and having fun, that's all. Please."

"That so?" the old man asked.

"Yes, I swear I'm telling you the truth."

Another smaller pang of pain threaded the back of Caleb's leg as he felt the screwdriver being pulled out—for way too long. Christ, how deep inside had it been? Once it was out, he allowed the side of his face to slump against the floor, and he lay there panting and relieved that the old man was starting to see reason.

"Please," Caleb said. "I just want to go home. I won't tell anyone about the house, I swear. Please."

"You stumbled into this house on accident." The old man's sentence was a statement, not a question. "You're not with private investigators?"

"No!" Caleb quickly said.

"Police? FBI? CIA?"

"No! I'm only eighteen!"

Caleb could almost physically see the cogs turning in the old man's head. He was realizing what a huge mistake he'd made tying up an innocent kid and questioning him about matters he knew nothing about. It might have been Caleb's imagination, but was it also regret and pity he detected in the old man's hesitation?

Caleb knew people like him. Tough men who were so used to dealing daily with scumbags that their standoffish attitude bled into their personal lives and every interaction turned into a power play. But they weren't without empathy. They just showed it in the form of tough love.

Too consumed by his anticipation for the old man's verdict and focused on the pain that made it difficult to think about anything else, Caleb didn't see the screwdriver until it was buried in his leg again. The precision with which it was buried in the exact same spot was verging on surgical. Caleb screamed louder this time, and he continued screaming because the pain was so much worse, and the screwdriver was digging into his flesh, the sensation being that of his muscles and tissue being excavated with a spoon. Between screams, he managed to hiss a solitary word.

"Stop!"

It did nothing to stop the old man. Even relaxing didn't help this time. It just made things worse. Only when the old man decided that it was enough did he stop. By then, Caleb was nauseous, dizzy, and sleepy, and while swimming in all of that, one realization superimposed itself against everything else—he was wrong about the old man.

"You obviously don't understand how this works." His captor presented the screwdriver to Caleb. To his horror, it was stained with blood almost all the way to the handle. "So, we're going to try this again."

Caleb knew what was coming. The wound in his leg screamed with agony even before the screwdriver went in.

"Who sent you?" the old man asked.

Thirteen

Basement Corridor

Quinn couldn't tell how long that tunnel stretched in front of her. All she knew was her battery was dropping—fast—and with it, her sanity as well.

Stumbling through the dark, she couldn't shake the feeling of being closely watched and followed, but whenever she looked over her shoulder, nothing but darkness greeted her. She traced the fingers of her free hand along the wall, afraid she was going to lose her way if she let go.

Her own voice and footsteps were deceptive inside the tunnel. They bounced back from the walls, resounded even moments after she went quiet, and it was enough to convince her there was another person somewhere in the darkness—another lost soul like her who was unfortunate enough to stumble upon this house.

Then there were the sounds she knew didn't belong to her. The ones that came just infrequently enough for Quinn to learn to dread them.

The sound of rattling chains.

She could never tell whether they came behind her or in front of her. They were far away, but not too much. Sufficiently to be on edge the entire time.

Ruts in the dirt and striations and scratch marks on the walls told stories of their own, ones that Quinn would have preferred not to know. Despite doing her best to shut her mind to the echoes of violence and screams that still lingered in the tunnel like noxious gas, she couldn't help but imagine scenes unfolding here. This was only increased by the red streaks and handprints her torch occasionally illuminated.

Innocent young women like her stumbling through the dark, bleeding, dirty, crying, begging to be out of here. They would be as confused as Quinn. They'd have a million questions about this house, about the old man, about…

About the thing that was chained in the basement.

What in the world was that? Was the old man…?

Quinn stopped in her tracks.

Of course. It all made so much sense. The thing, whatever it was, was either the old man's pet or imprisoned animal. Was animal the right term for it?

More like monster.

Tyler, Caleb, and Quinn entered the house, thinking it was abandoned, and the old man, fearing they would learn his secret, tried to kill them. But why would he kill them if they hadn't even seen the basement? Attempting to murder them would only bring the police to his doorstep, and then his secret would be exposed for sure.

He might have panicked. Or maybe he wasn't sure the basement secret had been uncovered by the intruders. Or maybe…

No, that's crazy.

What if the old man had intended to kill the intruders from the start in order to feed the thing residing in the basement?

In the outside world where things were normal—or rather, *relatively* normal—such a thought spoken aloud would earn a person a straitjacket, but here it didn't seem so outlandish. And yet, could Quinn really say it was crazy, given everything she'd seen in the house, especially in the basement?

Now it's your turn, the old man had said.

Quinn's turn to what? To feed the monster? To… maybe try to fight it? What if the old man was afraid of it as much as Quinn was?

Those thoughts were shoved aside when she lowered her phone and noticed a patch of light ahead. She gasped in a stifled hope and turned off the torch. She was at 11 percent battery.

Putting her phone into her pocket, she broke into a gait toward the source of the incandescence. She only slowed down when she was close enough to determine that the light was pouring in from a room.

She stopped to listen for any noise that would warn her of danger inside, and when none came, she was encouraged enough to peek. She couldn't immediately wrap her mind around the bizarre nature of the room. The sight would have been paralyzing in any setting. Here, emerging from the nightmarish tunnel clad in darkness in which a monster prowled, it was all the more bewildering.

The piss-colored illumination revealed a room that wasn't too cramped, but the clutter inside made it suffocating. Everywhere Quinn looked—the bed, the shelves, and lined up against the walls—the place was crowded with dolls.

Oh my God.

The hairs on the nape of her neck stood straight as she brought a trembling hand to her mouth. The dolls were all girls, some old and worn with cracked porcelain faces, others unnervingly pristine. The way they were arranged radiated an obsessive precision, each one placed as if it had its own designated spot, an unspoken rule that demanded perfection.

The yellow light did nothing to muffle the vibrant and too-bright colors of the dresses and the fake hair. It was all an incongruous contrast to the decaying wall, the cracked ceiling, and the dirt floor Quinn stood on.

It was overwhelming having so many lifeless eyes on her, boring into her, the inanimate smiles seeming to shift and elongate when she wasn't looking.

She had been taking steps backward inadvertently, which she hadn't noticed until her heel bumped into something. She twisted…

… and let out a shriek so shrill it made her own ears hurt.

She put both hands over her mouth and nose, let loose another scream, and when she was out of breath, she screamed once more.

Sitting in a rocking chair in front of a crude mockery of a tea party table was a desiccated corpse dressed like one of the dolls. Its hair, thin and matted, clung to the shriveled skull. Empty eye sockets stared back at Quinn above two punctures where the nose should have been. The lips had curled back, revealing blackened teeth and gray gums pulled too high up. The dress that might have been violet once upon a time stood faded, stained, and melded to the corpse's body.

Quinn felt something crunch under her foot. She looked down, moved her foot away, and another scream escaped her mouth. That wasn't just dirt she was standing on. It was bones.

Human bones.

After that, Quinn stopped seeing her surroundings completely. Only the corpse existed, along with the unshakable realization that the situation she was in was so, so, *so* much worse than she ever could have imagined.

She stopped screaming, pressed her palms into her head, and closed her eyes.

"This isn't real. It isn't fucking real. Okay," she said, trying to transport herself somewhere, anywhere but here because if she stayed in this nightmare a second longer, she was going to snap. "Wake up. Wake up. Come on. Just wake up."

She hit herself on the head with her palm. It was no use. Like trying to force her bladder to go loose in a public restroom.

When she opened her eyes, the panic had subsided, but an even worse feeling lingered: An indelible sense of defeat. She was stuck in this deranged place, and no matter how much she cried, how much she wished to get out of here, it wouldn't happen. She was stuck here, and no one was coming to her rescue.

She hadn't even considered the idea that things could become even worse, but a voice at the back of her head—some kind of a protective urge dormant in every human in the absence of danger—spoke to her.

You have to hide.

She easily could have chalked it up to her elevated fear, but that's when the sound in the distance snapped her attention. Heavy footsteps mixed with guttural grunting.

Oh God. It's coming back to its room!

Quinn turned to look, accidentally knocking a doll down.

"Ma-ma!" the doll exclaimed the moment it hit the dirt.

The footsteps outside stopped. A quizzical snort followed. That turned into growling as the heavy patter grew in speed.

Hide!

She didn't bother picking up the doll. There was no time. The bed was the only hiding spot in the room. She got down on her belly and crawled under the bed skirt that hung off the edges close to the ground. She completely ignored the things that crunched under her weight and the sticky stuff her fingers landed in because it was better for her own sanity.

Seconds later, the pair of footsteps skidded to a stop in front of the doorway, and Quinn suppressed a trembling gasp.

Time ceased to exist as Quinn stared at the bare feet kicking the dirt while entering the room. They were cloaked in coarse hair, matted in spots, dirt caked underneath the yellowed, chipped nails. As they stood in front of the bed, Quinn expected the curtain concealing her to rise any moment, for a grotesque head to appear inches from her face, and she knew, if it came to that, she would scream, and she wouldn't stop screaming until the thing forced her to stop by snuffing her life out.

A porcine snort came above her, followed by a frustrated squeal, and Quinn knew it was because it had noticed the doll on the ground, and in her mind, she slapped herself on the face hard because she should have taken the two extra seconds to put it back on the shelf, because now the thing in the room would know an intruder was present.

But even without that misplacement, the creature knew someone had touched its things. The manner in which it had perfectly arranged every single detail would make any deviation noticeable, no matter how small. All Quinn could do was lie still, be perfectly quiet, and hope to God and anyone else controlling the universe that the monster wouldn't drag her out into the open to replace the tea party doll with a real thing.

She watched as a hand as equally beastly as the feet scooped up the toppled doll along with a fistful of tiny bones.

"Ma-ma!" the doll said as it was elevated out of view.

Silence was followed by the shifting of the footsteps so that the toes faced the shelves. The longer Quinn stared, the more her confusion deepened. The feet looked almost human—five toes, familiar yet unsettling in their resemblance. The skin was too pale, stretched too thinly against the prominent veins. A multitude of shallow but visible scars crisscrossed the dorsum.

It was that similarity to human anatomy that unsettled Quinn the most. Teetering on the precipice of familiar, but not quite there.

The thing was breathing heavy, throaty breaths as if its larynx had been pressed. The footsteps moved alongside the bed, stopping somewhere out of view. There was a click, and a loud, tinny waltz began blaring in the room.

The feet shuffled, stopped, and then began traipsing in circles with crude and untrained coordination. Quinn lowered her head to sneak a peek at what was going on. Under the skirt of the bed, she saw the hem of the dead body's dress swaying and pirouetting around the monster. The creature was letting out clipped huffs that might have been sounds of happiness—Quinn couldn't tell.

The dance went on for minutes as Quinn stared in both horror and bizarre fascination—but mostly horror. Then the dancing became less vigorous, and the grunting turned into growls of frustration. There came a loud tearing noise like ripping up a piece of paper, followed by a hollow *thump* as a face appeared in Quinn's view, pushing the skirt of the bed slightly aside.

Quinn cried out into her hand, and had there not been the music, the monster surely would have heard her right then and there.

She stared at the face of the corpse gawking at her in open-mouthed terror, and in that instant, she swore she could see a bevy of images in her mind allowing her to gain a glimpse into the woman that once inhabited that lifeless body. Someone like Quinn, tear-stricken, crazed with fear, the eyeballs still intact, the skin not yet decayed and wilted, the teeth white, the hair lush and soft.

Quinn would have helped her. She would have crawled out from under the bed, and she would have faced this thing, and together, maybe she and the girl could overpower it. Alone, however, she was powerless against it.

Then she blinked, and the illusion was gone, and the corpse was just a corpse again.

Tears streamed down Quinn's face, both from the fear that burrowed its claws deep into her skin and the regrets of all her decisions that hit her once again, now stronger than ever with the proximity of death looming by.

Something dropped on the floor behind the corpse in front of the monster's feet. To Quinn's horror, she recognized the detached arm of the dead body torn from the shoulder. She couldn't stop the squeaking that came from her mouth as she sobbed.

The corpse was yanked away with an angry snarl, the skirt of the bed flailing upward just momentarily—just enough for Quinn to see the muscular legs belonging to the monster.

She braced herself for that hirsute hand to appear under the bed and grope the air in search of her face. What happened instead was the monster unleashed a vicious, high-pitched scream that contrasted its deep grunting, and it violently threw the dead body on the ground.

Quinn watched as the face of the corpse was smacked so hard the head turned to look at Quinn. A closed fist slammed on top of the cheek with a resounding squelch. Where the hit landed, the cheek caved in. But the violent outburst didn't stop there.

The monster kept screaming and hitting the corpse. Each new hit deformed the face further, making the features progressively unrecognizable.

Stop.

The monster grabbed the neck and squeezed. Something snapped under its grip.

Stop it!

It kept bringing both hands down on the corpse's face. Wet *thunk*s were interspersed with cracking, a sickening sound that reminded Quinn of walnuts. The music started repeating the same three notes over and over. Quinn pressed her palms over her ears as hard as she could and closed her eyes firmly.

Please for the love of God just fucking stop this stop it stop it stop it!

And it did. The squelching, the cracking, the pounding, the screaming. Only the music and the monster's husky panting remained.

Quinn didn't want to open her eyes, but she did. Her breath hitched in a hiccup when she saw the soupy remains of what was once the corpse's head. The floor was littered with wet, gray tissue and small, sharp fragments of broken bones.

The monster's erratic breaths turned to whining, something as close to a petulant tantrum as it could get. Standing from the corpse, it strode to the corner of the room and shrieked. The music stopped with a loud, startling crash. When it was done stomping all over it, the radio lay in pieces, the room enveloped in silence.

Perhaps in realization of what it had done, the thing wailed. It was a sound that quickly built to a crescendo, which caused Quinn's eardrums to pulsate. Dolls rained all around the room to the symphony of crashing and clattering and screaming as the monster was thrown into a frenzy. Carefully sorted dolls were thrown against the wall, breaking apart and occasionally uttering a discordant phrase like *I love you.*

The bars of the bed groaned and bent as the monster climbed on and off of it, throwing the dolls that were perched on top here and there.

Please don't flip the bed, please don't flip the bed...

Quinn couldn't tell how long the fit of rage lasted and how many times she winced while under that bed, waiting for the moment when she would be discovered. The unnerving silence was what made her go completely quiet.

By then, the dolls—both broken and intact—were scattered all over the floor. With its rage subsiding, the monster might have realized what it had done because it raised a foot and stamped it on the ground like a child before storming out of the room.

Quinn listened to the gravelly noise in its throat receding, and she couldn't help but wonder if it was the monster crying—and what a terrible thing that was, realizing that such a monstrous creature was capable of sorrow.

Fourteen

1F Staircase

It took Tyler way too long to find the stairs leading to the second floor. When he finally did, he didn't climb them right away. He stared at the top clad in darkness, one hand on the banister, knees slightly bent in case he had to run.

His mind played out a scene in which the old man—Rufus—appeared at the top of the stairs just as Tyler was halfway there, leaving him with no room to either run or charge the bastard. He'd be completely defenseless.

That's why he listened first. This house had a way of playing tricks on the mind, he realized. Sounds that the human ears weren't used to existed in this place as if it was an entirely different dimension. Creaking of the walls, muffled clanging traveling through pipes, footsteps that seemed to migrate from one end of the house to the other in seconds, ephemeral moans that could be both human and mechanical, and if one listened really closely, they could catch the faintest sound of a tormented scream.

The woman who spoke on the phone was upstairs. It sounded like she knew how to get out of the house. That meant Tyler had to find her. He tried not to consider the idea that it could be a trap. Right now, the woman was fueling him with the much-needed hope for escape. He'd worry about the rest when the time came.

With that, he ambled up the stairs, one hand on the banister, eyes fixated on the top. The wood underneath him didn't so much creak as it screamed. The slower Tyler tried to move, the more apparent the noise became, so he hurried up.

Once upstairs, he peeked both ways, which was enough to determine that the second floor was as circuitous as the first one. Numerous doors lined the corridor, all closed. Any one of those could be the bedroom where the woman was. Would she leave him some sort of hint at the door, or would he have no choice but to try opening each one?

With no way of knowing where to start, he turned left and began rattling each doorknob along the way. Most were locked. The few open ones were not the rooms he was looking for—a library, an office, a bathroom, an unidentified room cluttered with heaps of messes that left only patches of the carpet exposed.

At the end of the hallway, he noticed something that made his heart jump with joy. A window that hadn't been blocked.

He didn't care if the entire house heard him. He broke into a run toward the pane of glass, laughter choked in his throat. He stopped in front of the smudged glass and stared out into the sweet, sweet exterior of the house. It was dark, but he could see past the lawn of grass, across the road, and...

His car. It was there. Right where he left it. The sight of it made something unspool in Tyler's chest, flooding him with relief and joy.

Okay. Gotta find a way down. How do I...?

He couldn't find a way to open the window. There was no handle, no latch. Nothing. He looked down, but his hopes plummeted when he realized how high up the window was.

"Shit."

There was nothing to hold onto, nothing to soften his blow. Just the deceptive grass that concealed the hard ground. Even if he broke the window and jumped out of it, he would hurt himself badly. Break one or both legs.

One, he could go for. He would be able to drag himself to the car and drive away—maybe. But the glass shattering would surely catch Rufus's attention, and would Tyler be able to run to the car, start it, and drive off before the old man took him out with the rifle?

It was too risky, but if he could find a rope or a ladder...

Movement near the Chevy caught Tyler's attention. He thought it was his imagination at first, but then the scene crystalized. A scrawny old man was prowling around his car.

"Hey," Tyler said, even though there was no way for Rufus to hear him.

He watched as the old man peered through the driver's side of the screen, reeled back—

"No!"

—and brought the stock of the rifle on the glass.

The ensuing shatter was mute, but Tyler could hear it in his head and feel it in his gut.

"Stop, you fucker!" Tyler slammed his palm on the glass.

Rufus opened the door of the car, leaned inside, and a moment later, he was pushing the car across the road, guiding it toward the house.

"No. Dammit, no!" Tyler said, his voice tame again because Rufus was too close to hear him if he caused too much of a commotion.

Someone would have told him it was just a car, and it was, but not to Tyler. To Tyler, it was a loyal companion. Someone who took him out on the road whenever he had a bad day or needed escape from the house. Someone who could erase all his problems with one rev of the engine. Someone who stoically listened and never complained.

I don't know why you care about it so much. It's a piece of shit, his dad had said on more than one occasion.

Tyler didn't care. From the moment he laid eyes on it at the car dealer's shop, he knew it was love at first sight. It didn't matter that the Chevy was a rust bucket. It was *his* rust bucket, and even if he one day earned enough money to afford a better car, he'd never swap it.

And now, he was forced to watch as his loyal companion that had been with him through thick and thin for the past three years was hauled behind the house to join the other cars, where it would most likely be stripped for parts and left to rot.

The term "cemetery for cars" he'd coined earlier struck a different chord this time, sending a cascade of painful echoes down his ribcage. He and his friends had fallen right into Rufus's trap. They had been outside. All they had to do was turn around and leave. All they had to…

It was then that an even greater realization hit Tyler: The old man really had no intention of letting them live. That much had been clear right from the start, but the human mind was really good at rationalizing until the very last moment.

Seeing the Chevy taken away, however, was a sobering experience. The severity of the situation finally hit Tyler like a punch to the jaw.

We're going to die here.

And he didn't think it as a mere definition. He *felt* it. It was the closest he'd been to death in his life—and he was sure he'd dance even closer as the night dragged on. The sheer size of the situation cleaved his abdomen.

A stray voice had been shouting something for a while, but Tyler only heard it after it rose above the screaming in his head.

"Hey! Can you hear me?"

It was a croaky feminine voice, its location unknown. Tyler looked around but couldn't find where the voice was coming from.

"I'm in here," the voice said, now barely above a whisper.

"Where? I can't find you," Tyler said.

"Follow my voice," the woman said.

Tyler opened the closest door. It was a bedroom, but no one was inside.

"Where are you?" he asked.

"Over here!" The voice was coming from the adjacent wall.

How Tyler hadn't noticed the door that was ajar and the sickly light peering from it was beyond him. When he zoned in on it, though, he knew he'd found her.

He barged inside the bedroom and beheld her on the bed. And his hopes dropped off a cliff because she looked nothing like he'd imagined her. And he knew right at first glance that there was no escaping from this house.

He was going to die a gruesome death here.

Fifteen

2F Bedroom

"Close the door," the woman said.

Tyler heard the words, but he couldn't string their meaning together into a coherent sentence because the screaming in his head was deafening.

The woman reclined on her back, propped on her elbows against the gossamer embrace of the canopy bed. Strands of gray were woven into her otherwise blonde hair, which was frayed at the ends and jutted at angles. Her age lingered in curious liminality. She could have been in her late twenties or early forties—the mask of perpetual exhaustion carved into her face made it impossible to tell. Her eyes, two ashen orbs, hovered above the sunken valleys where her cheeks should have been. The lips were merely a faint suggestion of thin lines.

Tyler had registered all those features on a superficial level because he couldn't get his eyes off the lower part of the woman's body. Just below the panties where her legs should have been stood two mangled stumps, uneven and badly scarred.

She shifted, accentuating the bones in her shoulders jutting against taut skin. "You have to close the door before he comes!"

Her voice was ripe with fear, but not the kind that came with the novelty of a trauma. This was the ossified terror of repeated suffering. This woman used to know fear. Now fear had become her entire persona.

Tyler snapped out of his stupor, gently closed the door behind himself, and turned to face the woman. "Wha... what happ— Who are you?"

"Where is he?" she asked. "Is he close by? Hey, I need you to focus because we don't have a lot of time. Where is Rufus?"

"I, uh…" Tyler hooked a thumb at the door. He knew what he wanted to say, but he couldn't get the words out for the longest time. He cleared his throat. "I saw him outside. He was… he was… doing something with my car."

"Okay. That probably means we have a little bit of time," the woman said. "Who else is here with you?"

"Um… My friends." Tyler forced himself to look the woman in the eyes. "Two of my friends. Quinn and Caleb. But I don't know where they are."

"Forget about them. They're most likely dead. You have to run before he—"

She stopped, her eyes bulging at a sound she'd apparently heard, but when Tyler listened, there was nothing.

"Please, listen to me. If he catches you, you're dead. Do you understand me?" she asked.

Tyler didn't answer. His gaze drifted to the woman's ruined legs again.

"He did this to me," she said. "Wanna know how?" Tyler shook his head, but the woman explained it anyway. "When I tried to run, he tied me down and chopped my legs off with an ax. I was awake the whole…" Her voice trailed, but she quickly composed herself. "My boyfriend and I thought this place was abandoned. We went inside because he wanted to see it, and… We didn't… We couldn't have known."

Tears glistened in her eyes.

"Anyway," she continued. "Rufus came out of nowhere. He injured Ethan, and I was so scared I ran. But I couldn't find a way out. This house can be too confusing to someone who just came to it. He was searching for me the whole time. And when he found me… The next thing I knew, I was tied up right next to Ethan. Rufus was there, and he…"

She closed her eyes for a moment. Tears trickled down her cheeks.

"He made me watch as he strangled Ethan to death. Have you ever seen that happen? Do you know what facial expressions a person makes? You know how long it takes for them to die? Then he put me in this room."

"Why?" Tyler asked.

"Because he wants children," the woman said.

Tyler was about to ask her what that meant, but then it hit him, and it made him want to puke.

"There were more like me, but he kills the ones that can't get pregnant. Or just leaves them in the basement. It's the only reason why he's still keeping me alive."

"Holy fuck," Tyler exclaimed with a trembling voice.

The woman's jaw clenched and unclenched.

On the nightstand next to her was a landline phone, almost like her captor had put it here just to mock her.

"How long have you been here?" Tyler asked.

"Two years," she said.

Tyler felt a gut punch. *Jesus fucking Christ.*

"I already gave birth to two of his babies a while ago, but he always takes them away, and then I never see them again. I'm pretty sure they die because I heard him crying and screaming a few times, but he refuses to tell me. If I say anything I'm not supposed to, he hurts me."

"What the fuck." Tyler's mind was on overdrive, too much information to absorb.

"Ethan and I weren't the first ones to arrive. He kills the men. He keeps the women."

Quinn.

If the son of a bitch caught her, death would be a preferred outcome to living like this woman—crippled and used for breeding. Jesus Christ, what a monstrous thing to do.

"How do I get out of here?" Tyler asked.

The woman seemed to contemplate her answer before replying, "You can't. If you're here, then he won't let you leave."

"No. No. He's just an old man. I can beat him," Tyler said, but he didn't believe his own words. "If I… If I catch him off guard, I can…"

The woman shook her head. "You don't understand. He's not just an old man. He's been doing this all his life. He doesn't let anyone escape."

It was obvious the woman had been brainwashed by Rufus into thinking he was omnipotent, but Tyler knew better. He was human, and he could be stopped, no matter how resilient.

"You've been here for two years. Come on. There's gotta be a way out. We can both make it out of here," he said. "Don't you…?" he started, then stopped himself when he considered whether his question would bring pain to the woman. It was too late. She was already waiting for him to finish. "Don't you want to go back to your life?"

Her features went slack, and she looked exhausted enough then to add a few more years to her age. There was a lack of reaction at the mention of her old life, though. A look of numbness. Did she even remember her life before this, or were the house and this bedroom the only thing she knew?

"No." The woman shook her head. "I never want to go back."

"Why?"

"Look at me. I just want to die. That's all I'm good for."

Tears welled up in her eyes. She raised a veiny, skeletal hand to wipe them.

Tyler opened his mouth, but he was at a loss for words. He couldn't tell what the right approach was anymore. He could stand there spewing nonsense he didn't believe himself—that she had to fight for her life and that she would find a reason to live. When he looked at her, though—really looked at her—he saw only an irreparable brokenness in her eyes.

Even if she made it out alive, what then? She could spend thousands of dollars on therapy—and it would have to be an incredible therapist—and she would still suffer from depression and PTSD. To make matters worse, whenever she looked at her missing legs, whenever she closed her eyes, she would remember this house. Rufus. How he violated her. Put babies inside her then took them away.

What kind of a life would that be for her?

"Then help me get out. Before it's too late. Please," Tyler said.

She gulped, closed her eyes briefly as if she was trying to fend off a migraine, then said, "There's only one way out of this, and it's to kill Rufus. As long as he's alive, you'll be in danger."

"Okay. So, I'll find some tools, try to get a drop on him. There must be something I can use as a weapon in the basement or storage, right?"

At that, the woman straightened her back like an arrow, and her eyes grew wide. "Do not go into the basement! You must never go into the basement! You don't—"

"Whoa, whoa." Tyler raised his hands. "Okay. Okay. The basement's a no-go. All right."

That seemed to calm her down a bit, even though she was still hyperventilating.

"So then—" Tyler started before both he and the woman snapped at the door because his sentence was interrupted by the unmistakable sound of approaching footsteps.

"Oh no!" the woman said. "It's him. He's coming! Kill me! Please, kill me! Before he finds me! If he knows I want to help you—"

Tyler spun, looking around the room for an adequate hiding spot. The footsteps were growing louder by the second.

"Please! You have to kill me!" the woman begged through tears. "You don't understand what he'll do to me!"

The only adequate hiding spots were under the bed and in the closet, and the bed seemed like a bad spot. Now that the footsteps were approaching so rapidly and with such deliberation, however, the closet seemed just as terrible.

In the background, the woman's voice droned on, begging Tyler to kill her. With the footsteps almost at the door, he opened the closet, slid inside, and closed the door—merely two seconds before the doorknob rattled.

From here, he could see everything through the perforations of the latticed closet door. The woman's pleas for death had ceased, and her trembling gaze was fixed solely on the door. It didn't burst open in the violent manner Tyler expected it to. It rather groaned on its hinges, inching open with painful slowness until the figure standing in it was fully exposed.

The rifle was still in Rufus's hand as if the firearm was fused to his limb, though it dangled with a lack of caution. Moments of inattention like these were perfect to ambush the old man, except he was immune even then, too, because he was quick to jump from relaxed to fully alert within less than a second.

Rufus scanned the room in an agonizingly slow manner. His eyes lingered on the woman as he entered the room.

"Who were you talking to just now?" he asked.

"N—no one." The woman shook her head.

"Oh really?" Rufus asked. He bent down to look under her bed.

Shit, he's looking for you!

"You wouldn't lie to me, would you, Gretchen?" he asked.

"No. Never. I swear," the woman said, voice quavering violently.

"Because you know what happens when you lie to me."

"I'm not lying, I swear."

Rufus was still looking around the room. His hands—*oh God*—were drenched in blood to his wrists. Tyler didn't have time to question whose blood that was because Rufus's gaze inevitably locked on the closet—on Tyler.

Tyler couldn't move. Everything inside him screamed at him to burst out, tackle the old fucker while the shotgun was still not raised, while he still had the advantage.

But he couldn't. He was frozen with fear. Rufus was right in front of the closet, so close that Tyler could smell blood and stale sweat on him.

"It was me," Gretchen said.

Rufus stopped.

"I was talking to myself," she said.

The old man slightly turned his head, the closet no longer holding his interest. He faced Gretchen slowly. Every motion he made seemed rife with some sort of intention as if it served to amplify Gretchen's—and perhaps Tyler's—fear, and the glee on his face derived from it was almost palpable.

"Is that so?" he asked, slowly making his way to the bedside. "To yourself? Again? What did I say about speaking without permission?"

"I'm sorry. I'm sorry. I won't do it again. I swear I'll never—"

Rufus slapped her without a warning. It made even Tyler recoil. It wasn't a mild slap to make her shut up. No, this was a swing from the hip meant to hurt Gretchen.

She collapsed on the bed, hair falling into her face.

"You don't ever speak without permission, you hear me?!" he shouted in her face. "You have one job and nothing else."

"Yes. Yes. I know."

Rufus was facing away from Tyler. If there ever was an opportune moment to attack, it was now.

Come on. Attack him now. He'll never see it coming.

"You know?" Rufus asked.

"Yes. I swear. Please..." Gretchen said.

"No, I don't think you do know. And you know what happens when you lie."

Every fiber of Tyler's being wanted to jump out and tackle this old motherfucker to the ground, beat him to a pulp, and laugh in his face about it, but his feet remained entrenched. In the end, it was a good thing he didn't jump out because Rufus pulled something out of the back of his pants—something Tyler had somehow completely missed until then.

The long combat knife gleamed under the ceiling light as Rufus presented it before Gretchen. Tyler watched as her chest began rising and falling with shallow breaths, eyes wide as eggs.

"Give me your right hand," he said.

Gretchen instantly began sobbing in a manner that said she knew from past experience what was coming.

"Rufus, don't! Please!"

"I won't ask again," Rufus said.

"Please! Please! I didn't do anything, I swear! I'll never talk again!"

"Shut up, bitch!" He swung the blunt side of the knife at her forehead.

It connected with a sickening thud as Gretchen collapsed on the bed again, soundlessly this time. She wasn't getting up.

Tyler's heart was beating so violently he felt as though it would burst out of his chest. The entire time, his instincts screamed at him to do something, just fucking do something, help her somehow, stop this act of violence on a helpless woman, but the fear that held him rooted inside the closet refused to let him budge. Even if he wanted to, he didn't have the means to do it. What could he possibly do? Strangle her to death like Rufus did her boyfriend?

Rufus grabbed her by the hair and effortlessly pulled her off the bed. Gretchen, whose eyes had been fluttering open and unfocused, began kicking and flailing against Rufus. He shoved her to the floor hard then kicked her in the ribs. She cried out, held her belly, and sobbed while pleading imperceptible words.

Rufus flipped her over on her chest, knelt down on the back of her neck, and pinned her wrist on the floor. Gretchen's free hand and her leg stumps bucked, but she might as well have been a bug crushed under a rock. Veins bulged on her forehead.

Her mouth was open in a mute scream as Rufus's knee crushed her throat under his weight.

Help her!

"This is what you get!" Rufus said as he placed the blade of the knife on Gretchen's wrist. "This is all your fault!"

Gretchen stretched a hand out toward Tyler, her eyes fixing in the general direction of where he was hiding.

No, no, no! Don't! He'll see me!

Her mouth worked like a fish out of water, and she didn't need to speak the words for Tyler to understand she was begging him to help her. He wanted to help her, he really did, but when he saw the psychotic look on Rufus's face, the merciless way he treated her like she was not only a man but a mortal threat to him, he knew that would not be happening.

Tyler didn't believe Rufus would hurt Gretchen. Not really. Who could do such a thing? So when Rufus began slicing through Gretchen's wrist, and when Tyler saw the blood oozing out around the blade, something snapped inside his mind.

Up until then, he had been scared of Rufus. Seeing what he was capable of, the sadistic acts he was able to perform without so much as flinching, that fear turned into filtered terror that poured into his veins.

This old man wasn't a calculated murderer. He was a fucking nutjob who couldn't be reasoned with. Tyler knew a few people like those. People who would go from laughing to threatening to murder everyone in the room. Rufus allowed his impulse to control him, and when it did, beware those in the vicinity because his fury was indiscriminate.

One cut. That's all the old man did before stopping. Blood pooled on the carpet. Gretchen's entire body spasmed. A gurgle escaped her throat, a substitute for a scream. Tyler hoped she would die from asphyxiation before Rufus sliced her hand off.

"See? This is what happens when you disobey," Rufus said. "Next time, I'm taking your other hand, and when you're out of limbs, I'll start with your teeth. Then your eyes."

He slid the blade of the knife across her wrist once more. It produced a sickening grating noise like cutting through cartilage and bone. Gretchen spasmed harder before her eyes rolled to the back of her head. Her eyes were bloodshot, she was red in the face, and the veins on her forehead looked just about ready to burst.

"We're not done yet, sweetie," Rufus said. "Not by—"

A crash somewhere in the house made the old man pause. His gaze lingered on the door; then he stood from Gretchen. She inhaled a drowning woman's gasp of air, rolled onto her back, and scooted to the corner of the room, holding her bleeding wrist against her chest and coughing violently.

Rufus was still staring at the door. He pointed the bloodstained knife at Gretchen and said, "Don't you fucking move. I'm not done with you yet."

With that, he stormed out, shutting the door behind him.

Gretchen's coughs and gasps were interrupted by shuddering sobs. Tyler was no longer thinking rationally. Seeing Rufus's punishment on Gretchen, he wanted out of this room before the son of a bitch returned.

He stepped out of the closet, eyes mostly trained on the door. He only briefly looked at Gretchen in the corner of the room, staring at the wound inflicted by Rufus, the cut so deep the hand dangled from her wrist. She looked at Tyler, and she was no longer pleading with him. She was shooting an accusatory glance in his direction as if to say this was his fault.

"I'm sorry. I'm so sorry," he said as he inched toward the door. He wasn't just sorry for what happened. He was sorry because he planned on leaving her here. After seeing what he saw, there was no way in hell he was risking staying here any longer. "I'll come back for you. I promise I'll come back for you."

He didn't believe in his own promise, and as he ran out of the room, he hoped he would never have to see Gretchen again.

Sixteen

Basement Children's Room

Quinn waited until she could no longer hear any noise aside from her own sobs. That's when she crawled out from under the bed, slowly. The dolls rattled as she pulled herself over them, a noise too loud against the suffocating silence.

When she stood, her legs were wobbly, threatening to give out on her. Quinn tried not to look at the dead body—what was left of it anyway. The images of the skull getting crushed like a pumpkin flashed against the inside of her eyelids whenever she blinked.

Pull yourself together. You have to get out of here.

The room was a mess, a complete contrast to the sight Quinn beheld upon first entering. Dolls were all over the floor around and over the dead body, the hanging shelf was broken in half and held on the wall by a single screw, the radio lay in pieces, and the bedsheets were messed up.

Tyler and Caleb crossed Quinn's mind. She hadn't thought of them in what felt like forever. How long had she been in this basement, anyway? She thought back to the moment when she last saw Tyler, and she hated his guts because it was his fault she was down here. He had told her to run while he held the door, and she did, and look where that got her.

Meanwhile, all he had to deal with was a sadistic old man with a rifle—which seemed to Quinn like child's play now—not this... this...

"Fuck!" she shouted, and she didn't care if the monster would hear her in that moment because anger was getting the better of her.

She picked one doll off the ground and chucked it against the wall as hard as she could. It didn't even make a loud noise on impact. It just noiselessly fell on the ground, leaving Quinn with an even greater feeling of emptiness and frustration.

The fear would return soon, she knew that, so she needed to hurry up and leave before she became delirious with panic again. She checked her phone. Seven percent.

Fuck fuck FUCK!

She wanted to throw it against the wall, too, but she composed herself, speaking words of comfort to herself again, "You're going to get out of here. You're going to find a way out. This place can't be that big. Come on, Quinn. You got this. You got this. You *got* this."

Speaking to herself when she was distressed was something she learned from a high school psychologist. The lady was far from the epitome of a good counselor—too old, rough exterior, constantly smelled of cigarettes, and had a voice that was more appropriate for a position of authority than support. Quinn had made the mistake of opening up to her about feeling like an outcast, told her about problems at home, and the psychologist said Quinn was 'lashing out.' It was a nice way of telling her she was spoiled.

As shitty as she was at her job, the grounding and self-comforting techniques she'd taught her were something Quinn had been using ever since. Maybe it was placebo, but she felt that it helped her, at least a little.

And if it helped in a situation like this one, then it truly must have worked, right?

Peeking both ways in the corridor, Quinn turned right then stopped, trying to remember which way she had come from. It was so easy to get confused here, especially with fear constantly holding the reins. She thought for a second before coming to the conclusion that she had turned in the right direction. This was the part of the corridor she still hadn't explored.

She didn't need to go far to understand that the basement was a sprawling network with its own rooms. Right next to the doll room was a small, grimy bathroom. The smell of shit made Quinn's eyes tear up, so she quickly moved along.

Right after that was a room that might have been used as a storage or a garbage disposal. It was impossible to tell due to the nature of the creature residing here. After that, an empty room. No, not empty.

Jesus.

Not empty at all. Fucking far from it. Lined up against the wall were rows of cages, like the ones used in animal shelters. Dog bowls sat in some of them, crusted with something black that had hardened over the surface.

Quinn moved past it much faster than the others, but it was already too late. The images of bloodstained wire grids and unidentified slop inside which maggots crawled were drilling themselves into her skull already. The real horror of those images was just in her periphery, though, waiting for her to slow down just for a moment so it could catch up to her, bathe her in its glimpse of carnage.

"No," Quinn whispered, shaking her head, hoping that saying it out loud would help keep those thoughts away.

The following room was as bizarre as the one with the dolls. A desk was cluttered with stacks of tattered papers. Newspaper clippings were glued to the wall, their edges peeling away like corners of an old map. The accumulation of dust was an indicator that this room was rarely used, perhaps never, and yet its existence implied the monster might be capable of human-like thinking.

Quinn's gaze fell on the empty wallet on the desk. Next to it was a driver's license, turned in a way that Quinn could clearly see the owner. 'GRETCHEN SUMMERS,' it said under the picture of the cute smiling brunette. An Oregon-issued license.

Quinn leaned in to take a closer look. A chill caressed the skin of her back as she wondered if Gretchen was the dead body in the doll room. She hugged herself in an attempt to fend off the cold that was slowly nesting inside her bones.

Looking past the numerous newspapers on the desk, she opened the drawer that stood ajar. Something inside her died at the sight of all the faces staring back at her from the driver's licenses. Both men and women, old and young, not just from Oregon but other states, too, had fallen victim to this house.

Quinn was just another number to the ones living in this house. Just another driver's license to be added to the collection, a corpse to be played with.

The papers that were plastered to the wall seemed to be of greater significance due to their honorary location. Quinn noticed a photograph of a young man. The same one she'd seen in the hanged photo back inside the house. She squinted at it, trying to determine if it was the old man in his youth. If she tried really hard, she could spot some similarities in the contours, but then again, maybe she was just seeing things that weren't there.

Right next to it was a photo of the same man and a woman. They were smiling. He was holding his hand on her bulging belly. One didn't need to look hard enough to see the volumes the photograph spoke. The photo was important because it portrayed not just a moment of the couple's happiness but their hopes for a bright future—one that Quinn assumed was never realized.

The tragic ending was exactly why it was so significant. The people in the picture would look at it, and they would remember the days when they were free from worry and when life seemed perfect. This dingy room was exactly where it belonged. It was an appropriate representation of the couple's shattered life.

Maybe the old man was the way he was because he lost his wife and child. Maybe the way he was had nothing to do with it. Maybe the old man was not the person in the photograph but just another victim, and if that was the case, then he was not just a monster. He was way worse than a monster. He was the devil himself incarnate.

Quinn pinched the bottom of the photo between two fingers and pulled it free from the newspaper it was glued on. It came loose with a low tearing sound. She studied the face of the pregnant woman. Photographs could be deceptive, yes, but she looked so innocent and happy here. Like the kind of person who would be content with taking care of her baby and baking cookies. Someone who never wanted to be a bother to other people.

And the young man? His build and his bulky fingers suggested a blue-collar job, if Quinn had to assume, because what other jobs did people have back in those days? Maybe a construction worker. Maybe a firefighter. It was difficult to read anything past that momentary joy displayed in the photograph.

Quinn looked up at the newspaper pages on the wall. The headline printed in capital, bolded letters caught her attention.

MAN SETS FIRE TO MEDICAL FACILITY IN OREGON, CLAIMS DOZENS OF LIVES.

In a tragic turn of events this morning, a devastating fire engulfed the Riverpoint Medical Facility, leaving the building in ruins and taking the lives of at least 32 people. Rufus Fletcher (28), an electrician from Eugene, Oregon, is suspected to have tampered with Riverpoint's electrical appliances, causing a fire that claimed the lives of people inside. Fletcher himself is believed to have perished in the inferno.

"This is a great tragedy," Fire Chief Robert Lewis said. "No one could have expected something like this to happen to a place like Riverpoint."

Riverpoint Medical Facility was one of the first places where IVF (in-vitro fertilization) was introduced. Thanks to it, many women who had been unable to conceive by natural means were given an opportunity to have babies. Without it, women will be forced to seek IVF treatment outside the state of Oregon.

Rufus Fletcher's wife, Margaret Fletcher, was a patient at Riverpoint for IVF before she tragically died during childbirth due to complications. Authorities believe the fire was an act of revenge on Riverpoint for the death of Margaret Fletcher. Their newborn is also believed to have died in the fire.

A community support center has been set up to assist affected families.

"Christ," Quinn said.

There were many other articles, but most of them seemed irrelevant. They spoke about the grand opening of Riverpoint Medical Facility, the reputation it built, thanks to its medical innovation, but then things sort of became... weird.

RUMORS SWIRL AROUND RIVERPOINT MEDICAL FACILITY: ALLEGATIONS OF A SECRET EXPERIMENTATION SURFACE

The newspaper article was printed in such small letters that Quinn had to squint. Some of the text was unintelligible.

Date: December 4, 1992
Byline: Sarah Westbrook, Senior Reporter

In a stunning new development, rumors have emerged suggesting that Riverpoint Medical Facility, one of the nation's leading centers for fertility treatment, may be involved in secret, unapproved experimentation on patients. The facility, which has long been regarded as a trailblazer in the field of in-vitro fertilization (IVF), is now facing intense scrutiny after whistleblowers came forward with allegations of unethical practices.

Sources close to the investigation have claimed that certain treatments being offered at Riverpoint went beyond the scope of traditional IVF procedures and involved experimental methods that may not have been approved by medical oversight boards. While these [unintelligible], they have raised significant concerns within the medical community and among former patients.

"We've heard whispers for years, but now it seems that some people are finally starting to speak out," said Dr. Clara Montgomery, a reproductive health expert who has worked in the field for over 20 years. "If these allegations are true, it could be a massive breach of ethical standards in medicine."

One former employee of Riverpoint, who chose to remain anonymous for his own safety, described working at the facility as "bizarre," stating that certain patients were reportedly offered experimental [unintelligible] without their full knowledge of the consequences. The employee also claimed to have seen confidential documents indicating that some of these treatments were designed to push the boundaries of genetic modification.

Local law enforcement and the medical board have launched an investigation into the matter, though Riverpoint's administration has vehemently denied the allegations. "Riverpoint Medical Facility is committed to the highest standards of patient care, and we strictly adhere to all ethical guidelines and regulatory frameworks," said Dr. William Bauer, the facility's director, in a statement issued yesterday.

However, our sources claim that Dr. Bauer's statement is not true.

Howard Richards, a doctor specialist for IVF employed at Riverpoint, who has gained notoriety in the scientific community due to his extreme stances and unorthodox approach to medical experimentation, was said to be directly involved in treatment of patients despite his track record. Whistleblowers claim Richards was hired exactly because of his controversial background to help in the experimentation.

"While it is true that a former IVF specialist employed at Riverpoint was engaged in some unethical practices, these researches have been conducted by a party not related to Riverpoint," Dr. Bauer said. "We have since fired Dr. Richards because we believe the safety of our patients is our number one priority."

Rumors continue to persist despite the director's claim, with multiple former patients coming forward, though some remain reluctant to go public with their experiences for fear of retaliation. One anonymous source, who underwent treatment at Riverpoint, spoke of "vague" consent forms and unsettling experiences that gave her PTSD.

"There was always something that felt off about it," she said. "They kept telling me how lucky I was to be part of their 'exclusive program,' but I never fully understood what that meant, and the doctors didn't seem too eager to explain it to me."

"As soon as she was born, they took my baby from me," another former patient claims. "I never saw her again. I called the police and hired an attorney, but no one was able to help me. I think about her every day."

Other sources claim Riverpoint hides the number of patient deaths, as well as miscarriages and deaths of newborn conceived via IVF to make their success statistics look better. However, some of the patients *have had nothing but words of praise for Riverpoint and its doctors, causing others to believe they may have been blackmailed.*

Investigators are working to uncover the truth behind these claims. In the meantime, patients who sought treatment at Riverpoint are left grappling with questions about the integrity of their care and the safety of their procedures.

[rest of the article unintelligible]

Rummaging through the stacks of useless papers, Quinn found a photo album near the bottom. The protective see-through layers between pages were smudged with something old and sticky. At first, there were a lot of photos of the couple on the wall. Then, the woman ceased to appear, and the man's smile disappeared from his face. As he grew older, the ridges on his face deepened along with the pain in his eyes, and he resembled more and more the old man he was today.

Quinn licked her dry lips.

"Rufus Fletcher," she said to the air, perhaps hoping the name would help her understand things better. "You set the fire to Riverpoint. And then what did you do? You ran away?"

She flipped to the next page and got her answer. And she gasped so hard spit flew too fast down her throat and she started coughing. It took her a while to gather enough courage to flip through the remaining pages of the album, and with each new picture, new tears welled up in her eyes, and she felt like puking.

Her phone was at 4 percent. It was enough to snap pictures of everything important in the room. She also grabbed some of the articles and photographs with her, stuffing them into her pockets.

No sooner had she finished did she hear footsteps in the distance, accompanied by that disgusting grunting. She put her phone back in her pocket and bolted out of there.

Seventeen

Torture Room

"Hey! Don't you pass out on me!"

Caleb could hardly focus on the rough voice that sounded like it was coming from inside a barrel. All he knew was pain beyond description. Pain he never thought was possible. Pain that made him drift in and out of consciousness.

He tried to open his eyes, but the best he could do was raise them to a half-lidded position. Through a blurry image, he saw movement in front of himself, smelled blood and his own urine. A hard slap to the face cleared everything up and brought his tormentor back into focus.

"We're not done yet. Not by a long shot," the old man said, flashing Caleb something that probably should have been a smile, but the wild-eyed look made it look nothing like it.

He tossed the bloodstained scalpel aside, causing it to clatter to the floor in front of Caleb's face. Caleb must have passed out at some point because he didn't remember the scalpel being stained with blood. He was splayed sideways as well, he realized. When had that happened?

The door was right there. Open, like a mockery. Various other tools were scattered all over the floor. Most of them were bloodstained. A fresh coat of blood—Caleb's blood—spattered the old stains on the floor.

While the old man was rummaging through the toolbox, Caleb looked down, and an anchor crushed his organs under their weight. A high-pitched sound filled the room. It took Caleb a moment to understand it was his own scream. Before the horror even began subsiding, pain flashed in his entire body.

His hand was mangled beyond recognition, the fingers curved at odd angles, bones either jutting out or tented against the swollen skin. On three fingers, where the nails once stood, was disfigured flesh. Another nail was split down the middle, one half standing upright, detached from the cuticle. The old man had given up on taking all his nails off halfway through the fourth one.

His legs were striated with a bevy of slashes that intersected like roads. Some were so deep he could see the flesh splitting open into a crevice. On his thigh, Caleb could see a strip of the skin peeling back like a banana. That probably would have been the worst pain, but Caleb had started passing out around that time, so he wasn't present during the entire process. All he did remember was begging God for it to end and feeling the serrated blade of the knife vibrating against his flesh like when a well-done steak was being cut.

He didn't even see that the old man was in front of him again until he felt his hand slapping his face. Only then did he stop screaming.

"Please... Please..." Caleb begged.

He didn't even care about getting out of here anymore. He just wanted the pain to end. He hurt everywhere. His arms, God, his hand, his legs...

Even his face and mouth hurt. Earlier, the old man had carved Caleb's face by running a scalpel along his forehead and down his cheek. That was only a prelude to the pliers. The old man had knelt down on Caleb's back and face, held him down tightly, and pried his mouth open with the tool. When Caleb resisted, the old man threatened to pinch his tongue with the pliers instead, so Caleb relented through tears and pleas, which fell on deaf ears.

Then, the stranger tightened the pliers around an upper tooth—not one of the frontal ones, which were smaller, but his first molar because of course he wanted Caleb to suffer as much as possible.

Caleb couldn't describe the pain he felt during the extraction. The pliers had squeezed a part of his gum along with his tooth. There was a lot of grinding against the tooth as the old man struggled to pinch it properly. Caleb was pretty sure the pliers had chipped a part of his tooth in the process. Then came the tugging, and the sound of tearing that seemed to reverberate right from inside Caleb's skull.

Caleb already had a missing tooth. A molar on the lower left side, which he had to get extracted because the dentist had drilled the cavity so deep that removing the tooth was the only remaining option. But that was done under completely different circumstances. In a sterile room, under anesthesia, by professionals who did their utmost to make Caleb as comfortable as they could. By the time Caleb left the clinic, he was feeling only mild pain in the spot where he was biting down the gauze.

When the old man was done, he held the tooth out in the pliers for Caleb to see. The root of the molar—*Jesus, it was so much longer than the actual crown*—was completely drenched in blood, and Caleb saw a small, fleshy clump clinging to the sharp end.

The old man laughed at that as if he had just found gold. He tossed both the pliers and the tooth aside and went back to rifle through the toolbox.

Caleb's lower lip was swollen and bleeding from the punches, his mouth tasted like copper, and he felt one of his side teeth loose inside its gum.

If the old man stopped now, Caleb could still recover someday. He could go on with his life with minimal scarring on the surface. The real wounds would be in his head.

But his captor had no intention of stopping. Almost an hour into the torture—although it felt like much longer—the old man showed no signs of growing tired. The worst thing was Caleb knew this was only the beginning. The old man had made it pretty clear he would bring out the big guns if Caleb refused to cooperate.

At one point, Caleb caved and told him that it was true—that he was a journalist trying to find his next scoop. A badly thought-out lie just to make the pain stop. The old man wasn't buying it. He firmly believed Caleb was sent by someone else and kept mentioning Riverpoint, whatever that was.

"Still not willing to talk?" the old man asked as he raised a pistol-like tool Caleb couldn't identify. He brought the tip to the gash on Caleb's thigh—the deepest one—and said, "Try not to buck. It'll hurt more."

The captor pulled the trigger, and only when Caleb saw the blinding blueish blaze coming from the tip, and only when it felt as though his smallest, finest nerves were being snipped one by one, and only when he smelled the burning flesh did horror dawn on him at the understanding that it was a welding tool. Caleb screamed, and despite the old man's warnings, thrashed as violently as his tormentor's grip allowed him to.

Make it stop! Make it stop!

The old man was smiling at Caleb, eyes full of glee. Was he even doing this to extract information anymore, or was that simply an excuse to engage in the torture he obviously enjoyed so much?

Even as the world faded out of existence and Caleb stopped screaming, he heard the buzzing of the welding tool, and he was grateful that he was losing consciousness because the pain surpassed everything else he'd felt up until then.

He drifted in a happier place, away from the torture room, away from the house, from the old man.

Away from Quinn and Tyler.

He couldn't tell how long that lasted. It was the feeling of something sharp being jabbed right under his eye that jolted him back to the real world.

After that, his mind sort of went into overdrive, and he no longer fully understood what was going on.

House of Decay

Eighteen

Basement Corridor

At the end of the long corridor, when Quinn's phone battery was down to two percent, she ran into an old, wooden door. A dead end.

"No, no, no, please."

She looked back where she came from. She could still see the light peering from some of the rooms, but she didn't want to go back there. Anywhere but the doll room and the place where that monster was.

She took a step back and kicked the door as hard as she could. The reverb of the impact traveled up her ankle, warning her knee with a slight pang. She ignored it and kicked again. The entire door rattled, and that meant something. It had to. She kicked once more and the door yielded with a loud crunch and slam.

Yes!

She ran inside the room and almost ran into the wall directly in front of her. She swiveled, but to her horror, it was a small, empty room.

No!

Her phone let out a ping. She looked down to see a message informing her it would shut down in thirty seconds.

"No," Quinn said, tears welling up in her eyes.

She stared at the wallpaper, soaking up the final seconds of screen time she would probably ever see. Then, without another warning or indication, the screen went black, and the torch turned off, and Quinn was plunged into darkness.

She let out a sob. She looked back at the hallway because that was the only place that had any kind of light. Sniffling, she put her phone into her pocket and sat down. She hugged her knees, buried her head down, and began sobbing while rocking back and forth.

I'm sorry. I'm sorry.

But she didn't know who she was apologizing to or what for. Erin, for ruining their friendship? Her parents for not being the daughter they wished for? All the people she hurt for not being a better person? Herself for not making better decisions?

Quinn contemplated her life. She'd never even had a relationship. She kissed a few guys (not counting truth or dare) and allowed a few of them to touch her in inappropriate spots, but it never went beyond that, and she never experienced the emotional crap that all her female friends were so happy about—holding hands, sending each other goodnight and good morning texts, cuddling together, all that stuff.

When her friends talked about the emotional stuff in their relationships, Quinn always pretended to gag at those things, but the truth was—and this was something she'd been aware of for a while now—she wondered what it felt like to be in a relationship. To know someone accepted her wholly for who she was, to wake up next to someone she admired. Someone who would help pick her up when she was down, someone who she could give all her love to.

She wanted to experience it someday, but she was also running from it because having a person next to you wasn't always flowery. To have someone care about you required opening up, sharing your weaknesses and imperfections, and Quinn didn't think she was loveable. Not with all the flaws she possessed. So, it was easier to pretend she was an ice-cold bitch who didn't need anyone in her life.

One reason why she hadn't entered any relationships yet was because of something she'd been grappling with for a while but refused to admit to herself because of social norms, and because she knew that if she ventured down that path, her identity would be defined by it, transforming her entirely.

Trapped in this darkness, it seemed liked the stupidest, most insignificant thing ever, and Quinn had no trouble admitting it to herself.

She liked girls.

No matter how hard she tried to make herself attracted to the opposite sex, it didn't work. It made sense, didn't it? It was why she preferred hanging out with guys. Why she liked activities for boys. Why she stuttered when she was in the presence of a cute girl.

It was so simple coming to terms with that here, away from judgmental eyes, and that made her realize how stupid she had been for allowing society to define what she should be. It also made her jealous of the gay people who were not shy about their sexuality. They got to be themselves during the best years of their life.

She lived in Oregon, for Christ's sake, one of the most liberal states in America. Why hadn't she been more open about it? The answer presented itself to her immediately.

Because parental raising and past experiences did wonders when it came to molding a person.

And now she would never get to feel love, never get to show her scars to a person willing to see them. She would die down here—or be subjected to a fate worse than death—and no one would ever know. Her parents would spend years wondering where she had gone. The police would convince them she ran away, given her history of delinquency. Maybe they would ask themselves if they could have done anything and why Quinn would do that to them. Maybe the false closure would be enough to help them move on. Maybe they would always wonder what really happened.

All in all, they would never get the answers they were looking for, and Quinn would be just another forgotten victim in a world full of cruelty, just another ID to be added to the stack in the drawer of this fucked-up place.

That made her cry harder. She didn't care if the monster heard her. She just wanted all of this to be over, no matter the result. She wept until tears stopped coming out of her eyes and her sobs turned to dry hiccups. That's when she looked up at the corridor in front of her. The light in the distance was still on, a taunting IV to keep her alive but not help guide her out of this place.

She looked farther up, and her breath caught in her throat.

High up, pale light speared the darkness. Quinn jumped to her feet. She turned to look at it from various angles. It wasn't just a small crack letting in a sliver of light. It was a *passage* up there. She'd somehow missed that, despite the cramped space of the room, the ceiling stretched upward at least... She calculated at least enough to get her out of the basement.

Her heart danced at the prospect of getting out, but it felt like staring at the exit blocked by an electric fence. If she returned to one of the previous rooms, maybe she could find a rope or something. Had she seen anything like that? Anything that would—

Her gaze fell on the craggy wall in front of her. Those weren't crags at all. She felt so stupid she wanted to hit herself in the forehead and laugh.

A freaking ladder leading up!

In her panic, she must have missed it when she first entered, before the lights went out. Now that her eyes were adjusted to the dark, she could see just clearly enough to tell that the ladder led all the way up—and hopefully out of the basement.

The wooden rungs were in a far from ideal condition. Some were rotted, some outright missing, and she didn't even want to think about the bugs that might be crawling all over it. It led out of here, away from the monster, from the doll room, from the dead body, from the photographs and newspaper articles, and Quinn didn't care that she would have to face that old fart with the rifle.

That courageous attitude diminished when she wrapped her hands around the rung that was at eye level and heard it creak. The ladder might not have been used in years. The door she'd broken through certainly caved too easily, so who was to say the ladder would be any better? She hoped her small frame would work in her favor.

"Okay. You got this, Quinn. Come on. You can do it."

She took a step on the first rung, shifted her entire weight on it, and it snapped in half loudly.

"Jesus!" she said, heart beating fast.

Well, at least it happened while she was still close to the ground. If it had happened somewhere higher up...

She tried to estimate the distance to the top. Fifteen feet, maybe? That wasn't too bad, right?

"Okay." She found the next closest rung, placed her foot on it, and craned her head to look back at the corridor.

And wished she hadn't done that.

The human brain is an enigma. It works miraculously when it comes to noticing small, subtle details that we don't actively register. It comes in the form of a gut feeling. Something that tells us we shouldn't take a turn into that alley, or that something is off about this person, or that we're being watched.

When Quinn looked at the corridor, she didn't right away notice anything wrong with it. It was just that feeling that told her something in there had changed, that something was... *wrong*.

She tried not to blink, but the burning in her eyes forced her to. And that's when she noticed it.

The way the shadows moved against the light seeping in through the closest room. That's when that strange shape in the corridor began to coalesce in her mind, gaining a form her brain was able to put together.

And that's when a chill prickled the entire length of her spine.

A silhouette of a bulky figure stood stock-still against the light, facing Quinn. A smooth, round head towered over wide, sloping shoulders. Arms hung too close to the ground, muscular, the fingers abnormally long and sharp.

Even as she stared at it, Quinn's mind somersaulted in attempts to create a scenario in which she could rationalize that the thing out in the corridor was just a trick of the light and nothing more. As if to confirm her suspicion, the fingers of one hand contracted, ever so subtly, enough for Quinn to continue staring, still in disbelief.

When the shadow began sprinting toward her, and when she heard the heavy patter of footsteps mixed with that familiar grunting she'd come to hate so much, she knew that her gut feeling had been warning her all along of a dangerous presence, and she'd lingered at the ladder too long.

Quinn screamed and raced up the ladder. The unstable rungs were not even in the back of her mind as she clambered up, up, up, just as a heavy body crashed into the wall below her. A frustrated bray filled the tiny room as Quinn heard the creature clawing its way up after her. She could hear wood snapping below her, one after the other, and she thought, *Good, that's going to stop him*, but the growling was only coming closer to her.

She was climbing as fast as she could, and she was aware that, at any moment, the rungs she was holding and standing on could break, and if that happened... *oh God* it would be game over for her because she would hurt herself so bad in the fall that she wouldn't be able to run anymore and that thing would be able to do with her whatever it—

Climb faster! Faster!

She expected to feel a hand wrapping around her ankle, pulling her away from the light she was so close to, back into that damp, dark place where she would meet her doom.

Climb!

The panting of the monster behind her was loud enough to drown out her own. In certain instances, it sounded like the thing was clearing its throat. In others, the sewage pipe noise its throat was making made it sound like it was choking on its own phlegm.

Quinn looked up. She was so close now. Just a few feet away from the ledge where the light peered from the open door.

Yes! Please!

The monster was still behind her—*how the fuck?!*—and unrelentingly climbing despite the persistent snapping of the wood.

Of course, it would have been too easy if this place didn't have obstacles to prevent her escape. Near the top, the rung Quinn was standing on with both feet broke under her weight. The only thing that stopped her plummeting straight down on top of that monster was the fact that she was gripping the ladder firmly with both hands.

She let out a small scream, legs dangling, knees banging against the wet wall. The thing let out a satisfied grunt. It was gaining on her.

Back in high school, she used to have a classmate who would put all the girls—and boys—to shame with her strength. Josie Sanders didn't look buff or anything, but when pull-up tests were being done in P.E., she didn't just hang from the bar as long as she could like it was meant for girls. No, no. She did actual pull-ups like the boys. She could do at least six before growing tired. She made it look so easy, too, pulling one's weight effortlessly using the arms.

But Quinn was never good at sports. She skipped P.E. as much as she could unless volleyball was being played, hated breaking a sweat, and the only times she used her muscles was when she had to carry a stack of plates.

She hoped that at least the adrenaline electrifying her veins would give her the necessary strength to hoist herself over the top, but one feeble attempt was enough to convince her otherwise. She couldn't even make her arms budge at the elbows.

She kicked the air, searching for a foothold, but all the rungs seemed to have disappeared. The top of her shoe found a broken edge of the rung, barely enough space for her toes, but that was just how much she needed.

With her leg assisting, she was able to pull herself up to the next rung, then the next one, and then finally, the ladder was no more, and she was elbowing the floor in front of the open door, basking in the beautiful, beautiful light in her face.

She would have let out a hysterical laugh right then and there had she not been clenching her jaw so tightly. She propped her foot against the final rung, and—

Sharp pain tore through her calf. The momentary pain that blinded Quinn was enough for the worst thing she could imagine to happen.

The monster squeezed her foot. Hard. Immediately, Quinn was sliding back toward the lip of the floor, all the while screaming. The hem of her shirt caught on something, and that was what stopped her from falling off the edge.

No!

A raspy sound escaped the monster's mouth. Quinn could smell it. It was the same smell from the doll room—a fragrance of cruelty and death crawling all over her.

Feeling the monster's touch on her foot was like feeling a cockroach crawling over her face, and she bucked against it as if she had been electrocuted. The monster's grip was iron, and he was not letting go. Realizing she would not be able to get rid of it like that, she focused on crawling toward the door instead.

She managed to get one knee up, but her other leg was firmly being held down—and the creature was getting ever closer. Quinn rolled over on her rear. She could see it from here—the veiny, hairy hand with claw-sharp nails emerging from the darkness, holding her firmly by the foot.

"Let. Fucking. Go!" She used her free heel to kick hard at the fingers, over and over.

The monster was unrelenting. Then the other hand appeared. Fingers wrapped around the top of the ledge, slowly, almost graciously. Quinn pulled her foot, again and again, and her shoe began sliding off.

Then, her foot slipped out of the shoe, hard. One second, the monster's hands were there, and in the other, she heard a rapidly receding scream before the crash at the bottom silenced it entirely.

Quinn was panting, staring at the scratch marks at the edge where the monster's hand was, half not believing that just happened. A triumphant joy came over her, and she screamed complacently, "Take that, you motherfucker!"

Just because she could, she crawled over to the edge, peered down into the darkness, and hoped she would see the thing broken-bodied at the bottom but still alive so the piece of shit could suffer. If there was a pair of eyes staring back at her from that pit, then Quinn didn't see it from the drowning darkness.

Then she realized how foolish she was being by gloating to the creature, effectively putting her life further at risk. She pulled herself away from the edge, stood, and once she was through the door, she shut it tightly.

Starve down there, you piece of shit, she thought to herself, hoping the lack of lock on the door wouldn't be a problem.

She turned around and began walking down the hallway. The pain that blitzed through her calf made her yelp. The burning sensation had been here this entire time, but she hadn't become aware of it until then. She tilted to take a look at the damage. A long, vertical gash ran through her leg.

"Ah, fuck."

Now that she'd become aware of it, she could no longer ignore the pain. It hit her with a debilitating strength, forcing her into a sitting position. She was bleeding. She had to take care of the wound as soon as possible. She'd probably need some treatment at the hospital later. For now, she just had to make sure not to pass out from the loss of blood.

A single door stood at the end of the corridor. Quinn forced herself on her feet and hobbled to it. The injured leg was the same one where the monster had taken her shoe. She opened the door, looked both ways, and was relieved to see a bathroom nearby.

She locked the door, leaned on the sink, and opened the medicine cabinet. She rifled through pill bottles, knocking some of them down into the sink. The loud clang made her remember the old man, so she forced herself to slow down before continuing.

All the pill bottles were empty, no sign of painkillers. There were alcohol swabs, which she snatched, and in a plastic cup, she found scissors and tweezers. No gauze or bandages in any of the cupboards, though.

"Shit."

The pain was pounding into her head, making it difficult to focus on anything. She grabbed the scissors, plopped down on the toilet seat, and sliced off the torn pant leg. It was drenched in blood. Next, she cut two strips off the hem of her shirt horizontally, set it aside, and opened an alcohol swab.

This was going to suck.

The moment she pressed the swab against her calf, her leg twitched from the pain. She pushed down a squeal that tried to come out of her mouth. Once that initial jolt of agony subsided, wiping down the rest of her leg wasn't difficult. By then, the pain had decreased to a steady burning.

She wasn't bleeding too much, which was good. She took one strip of the cloth she cut, folded it, and pressed it against the wound. She used the other strip to tie the first one around her leg. With that done, she tilted her leg and admired her handiwork.

Just to be on the safe side, she flexed and extended her calf, then stood to put some weight on it. After taking a few steps, she realized it was harder walking with one shoe on, but she still kept it on because she feared the socks would not give her traction against the wood flooring in case she needed to run. The burning sensation in her calf was still there, but it was manageable.

"Okay. This is good. It's fine," she said. "Now, just gotta find my way out of here."

She took the scissors in one hand and tested out which way would be the best way to hold it. They wouldn't do a lot of damage unless the old man was right in her face and she managed to stab him in the eye. Otherwise, they were useless, but she still felt safer than running around the house empty-handed.

She unlocked the door, her hand lingered on the doorknob, and when she finally opened it, a tennis ball wedged itself inside her throat. The scissors were uselessly clutched in her hand because the fear made her completely forget about them, although they probably wouldn't do much against the tall figure standing in front of her.

Just as she started to scream, the person rushed at her, clamped one hand over her mouth, and pinned her against the wall. Quinn clawed at the figure's hands, batted at its face, and when it spoke, it took Quinn a long time to recognize him.

"Quinn, it's me!" Tyler said.

Nineteen

2F Bathroom

When Tyler saw the terror in Quinn's eyes transforming to confusion and finally realization, when he was sure she would stop screaming, he let go of her mouth.

"It's me. It's me," Tyler said.

"T— Tyler," Quinn said in an exhale as if the name was a foreign word she was trying to remember.

"Tyler." She pressed her head against his chest and wrapped her arms around his waist, shuddering and sobbing.

Tyler stroked her back. "It's okay. It's okay."

But it was not okay. Nothing was okay about this. Fucking nothing. Whenever he closed his eyes, he saw that scene. The knife slicing through Gretchen's wrist, her choked sounds, the way she twitched...

Seeing Quinn sobbing broke something inside him, too. Tears blurred his vision.

Jesus, what did they do to deserve this? Why them? Why was it happening to them? Why did people like Rufus exist in this world? Wasn't it cruel enough already?

Quinn cried for minutes, and when she finally composed herself enough, she asked with a broken voice, "Where's Caleb?"

Tyler peeked into the corridor before locking the door.

"I don't know," he said. "I haven't seen him."

Quinn sniffled and wiped the snot from her nose with her forearm. She swept her palms across her cheeks, let out a stuffy-nosed exhale, and much more calmly, said, "We have to get out of here."

"What about Caleb?"

"No offense to Caleb, but I'm pretty sure he'd do the same if it was him. For all we know, maybe he did. Help might already be on the way."

Tyler shook his head. "We don't know that."

"That's right, and the longer we stay here, the more danger we're gonna be in, and I'm not gonna stay here playing hide and go fucking seek in this house in the hopes of—" She stopped herself and pinched her nose bridge. "Okay. Tyler, listen to me. The old man is not the only thing we're up against here. Okay? I was down in that basement, and there's something down there. Some… some kind of monster."

She hesitated before saying that last word.

Tyler chose the following words carefully. "Quinn, you've been through a lot. You're scared. I get it. This place tends to play tricks on our minds."

It probably didn't matter how he phrased it because Quinn snapped anyway.

"You're not fucking listening to me!" She gestured vigorously with her hands. "I was attacked by something down there!"

"Shh!" Tyler raised a finger to his mouth, eyes drifting to the door.

"Something down there did this to me." She pointed to the makeshift bandage on her leg. "So, if you want to stay here, fine. Be my fucking guest. I'm getting the fuck out of here."

"Let's just calm down, okay? We both want the same thing, and rushing is gonna get us killed. You think I *want* to stay here?"

Quinn crossed her arms and pressed her lips together.

"I want out of here as much as the next person, but in case you haven't noticed," *because you were busy chasing ghosts in basements,* "there's no way out of here. Every goddamn exit is blocked. There's no way out of this house. And that old man is crazier than you think. You have no fucking idea what he's capable of, Quinn. I saw a woman with her fucking legs chopped off. He's been keeping her here for years as a prisoner, using her for breeding like she's some fucking cattle."

At that, Quinn's features softened. "Oh my God. So it *was* him."

"What?"

"Rufus. That's the old man's name," Quinn said.

"Yes. How do you know that?"

"Because I found this."

Quinn pulled crumpled pieces of paper from her pockets and handed them to Tyler. When he saw how much text there was on it, he said, "What is this? Are we play-pretending that we're in Ms. Schmidt's class again?"

"He and his wife tried to have babies, but they couldn't," Quinn said. "They signed up for some IVF trials in a medical facility, but Rufus's wife died, so he set fire to the center, killing a bunch of people, including his newborn."

"Jesus."

"But here's the thing. Rufus was never found. They believed he died in the fire, but I saw his photo album. He made it out, with his baby."

"What?"

"Look."

She pulled out old photographs from her pocket. Tyler could see the resemblance between the young man in the photo and Rufus. That was him, all right. And as he sifted through the photos, they became progressively more disturbing.

Rufus holding a newborn bundled in some blankets. The man's expression was as devoid of life as it was in his old age. Then came a close-up shot of the baby in the crib in a dark room.

"What the fuck…" Tyler said.

The baby was all… wrong. The limbs seemed too long, too wavy. Large lumps covered the face partly obscured by the dark. The bones of the torso tented against the skin at odd angles. Subsequent pictures revealed the baby as it grew older.

A toddler with a hunched back and arms sagging to the floor. A few strands of greasy, black hair stuck like seaweed to the scalp dotted with brown spots.

A little boy crouching, body and face hidden by the darkness, eyes gleaming red from the effect of the camera.

A lanky... Tyler wanted to say creature because the word seemed more fitting than human. A body covered in patches of hair, completely naked, muscular, the exposed chin too long and too wide.

The rooms were always dark where the photo was taken, save for one where there was a close-up of the creature's face, eyes bloodshot, mouth wide open in a mute, rabid scream Tyler could almost imagine in his mind, spittle flying in all directions.

"That monster that attacked me in the basement," Quinn said, "I don't think it's a monster at all."

Tyler looked up at her from the photographs.

"I think it's his son," she said.

Twenty

2F Bathroom

"His son?" Tyler asked.

He hadn't taken his eyes off the last photo in at least a minute.

"What the fuck kind of…?" he asked before his sentence trailed. He returned the photos to Quinn. "You keep these. I don't want them."

She gladly accepted them. It made her feel a lot safer to have some kind of evidence on her even if she never got the chance to present it to the authorities.

She stuffed the photos in her pocket and said, "There are articles that mention secret experiments at the medical facility where Rufus and his wife did IVF. Maybe those experimentations made the baby that way. I can only piece the story together based on what I read, so I assume the medical center didn't want to allow Rufus to take his son home, and he set fire to the place and made it look like both he and the baby died," Quinn said.

"And then he ran away? Here?" Tyler asked.

"Yes. I think so. Maybe he went into hiding first, waited for the dust to settle before coming back to the house. If the police thought he was dead, they wouldn't be searching for him, I guess."

In Quinn's mind, that story made perfect sense. It explained why the old man was so hellbent on killing them, too. He had been in hiding all these years, and he thought Quinn, Caleb, and Tyler would expose him.

Except, one thing didn't fit.

"He's been doing this for years," Quinn said.

"Doing what?"

"Killing people. I found a drawer full of IDs and driver's licenses. People like us accidentally found this house and got killed by him. He's probably scared of getting caught, so it's easier to just kill people."

"No, that's not why he kills them," Tyler said.

"He kills the men. He keeps the women to give them babies. That's what Gretchen said."

"Who?"

"The woman who Rufus… she's a prisoner here."

Quinn gulped. "Where is she now? Is she still alive?"

Her first thought was that they had to help her, but then those two gleaming eyes from the darkness came into view, and the gash on her leg pulsated just a little stronger, reminding her what she was up against.

"I don't know. I think so, but we won't be able to help her," Tyler said.

"Why not?"

"Rufus cut off her legs. I watched him chop her hand off. She'll only slow us down. We need to get our priorities straight."

"What do you want to do?"

"We're going to have to kill Rufus."

Blinds fell behind Quinn's eyes.

"Kill him?" she asked.

"I know. I hate the idea as much as you do, but I don't think we have any other choice here."

"What you're suggesting is murder."

Only when Quinn said the word did she feel its full weight. The implications of such an action were never light. Even if it was ruled out as self-defense and they got to walk away free, they still wouldn't be free.

"I know, but I think we're past that now. It's us or him. And trust me when I say that, if we don't kill him first, he'll kill us."

Quinn licked her lips. It didn't matter what they did from this point onward. The events of tonight would haunt them forever. Quinn would wake up covered in a cold sweat, glancing around the darkness in her room, and she would think for a moment she was still stuck in that basement, and the heap of clothes on her chair would deceive her into thinking it was the monster.

"Fuck it. All right," she said.

Because what was added murder on top of a night full of trauma?

Twenty-One

2F Game Room

It was insane how such a big house had so few items that could be used as weapons. Even the cue sticks and the balls had been removed from the pool table in the game room. The dartboard was empty, too. Rufus must have removed all the objects Gretchen and the other victims would use against him, therefore eliminating the threat to his life.

Quinn was equipped with the small scissors, which Tyler wasn't confident would help a lot, and he himself was empty-handed. After searching a few rooms, it became clear they weren't going to get lucky with a weapon, so they had to make a plan B. It was a shame because Tyler had hoped there would be another firearm in a drawer somewhere.

Despite the house being in disarray, it would appear that Rufus had meticulously planned the layout of every room. This was his playground, and he knew it like the back of his hand. Quinn and Tyler were mice stuck in a maze.

"I don't understand how he never got caught," Quinn said, throwing her hands in the air after they were done searching a room with a baby's crib inside.

Tyler wished she hadn't said that because that made him consider it, too, and he didn't like the conclusion he came to.

"I guess he's just really good," Tyler said. "That's what Gretchen said about him, too. I didn't believe her, and…"

"And what?" Quinn asked.

And I thought it was fear speaking instead of Gretchen because Rufus had fucked her up so bad, but she wasn't exaggerating. It's the truth.

"Nothing," Tyler said because it was easier to keep his worries down. That way, they were less real. "I don't think we're gonna find any weapons, Quinn."

"What about a phone, then? This house looks like it might have a landline."

"It does, but calls don't go out."

"Are you sure?"

"Yes, I tried it."

"Maybe you did it wrong."

"Quinn…" Tyler raised a hand then stopped himself from continuing because he was at a snapping point. "No, I didn't do it wrong. I did it right. Gretchen said the calls don't go out."

"Okay, who the fuck is this Gretchen?" Quinn spread her arms and let them slap her sides. "Why are we even trusting her?"

"She doesn't have a reason to lie to me."

"How do you know that?"

Because I saw the broken look in her eyes, heard her pleading for death.

"She's not lying, Quinn," Tyler said.

Maybe it was his tone that made her understand he wanted the discussion to be over. Maybe she herself was tired of arguing.

"Let's…" she started before grimacing. "Let's make a plan then."

"How's your leg?" Tyler asked.

"Fine," she said, but it was clear she was in pain. "How do you want to take down the old man?"

"I don't know, Quinn. With that gun he has, we're gonna have to sneak up on him. He's bound to drop his guard at some point." *Isn't he?* "What time is it anyway?"

"My phone's dead, remember?"

"Oh, right."

Tyler checked the time on his phone. A little after midnight. A part of him momentarily got excited because he subconsciously thought he would get to go home soon because it was late—just like with any party he'd hated attending—but then he remembered where he was. No curfew in this place, no appropriate time to bounce without seeming too rude.

"So, the plan," Quinn said. "How exactly did you want to sneak up on him?"

"Just get behind him and knock him the fuck out," Tyler said.

"Great plan. You come up with that on your own?"

"What do you want me to say, Quinn?"

"Something better than, 'get behind him and knock him the fuck out.'" Quinn mimicked.

"You're free to think of something more creative."

That shut her up. She crossed her arms, pursed her lips, then said, "Fuck this fucking place. And where the hell is Caleb? What did Rufus do to him?"

"I don't know," Tyler said.

"This house is too big. I mean, who the fuck even builds a house like this?!"

People like Rufus, Tyler wanted to say, but he didn't respond to Quinn because he knew nothing he told her would calm her down. She needed to voice her frustration with their life-threatening situation—as long as it didn't draw unwanted attention.

She opened her mouth and sucked in a sharp breath of air in what Tyler was sure was going to be an ear-splitting scream. Quinn slumped into a sofa, exhaled, and massaged her nose bridge.

"Truth or dare," she said.

Tyler sat across from her. "I don't think dares are safe here. So, truth."

"If you could change one thing from the past, what would it be? Not counting tonight."

"I'd…" Tyler thought, and he already knew the answer because he'd spent countless sleepless nights because of it. He just didn't know how to phrase it. "I'd call my mom more often."

I'd tell her... tell her that I love her.

The last text messages between Tyler and his mom flashed in his head, and tears suddenly burned his eyes.

I miss you. I'll be home soon, she had sent him.

He never responded to it. Or the two messages before that. About a year prior to that, she'd moved away for a job to earn more money. That meant Tyler had to go live with his dad, and he only got to see his mom during the holidays, if she even got time off then. He kept telling her she didn't need to work there, and that he would get two jobs if he had to, but his mom did what moms always do—sacrificed herself for her child.

No one could have expected her to die so abruptly. The doctors had said she had "something" on her heart, but that it was most likely harmless. Then one day, she just fell asleep and never woke up, and Tyler was left reeling, alone, because his parents had not spoken in over a decade and his dad didn't care so much. He did try to be supportive, but the lack of genuine sympathy was more harmful than helpful, so Tyler ended up bottling emotions.

She's gone, and I'll never get to talk to her again. That knowledge clamped his skull with newfound potency.

He wiped his tears. "Your turn, cupcake." He didn't want to give Quinn the time to ask follow-up questions. "Truth or dare?"

"Truth," Quinn said.

"Same question," Tyler said.

"You can't ask the same question. You have to make your own up."

"Says who?"

"Those are the rules."

"Bullshit."

Quinn rolled her eyes. "Fine."

She paused, then said, "Considering I asked the question first, I don't know what answer to give you. There are so many moments in my life I could change. So many events that could shape me differently. For some people, it's a single thing. For me, it's about choosing whichever one did the most damage. You know?"

Tyler nodded.

"Remember Erin?"

"Your high school best friend? Sure. What about her?"

"I told you she and I grew distant, but that's not entirely true. The truth is…" Quinn hesitated. "The truth is I might have told her I liked her, and she… Yeah, she didn't like that."

"Oh," Tyler said, realizing the weight of Quinn's words.

What she had just confessed to him was a huge freaking deal.

"Maybe I'd go back in time and never tell her I liked her," Quinn said. "Maybe our friendship would still be okay. We thought we would be friends forever. We even gave each other friendship bracelets. I thought she would be able to look past my… difference, I guess, that she would accept me for who I was. But I underestimated Erin's religious upbringing."

She let out a chortle and her trademark snort.

"So maybe it wasn't a loss after all," Tyler said.

"Maybe. Her parents had polluted her mind. But in the end, she was old enough to decide for herself. And she'd made her choice. God fucking forbid that you hang out with someone just because of their… Anyway, there are far more important things I could change."

"Like what?"

"I would have taken school more seriously," she said. "Would have tried to get into a good college."

"Really?" Tyler asked. "Why?"

"Because I feel lost now. Caleb knows what he wants from life. At least for the foreseeable future. You seem to have everything figured out, or you simply don't care if you don't. I don't know what I want from life. I don't know where I'm gonna be in a few years. And it's terrifying."

"It's okay to not have things figured out, you know? I mean, just look at Patrick. He decided to turn his life around, so he did some courses for programming, and now he works for a good company. Last I heard he was also engaged. We're talking about a guy in his late forties with two ex-wives and a long history of drug abuse who kept bouncing from job to job all his life.

"It's never too late, Quinn. Sometimes, you need to wander for a while to find what you want from life. And you're right. I don't have anything figured out myself, and I don't care. I just go with the flow, and I worry about problems as they come."

"You won't be able to deal with shit as it comes all your life."

"That's a problem for future me. I'll deal with it when it happens. Why worry about something that may or may not occur?"

Quinn leaned her palms on the sofa seat. "Yeah. You're right."

"Caleb and I knew, by the way," Tyler said. "And don't worry, we aren't going to be like Erin."

"What?"

"About your... sexual orientation. We knew about it."

He didn't want her to think he was ignoring the topic, especially not one that was so important.

"How did you know?" she asked.

Tyler snorted. "Come on, Quinn. We're your friends. It's our job to know."

Quinn smiled. Even though she didn't voice it, she looked like she was feeling better.

"Truth or dare," she said.

"Fuck it. Dare," Tyler said.

Because could they really put themselves in any more danger?

"Okay. I dare you to get us out of here."

"That's a tough one."

"You can do it, or you can accept the penalty for failing."

"Not giving me much of a choice here, are you?"

Quinn shrugged.

They stood.

"Let's just—" Tyler started before a dull bang nearby interrupted her sentence.

Both Quinn and Tyler froze, staring at the door. A door somewhere creaked open and gently closed. It was him. Rufus. Now was their chance to ambush him. Tyler started toward the hallway, but Quinn grabbed him by the arm and shook her head. Now that it was actually happening, the fear was back on her face, a vast contrast to the display of anger just moments ago.

"Tyler, wait," she said.

"Come on, Quinn," he whispered.

"I can't." Tears filled her eyes.

"We can do this. We're going to end this now. Okay?"

He wanted to add some words of encouragement. Something that would reassure Quinn that this was no big deal and that they would take care of it quickly and be able to get out of the house, but even he didn't believe that. He knew well that they were reaching a point of no return—that they might have already crossed it unwittingly.

"He tried to kill us. We take care of him, and then we can leave this house," he said.

Maybe the promise of escape was what eventually convinced Quinn. Maybe it was the fact that they had no other choice. When she gave him a series of nods, he knew they were good to go—or as good to go as they could ever be, given the lack of preparation time they were allowed.

Tyler peeked out into the hallway just as another doorknob turned and footsteps followed. The direction told him it came from the room at the end of the corridor. The door was open halfway there, and the dim light inside that hadn't been there earlier confirmed that the old man was indeed present.

Tyler didn't move. Not yet. He waited to see if the old man would come back out. There was some kind of sound coming from that room, some kind of intermittent scratching or groaning, Tyler couldn't tell.

"Well?" Quinn asked behind him.

He raised a hand at her. He continued staring at the room, waiting for the old man to come out again. It was the way the door stood ajar that told him Rufus had entered the room to retrieve something and that he should come strolling out any moment now.

The longer he waited, the more he became convinced that wasn't going to happen. It must have been minutes, and the faint scratching was still persisting.

Tyler looked at the adjacent rooms. Some were open. He turned to Quinn.

"Okay, listen," he said. "If he comes out while we're in the hallway, run to the closest open room. Always have your eye on the room you'll run to in case he catches us off guard. Okay?"

Quinn's jaw tensed up. Her eyes flitted to the door, but a moment later, she gave Tyler a firm nod.

Tyler nodded back. "Let's take that fucker down."

Twenty-Two

2F Hallway

Quinn walked behind Tyler, giving him three feet of space. When they first stepped out of the room, she was practically stuck to his back until Tyler warned her it was not a good idea to be too close to him. If the old man came out and panic took the spotlight, Tyler and Quinn would be bumping into each other, giving Rufus an easy chance to shoot them both.

Tyler had also told her not to stand directly behind him. Spreading out was the best way to go when dealing with someone equipped with a firearm, he had said. Why that was, Quinn wasn't sure. She assumed it was so that Rufus would have a harder time shooting both of them.

As they crept closer to the door, Quinn became more and more aware of her own trembling breaths, which she forced herself to calm down. Something was creaking on and off in that room, a steady *creeeak-craaaak-creeeak-craaaak*.

Tyler showed no signs of stopping, and Quinn wanted to pull him by the hand, to tell him to slow the fuck down because it felt like speeding on a backroad. The steady creaking was right in front of them. In the room. A rocking chair, Quinn realized.

Tyler gave Quinn an encouraging look. He nodded, waiting for her to nod back, and the way his lips stiffened told her it was time. He was going to barge inside the room, surprise the old man. Then, all hell would break loose.

Except, before he could do that, the creaking suddenly rose like the person sitting in the chair suddenly jumped from it. After that, the sound wound down to a waning momentum.

Cree-craa. Cree-craa. Cree. Craa.

House of Decay

Tyler looked inside the room. Quinn couldn't tell what it was he was looking at. When he entered, she followed, eyes fervently scanning the darkness. By the time they reached the chair, it was still rocking, an echo of someone's presence having left just moments ago.

Giving the chair a wide berth, Tyler scanned the room for any signs of a threat. Quinn was clutching the scissors so tightly the rings were digging into her skin. Her heart was jackhammering against her ribcage as she waited for something—anything—to just happen because she couldn't take the suspense.

When Tyler's shoulders sagged, she relaxed, too. She could see the defeat on Tyler's face, but she was glad Rufus wasn't here. It didn't matter that they were delaying the inevitable. She was not ready for this.

She exhaled and looked at the chair. It had stopped rocking.

Quinn watched as Tyler's look of disappointment transformed instantaneously. His mouth and eyes shot wide open, and Quinn didn't even have time to turn to see what he saw. She already knew, though. Even before the concussive slam to her head knocked her off her feet, she knew what was coming.

Before the ringing subsided in her ears and the room spun back into view, Quinn saw a figure in her periphery running past her. Then there was a deafening *pop* right next to her ear that caused the ringing to renew. The smell of gunpowder that filled the air confirmed her suspicion that a shot had been fired.

When she blinked the vertigo away, she realized she was on the floor, head throbbing hard, and above her stood the old man himself, a wry smile on his face that confirmed her suspicions—she and Tyler had been outplayed by him.

"Thought you was gonna fuck with me, huh?" Rufus asked.

He didn't even bother pointing the shotgun at either of them. Some distance away from her, Tyler was lying sideways, clutching his—*Oh Jesus God*—mangled and bleeding hand.

Quinn quickly looked away, but she couldn't get rid of the sight of Tyler's few missing digits.

"Thought you was gonna turn that bitch against me, didn't you?" the old man asked as he stepped closer to Tyler.

Quinn couldn't stop her gaze from drifting to her friend. She saw details she wished she didn't see, but she also couldn't look away. A concave space stood where Tyler's ring finger should have been. That one took the worst damage. The tip of his forefinger was an exposed bone. His little finger was badly cut, but that hardly seemed like a wound worthy of attention compared to the rest of his hand. He was bleeding badly. The carpet was already saturated with his blood. His face was pale. He was going into shock.

"You come into my house, and you try to expose me?!" Rufus asked. "Oh, sweethearts, you have no idea what you got yourselves into."

His gaze fixated on Quinn, and she had to look away because there was something unapologetically hungry in those eyes, something that belonged on posters for women's self-defense classes. A predator exaggerated by photo manipulation come to life.

It didn't matter that Quinn refused to look at him because he knelt down in front of her, so dangerously close that she could smell the stale sweat on him. He grabbed her by the chin and forcibly made her look into his eyes.

"No!" she cried out.

"You came here at the best possible time. If you behave, I'll treat you well. And if you don't…" He smiled again, and Quinn caught a glimpse of his too-perfect teeth.

He grabbed her under the arm and, with one hand, effortlessly hoisted her on her feet. "You're coming with me."

"No!" Quinn said, pushing against him, but he was too strong for someone of his age and frame. This was the kind of raw strength that came with years of heavy labor, the unbeatable kind of power that no gymgoer could surpass.

Rufus pointed the barrel of the shotgun at the bottom of Quinn's chin. "You shut your whore mouth, you slut! You hear me?! You're gonna do what I say, or..." The barrel trailed down Quinn's chest toward her crotch. It lingered in the space between her legs. "I'm going to make your life here a living hell."

Quinn was crying again. The old man was talking as if it was already decided she would be living here from now on. Because it was. The corpse dressed as a doll in the basement came to Quinn's mind, and she cried harder.

"Please don't do this," she said. "I just want to go home. I promise I'll never come back here, I swear. I won't tell anyone about this place. Please, please, just let me go home."

The corner of Rufus's lip curved into an amused smile, and he curiously cocked his head. "You won't tell, you say? And I'm supposed to take your word for it and let you go?"

There was no sympathy in his voice. No understanding. Only mockery.

No, not only that. There was joy, too. Immense satisfaction he took from Quinn's fear. Seeing that, Quinn swallowed her suffering down. She decided she wasn't going to let him take delight in her agony.

"Fuck you, you ugly old piece of shit," she said because it was the worst insult she could think of in that moment.

If the old man took any offense to that, he didn't show it.

Footsteps rushed at them. The old man saw Tyler charging before Quinn did. Rufus shoved Quinn onto the floor and even had enough time to pull out a knife that seemed way too long before Tyler managed to reach him.

The scene in front of her eyes seemed to unfold in slow motion: Tyler bull-rushing the old man, elbows poised for collision in front of himself; The old man reeling the knife hand back and thrusting the blade forward.

The old man tottered backward as Tyler crashed into him, and for a modicum of a moment, it seemed as though Tyler was successful. But then Quinn saw the red blooming in his side where the knife was embedded, and terror dawned on her.

Tyler looked down, and only when he saw the blade sticking out of his abdomen did he careen away from the old man, crashing onto his back.

The invisible chains strangling Quinn released their grip, and she let out an ear-splitting 'No!.' Meanwhile, the old man stood above Tyler, the knife in his hand, half of the blade stained red.

"Dumb kid," Rufus said.

He stepped over Tyler, who was groaning in pain and holding his stab wound, and walked over to the door on the other side of the room. Quinn crawled over to Tyler and assessed the situation, but she had no idea what to do.

"Tyler, we gotta run. Get up!" she said.

Tyler raised his head and let out a moan, and it became clear he was not going anywhere. The human mind wasn't always practical. Even in hopeless situations, a small part of us keeps hoping for a miracle. It opens doors to crushed hopes and renewed pain.

Quinn kept shaking Tyler, begging him to get up, please just get up. By then, Rufus had opened the door that seemed to lead into darkness and was strolling back to them. It still wasn't too late. They could still run if Tyler just got up. They might be able to…

The old man grabbed Tyler by one wrist and began pulling him across the floor. Quinn had no idea what he planned on doing until she gave the dark room a better look and realized it wasn't a room at all. It was a shaft of some sort.

She jumped to her feet and lunged at Rufus. She might have screamed something to the old man about letting Tyler go, but she was too focused on delivering hits to pay attention to the words.

Rufus blocked most of Quinn's hits, and when he found a moment of room, he backhanded her across the face so hard she fell to the floor again. The burning in her cheek brought her back to the days when her dad was hitting her, a reminder that Quinn promised would ignite an inferno of anger should it ever come to that again, but instead, she just lay there, as defeated and as terrified as when she was a kid.

Rufus dragged a half-conscious Tyler to the dark door. Tyler's head lolled as the old man pulled him up into a sitting position by the collar of his shirt.

Tyler!

Tyler's eyes fluttered open, only halfway. He feebly put his hands over the old man's, but he was powerless to fight him off.

"You wanted to see what I'm hiding? Well, here you go. You can feed it," Rufus said.

With that, he pushed Tyler down the shaft.

Twenty-Three

2F Guest Room

By the time the hollow clangs that echoed throughout the walls stopped, Quinn couldn't get them out of her head anymore.

Tyler hadn't even screamed when he was pushed down. He didn't let out a single yelp as he fell through the utility shaft. That's what bothered her the most. Not knowing whether he died while he was unconscious or if he opened his eyes just before the impact that killed him.

With the silence taking over, it became abundantly clear to Quinn how utterly abandoned she was. Abandoned, but not alone.

Rufus stood in the room with her, the door to the shaft closed, all his attention diverted to her. She'd had her chance to escape, and she'd squandered it. It was too late. The only thing left to do now was to hope she would stay alive long enough to consider an escape plan in the future.

In what future, though? Would she even get a chance to escape? If so, when? In days? Weeks? Months? Longer?

She couldn't wait that long. She just couldn't. She had a life outside of this house. A job she needed to attend, friends and family she needed to see. If she stayed here, then…

The lid she'd been pressing down on the brewing panic this entire time popped out. Quinn scrambled to her feet and ran to the door leading to the hallway. She didn't care if she had to bust through concrete walls to get out. She just wanted—*needed*—to be as far away from the house and the old man as she possibly could.

Right before she reached the door, Rufus's arm wrapped around her waist. She bent forward and reached toward the doorframe, just barely grabbing onto the edge before Rufus raised her into the air and pulled her away.

"Not so fast, sweetheart," Rufus said.

She balled her hands into fists, but no matter how many times she swung at him, all she managed to hit was his back because he hefted her over his shoulder like a bag of sand. She continued hitting him even as he dragged her through the hallway. Then, she just gave up, acceptance descended on her, and for the time being, at least the panic was gone.

Quinn stared at the numerous rooms Rufus took her past, contemplating the helplessness of her situation.

"You done fucked up coming here," Rufus said. "But works great for me."

His hand was resting on Quinn's ass, squeezing it with a little more than just precaution. She catatonically remained slumped over Rufus's shoulder until he took her inside one of the rooms on the second floor. There, he threw her on the floor with such carelessness she slammed her elbow on the wood flooring hard enough to think she might have broken it.

"Don't move. I'll be right back," Rufus said before exiting the room.

Foolishly enough, Quinn hoped he would forget to lock the door until she heard the disheartening *click* of the lock. She didn't think she could feel any worse than she already did, but the silence in the room made the terrible finality of her imprisonment crash on top of her.

She was about to allow herself to cry until she could cry no more, but that notion was interrupted when she noticed the sticky blood on the floor at her feet. Her gaze followed the trail and…

Quinn let out a scream, which trailed to hyperventilating breaths muffled by her hand over her mouth.

A dead woman sat against the night stand next to the canopy bed.

Oh Jesus. Oh fuck. Oh God, God, God, God—

She was missing both legs. One of her wrists was dangling by a thread. Where the trail of blood ended, she was sitting in a thick, glistening pool, her clothes drenched. A horizontal ravine split open her throat. Her head was cocked sideways, eyes wide open and staring at Quinn.

Gretchen.

A landline phone stood above her. Quinn gingerly approached it, careful to avoid stepping into the blood and on the dead woman. She thought she could feel Gretchen's eyes judgmentally following her. With her eyes darting to the door every few seconds, Quinn picked up the receiver. She dialed 911, hoping for a miracle that never came. She let out a whimper at the sound of the dead line before putting the receiver back down and stepping away.

The door unlocked, and Rufus entered. He tossed a long yellow dress on the bed and said, "You'll be wearing this from now on. If you get it dirty, you get punished."

Her gaze alternated between the dress and the old man. Impatient, he added, "Trust me, you don't want to be like her. So when I say you put the dress on, you put the dress on. But first, you're gonna have to clean this shit up, and it better be spotless because this is your room from now on."

He was about to leave, but he lingered at the door with his hand on the knob and asked, "You hungry?"

As if the false courtesy would somehow erase the fact that he was keeping her imprisoned here. That he killed her friend. Both of them most likely.

"Suit yourself," he said before exiting.

Minutes later, he returned with cleaning supplies that he left by the door.

"I'll be back in the morning. I expect this room to be clean by then," he said.

The click of the lock was too loud, too final. This was Quinn's new home, it seemed.

At least, for the foreseeable future.

Twenty-Four

2F Bedroom

How long had passed? Minutes? Hours? With panic running wild and no clock to check, time warped inside that decrepit room. Quinn spent a long time huddled on the floor, rocking back and forth, praying to God to tell her what to do, how to fix this, how to put all of this behind her.

This was after the multiple panic attacks and after she tried using the phone a few more times to make sure it really was dead and after she finished checking every nook and cranny in the room in the faint hopes that there might be a way out of here. The only window in the room was covered by bars from the inside. She tried to unscrew them from the wall, but they were tightly bolted and apparently welded, too.

She would have thrown things around the room in a fit of rage if she weren't afraid of the old man's retaliation, so instead of causing a mess, she screamed her lungs out before dropping to the floor and continuing to sob.

At some point, her head began to slump from exhaustion, but every few minutes, she would jerk back awake because of the images plaguing her in her half-asleep state. The old man barging inside the room and threatening to shoot Quinn, her waking up to him caressing the inside of her thighs with his coarse hands, The dead woman blinking at Quinn from the corner of the room—just subtly enough for her to question her sanity.

The weight of her eyelids kept forcing her eyes shut, but every time she stopped fighting it, her brain would find ways to keep her awake. Then there was the sight of that yellow dress on the bed. An ugly thing that looked like it belonged in the sixties or something, but still pristine despite its antiquity.

Quinn picked it up and held it out in front of herself. It seemed as though it was her size, too. Something about that made anger pound against her temples. Her hands crumpled the dress and she tossed it at the door. The mild fit of rage did nothing to alleviate the emotions that had built up inside her.

The springs of the mattress groaned when she sat at the edge of the bed, defeated. She stared at the wall ahead of her then searched the room again without any particular hope. Nothing in this room even closely resembled a weapon. If she wanted to off herself, she wouldn't be able to do it, and that was probably exactly what Rufus had planned all along.

If the dead woman… Gretchen, had been here a long time, she probably tried every trick in the book she could think of. In the end, it didn't matter, it seemed, because Rufus had won.

Was this how Quinn was going to end up someday, too? Without legs? A dead body in the room greeting the next victim?

God, please no. Please, please, please, please.

The vise squeezing her chest warned her of another wave of panic. Quinn's gaze was pulled to the door, her first instinct being to bang on it and scream at the old man to let her out just so she could get some fresh air, please, she just needed some fresh fucking air, Jesus, she couldn't breathe in this room without feeling like she was inhaling noxious fumes.

She rattled the doorknob with both hands, tugged at it hard over and over, but it was no use.

"Let me the fuck out, you perverted piece of shit!" she shouted and banged on the door purely out of anger.

She kicked the door three times, letting out a shriek at the final one. The room seemed to absorb both her emotions and the noise she was making, trapping them inside this hellish vacuum. The silence was quick to follow. The only thing that interrupted it was an occasional rattle that seemed to come from the pipes in the walls.

Quinn sank into a sitting position next to the bed and hung her head down. She needed to cry, but her eyes refused to produce any more tears. Her head was killing her. Her ear was still ringing slightly from the earlier gunshot.

That fucking rattling sound. It just wouldn't stop. It had gone from occasional to persistent. A hum that slowly filled the room, grew in volume, and...

Wait a fucking second.

Quinn raised her head. The sound was much louder now and growing by the second. It had transformed from a hum to a... to a...

She looked at the window, and the light that washed over it made her heart skip a beat. She hopped to her feet and ran to the bars, fully aware of what that sound was. A beautiful, familiar sound that sang of normalcy, of civilization, of anything other than the unnatural cacophony this house made.

Quinn stared at the truck lingering on the road. She watched as the beams turned off and the engine stopped whirring.

"Hey! Hey! Over here!" Quinn banged on the bars. "Hey! Help me!"

It quickly became apparent that the driver couldn't hear or see Quinn, no matter how loud she was. Of course not. Of fucking course not. It was pitch black, and the driver was too far away.

She stopped trying to get his attention and waited instead, watching like a hawk. It had been minutes since the truck stopped there. Had it? Or was time simply too diluted in this house?

Please don't leave. Please, please, don't leave me here. Come on. Just step outside, please, dude.

Any second, she expected to hear the truck's engine coughing before it roared to life and then for the vehicle to roll out of sight, leaving Quinn all alone in this house once again.

Please please please.

He had to have stopped for something, right? If he stepped out for a smoke break, maybe he would see her. She wouldn't need to explain what was going on. Men were usually not good at taking hints, but if a woman screaming for help in the window wasn't an obvious enough sign to call the cops, then that person seriously needed to do some self-reflecting.

The trucker still hadn't left. That was a good sign, Quinn hoped.

Please God, let it be a good sign.

Maybe he just stopped to double-check his GPS before he left. Quinn knew this was probably the only chance of a rescue she would ever get, and she knew she was wasting time standing at the window like an idiot, not doing anything to get the driver's attention, but she was afraid that, if she moved even for a second, the truck would disappear. That, and her brain was mush.

Luckily, she didn't need to think of a grand plan because the door of truck opened, and a man stepped out. She couldn't see the features of the driver clearly from here. He was wearing a baseball cap and was slim, but anything beyond that was lost to the darkness.

Quinn watched as the driver placed his hands on the small of his back and stretched. He pulled something out of his pocket, and the glow that followed confirmed it was a cellphone. Quinn was gripping the bars so hard her hands were cramping up. What was the driver going to do?

"Hey!" she shouted and slammed her palm repeatedly into the bars.

The driver gave no indication of having heard her. His head hung down toward the screen of his phone before turning in the general direction of the house.

"I'm over here!" Quinn waved.

The driver's gaze froze on her.

Yes! I'm here.

Then he looked down at his phone again. His eyes lingered there for a little bit. Quinn thought she noticed his thumb moving across the screen. She knew—just knew somehow—that he was about to leave and that her only means of getting rescued would be gone.

Before she could process that thought properly, the driver put his phone into his pocket and began striding toward the house.

Twenty-Five

Unknown Room

From the shards of tattered, undefined dreams, Tyler rose into darkness. The lack of oxygen his brain was screaming warnings about made him gasp for air—and that breath was stifled by a coughing burst. Every spasm and contraction made his body flare up with inconceivable pain.

He clenched his teeth so hard his jaw hurt, and he groaned in pain. A rotten stench invaded his nostrils, lingering on his lips and tongue. He was lying face-down on a gravelly ground. The pain migrated from his entire body into three concentrated areas: his head, his right hand, and his side.

His hand suffered the worst of it. It felt like he was holding it in fire, and even the tiniest movements sent needles to the wound. He was starting to remember fragments of what had happened before he blacked out, and the only thing that stopped him from screaming was that abundance of phlegm stuck in his throat, forcing him to cough and clear his airways.

He was still alive—was he?—and that was more than he could count on right now. Or maybe the old man hadn't intended on killing him just yet. Maybe Tyler's torment was only beginning.

I need to look. I have to see the...

A part of him believed that it had all been a dream, that he wasn't really hurt. No way. The pain was there to convince him otherwise. He rolled over to his back, causing a momentary jolt through his side. The gravel crunched under him.

He couldn't reach his phone. Not with his hurt hand. He tried the left hand, but just getting it across to the right pocket caused an explosion of knives in his side.

"Fuck," he said.

He took a few deep breaths, bracing himself for another attempt. He knew the longer he stayed here motionless and the colder his body became, the more pain he would later find himself in. It was always worse later.

Come on.

Holding his breath, he managed to get his left hand across to the pocket where his phone was. He wiggled his fingers inside, managed to scissor the edge of it between the forefinger and middle finger, and pulled. Goddamn jeans were holding it tight like a vise.

By then, the wound in his abdomen was leaking onto surrounding areas, a warning of overexertion he could not afford. He refused to give up. He pulled the phone, little by little, and finally, it came loose. The residual pain in his side refused to let go right away even when he was relaxed on his back again. He ignored the gravel jabbing into his shoulder blades.

Tyler unlocked the screen and turned on the torch, illuminating specks of dust dancing in the beam above him. His hand was gripping the phone too hard to compensate for the tremble. He knew what he was about to see, and as much as he braced himself, he couldn't be ready for the horror that he was about to face.

He raised his right hand but didn't point the torch at it right away. The cone of his light was shaking as if he had Parkinson's disease. Inhaling a hissing breath through his teeth, he swiveled the torch at his wounded hand—and stifled a cry.

Although it was not as terrible as it looked right after sustaining the gunshot, it was still pretty nasty. Tiny pellets were stuck in the little finger, which was tolerable. His ring finger, however, was completely gone. Blown off right down to the base. The tip of Tyler's forefinger ended in a chipped bone where the last joint should have been. Miraculously, the thumb and the middle finger were intact.

Good. I can keep flipping people off and fingering girls, he thought, suppressing a hysterical laugh.

He was handling the shock of his mutilation quite well, he thought. Maybe that part would come later.

Shining the torch on his side, he noticed the congealed blood where he had been stabbed. He put his phone down on his chest, touched the back of his head where pain was radiating from it, but there was no blood.

At least, it wasn't all that bad.

Tyler thought about his life after this—a life with a mutilated hand. He would be earning gawks from people in public. Whenever they looked at his hand, they'd wonder what happened. Maybe he was a war veteran. Maybe it was a factory accident. Maybe he was born that way.

It wouldn't be all curiosity, though. Some would pity him. He knew that because he was the one who did it. When he saw people with missing hands or feet in public, he didn't see just the mutilation. He saw an individual who was too visibly different, too much of an outcast just because of his appearance.

He hated that for himself, but now that he was about to join those ranks, his mind was working overtime to find a rationalization for what his future was going to be like. Maybe he wouldn't need to be a victim after this. Maybe he would be a survivor.

The gravel was jabbing into his back too sharply. He turned on his side. Any thoughts of what would happen later were interrupted when he shone the light on the ground he was lying on.

Twenty-Six

2F Bedroom

Quinn could see him clearly from here. Despite the visor of the baseball cap concealing much of his face, it was clear he was in his thirties. He had a kind face, or maybe Quinn was manifesting that because she wanted to believe that anyone who could help her was kind.

"Please!" She banged on the bars one final time before the man disappeared out of view below the window.

He had approached the house. Oh God. Rufus was going to kill him!

She spun, eyes falling on the door before she remembered it was locked. There had to be something in this room she could use to get the driver's attention, before… before…

Four muffled raps reverberated from downstairs. Quinn froze. About ten seconds later, the knocks repeated, louder this time. This was followed by a heavy patter of footsteps through the house.

Shit shit shit shit!

Quinn pressed her face against the bars and peered down. She couldn't see the trucker from here. The *tap-tap-tap* of the footsteps changed to a deeper and slower tune suggesting a person descending stairs.

The knocking came again. After a few seconds, the driver came into view in the corner of the window, his back to the house. He stopped in the middle of the lawn and stared at the screen of his phone. The way he was using both thumbs indicated he was zooming in or out.

"I'm in here! Please! Help me!" Quinn slammed her fist on the bars over and over.

The man spun around abruptly. He saw her! That hope waned when she realized he was staring at the entrance, not the window. She saw him smiling as Rufus approached.

"Hey! Hey!" Quinn resorted to jumping up and down and waving her arms.

The trucker was pointing to his phone and talking to Rufus. Rufus briefly looked at the screen; then he put one hand on the driver's shoulder and spun him away from the window, pointing down the road and explaining something.

"Fuck!" Quinn shouted.

She looked around the room again. She grabbed the footpost of the bed and tugged at it. If she could break it away from the bed, she could mash the window and signal for the driver to get out of here and call for help. It was no use, though. The pole remained firmly fixed to the bed.

"Come! On!" Quinn's muscles strained.

When she realized it was a futile fight, she let out a frustrated groan and raced back to the window. The trucker was nodding while Rufus was still explaining something. When the old man reached behind his back, Quinn's heart stopped.

Rufus scratched the small of his back before continuing to point here and there in the general direction of the road. From here, he seemed anything but hostile. He was invasive of the trucker's personal space, yes, but his features had softened to something Quinn didn't even know he was capable of expressing.

Quinn banged on the bars again then rattled them hard, to no avail. If the driver could just turn around, she could try to signal him again. He just needed to look up, just for a moment. Come on, anyone normal would look up at the windows purely out of curiosity, right?

The trucker nodded, smiled, and Rufus slapped the man's shoulder. The driver put his phone into his pocket, waved to Rufus, and started back toward the truck.

No!

"Don't leave! No!" Quinn shouted.

Rufus looked up at the window, flashed her a wry smile, and sank out of view. The driver was halfway down the lawn.

Come on, Quinn! Fucking do something!

If she at least had her phone on her to signal to him with her flashlight. She had to do something. Except, it was too late already. The driver was already crossing the road. He was about to enter the truck, and Quinn doubted he would give the house another glance when that happened. It was over. She was stuck in…

The lights in the room!

Quinn ran to the light switch and flicked it on and off over and over. She had a perfect view of the driver from here. He was in front of the truck's door, doing something on his phone.

Oh come on! Fucking look up, dude!

She kept turning the light on and off, on and off, the clicking of the switch incessant. The lights in the room were too dim, but it was night, and the driver shouldn't have trouble seeing the flickering if only he would look the hell up.

"Come on!"

Rufus was on his way up to her room right now. She was sure of it. He was going to make her pay dearly for misbehaving like this, but it didn't matter. If she could get the driver to call for help, it would all be worth it. Even if Rufus decided to kill her before the cops came, at least, they'd know what happened, and the fucker would never hurt another soul.

Click-click-click-click-click-click, the light switch went, on and off and on and off.

The driver was still on his phone, still scrolling or doing God-knows-what. He put his phone into his pocket—

No no no no—

—took a step up toward the door—

"Look at me!"

—and as if he could hear Quinn, he looked at the house.

And he froze.

And he squinted his eyes.

Yes!

Quinn ran to the window so hard she almost smashed her face into the bars. He was looking directly at her. Finally!

"Please!" Quinn alternated between jumping, waving, and banging on the bars. "Police! Help me!"

The driver took his hat off. His eyes grew wide. He stood there on the step leading up to his truck, frozen, a look of shock and disbelief so clearly written into his face that Quinn could almost read the thoughts in his mind.

"I need help! Call help! That man's a murderer!" she shouted. "Please! He's keeping me imprisoned here! You need to call the *police*! *Help me*!"

She kept saying the words help and police by opening her mouth as much as possible because maybe he would be able to read off her lips. Maybe the look of terror on her face would be enough to get him to understand what was going on.

"Please! Police! Call the police! Call the po—"

The loud bang tore through the air even before the last interrupted sentence. Things happened in slow motion, and it took Quinn's brain a moment to catch up. As the gunshot occurred, the driver's head kicked back, slamming into the door of the truck. His eyes rolled to the back of his head as he languidly fell to the ground. Where his head had been, blood spattered the door.

Quinn caught sight of a smoking gun barrel under her window. Rufus lowered the rifle and strode toward the truck.

"No!" she screamed.

The driver was lying on his back next to the truck. He was still moving. His hand rose before falling back down. A pool of blood was expanding beneath his head. Quinn was sobbing and shaking the bars as Rufus approached the driver. He stood above him, rifle held in both hands.

Quinn couldn't see it from here, but she imagined Rufus staring down at the driver with a blasé expression. She imagined the driver's eyes wide in fear and realization that he was dying, unable to plead because he was choking on his own blood.

Rufus pointed the rifle at the driver's head.

"No!" Quinn's voice trailed through her sobs.

She turned around and pressed her palms over her ears, but it hardly did anything to muffle the second gunshot. She didn't need to look to know that the driver was dead.

Twenty-Seven

Basement

Quinn's words wafted into Tyler's head at hyper-speed.

I was down in that basement, and there's something down there. Some kind of monster.

He hadn't believed her. Had chalked up her words to imagination fueled by panic. Now that he was staring at the ground, he was becoming a believer, and one sentence ran through his mind over and over.

I'm not lying on fucking gravel.

He was lying on a pile of bones. He could have convinced himself they belonged to animals. Big animals, but that didn't matter. They were animal bones. Then he saw the half of the human skull that stared at him from the empty eye socket.

Human bones.

He had to repeat that sentence in his head multiple times because he felt that it was the only way he'd make it real. Like a slow-rendering image, the scene in front of him crystalized.

These are human fucking bones.

Wherever Tyler looked, they were scattered on the floor like confetti. Broken ribcages with morsels of decomposed meat still stuck to them. Mandibles with missing teeth perched on top of a pile of discarded bones. Humerus that looked too white compared to its tarnished counterparts. Unidentifiable shards decorating the floor like sharp snowflakes.

No matter where Tyler pivoted the light, all he could see was an ocean of bones. Dozens, maybe even hundreds, of people thrown into this pit like an amalgamation of a shattered skeleton puzzle.

Tyler inhaled for a scream, but it was as if he'd smelled chloroform. The stench made him gag and closed his airway. He noticed movement on the bone his eyes were fixed on.

Maggots.

Something tickled his ankle. He swatted it away. His finger came off as slimy. Flies buzzed too close to his wounded hand, probing whether they could land and feast on his flesh. His ears, the nape of his neck, his arms, all felt itchy all of a sudden.

He was crawling over the bones. He didn't know when he started doing that. All he was aware of was the morbid xylophone rattling of the bones parting in a path in front of him and the never-ending darkness, along with the realization that he was going to become just another skeleton added to the pile, each bone separated and his own body lost to oblivion.

A wall. He found a wall. He crawled over to it and pressed his back against it, the torch pointed at the mass tomb as if he was afraid he'd see the bones moving, assembling to their former shape.

"I gotta get the fuck outta here," he said aloud because he didn't trust his own thoughts unless he could hear them clearly.

Upon shining the light in all directions, he noticed that the room—to his relief—was much smaller than he initially thought. A trail of bones led toward a passage expanding into more darkness. That was going to be Tyler's way out of here.

He stood up but then suddenly felt dizzy from the pain. His side was on fire, and the pain in his hand returned, too. He leaned on the wall and waited to see if the wave of nausea would pass or if he would throw up. He spat the pre-vomit acid he could taste in his mouth and decided he was okay enough to move.

Two steps forward, and the pain throbbed hard enough to immobilize Tyler. This was it. He was not going to be able to move. He was going to die in this place. A slow and painful death where he would be aware of everything that was going on.

But then the pain faded slightly, and he felt good enough to keep going. The trail of bones grew thinner as he emerged into the passage. Blood smeared the floor and the walls, and it streaked the passage long after most of the bones were gone.

Someone got dragged through here a long time ago. Someone who was either freshly dead or still alive and bleeding abundantly.

And Tyler was heading straight into the lair of the person responsible for the deaths.

This is crazy. This entire place is crazy. I must be hallucinating. How the fuck else could this be real?

But then he looked at his injured hand, feeling the burning in his missing digit, and he knew he could no longer fool himself into thinking this was a drug-induced hallucination.

He stopped in his tracks when a thought occurred to him.

He could be dead, and this was hell. Or maybe the car crashed and he was in a coma somewhere, trapped in a dream state he couldn't wake up from.

Yes. That makes sense. It has to be that. It's gotta be.

The more he thought about it, the more relieved he felt. That was only a momentary passing thought, though. The chances that he was in a coma were not non-existent, but Tyler deemed them to be pretty low.

A car crash in the middle of the empty road they drove on? Not a chance. Tyler might have been a fuck-up for many things, but he was an excellent driver. Maybe he ingested something that put him in a coma then. Maybe it—

All subsequent thoughts were suppressed when he heard the growl followed by shuffling footsteps. He froze, and although a part of him screamed that whatever was down there with him would be attracted to the light, he couldn't force himself to turn it off.

Something snapped in the distance. Outside, Tyler would have likened the noise to a heavy weight being pressed on a twig. Here, the twig could only be one other thing, and he tried not to imagine it.

He could see how this place had gotten to Quinn so quickly. Things that couldn't linger in sunlight thrived in this viscous darkness, amplified by the eyes' inability to give them form. That's how superstitions were born. The human imagination had no limits. But everything—every myth, legend, stereotype—stemmed from a granule of truth.

That meant that the growl...

Tyler could have dismissed the noise as his imagination the first time he heard it, amplified by his fear. The house was old. The walls creaked, and the basement was full of distorted echoes. The second time the sound came, he could no longer continue to fool himself.

He listened, waiting for a monstrous face to appear in the domain of his light, but it soon became apparent that the footsteps weren't approaching him, but rather circling the area. Just before the shuffling faded away, he heard that throaty groan one final time, confirming that there was indeed *someone* down here with him.

For the moment, though, he was alone, and he never thought he'd appreciate it as much as he did then.

Tyler breathed a sigh of relief before his breath hitched. Something was wrong on a very foundational level. Something he couldn't put into words because he never had to use it but recognized it like the back of his hand.

The modern age put some evolutionary instincts to sleep because it propagated laziness. A sense of danger, the instinct for survival, knowing when we were being watched. Those were on standby throughout most of our lives because, unlike our ancestors, we didn't need to watch our backs every minute of the day. The echoes of those instincts remained, though. Dormant, but not eradicated. They were embedded too deeply in the human psyche to be erased.

As Tyler stood in that darkness, those instincts awoke. They weren't foreign to him. It was as if he simply hadn't used them in a while.

The hairs on his forearms stood straight. A shiver ran down his spine. Heat drained from his face, and he felt an undeniable presence lingering in the darkness next to him.

He couldn't move. He felt as though every small motion could trigger an avalanche-like reaction. But in the end, he had to look. He had to see what the source of that putrid stench was hitting him in the face on and off. He had to see whether the malice he felt in the air matched the watcher.

He pointed his torch to his left and immediately noticed the two orbs hovering in the darkness—mere feet from him. And when he pointed the light farther up...

The next thing Tyler knew, he was blindly running through the tunnels, his phone intermittently illuminating the path and plunging it into darkness. Snarling and the patter of bare, heavy feet were at his heels, but he could hardly hear them over his own hyperventilating.

Oh shit oh fuck oh fuck fuck oh shit—

He became aware of a voice inside his head teasing him.

If you think this isn't real, then why are you running for your life?

Passages began opening on both sides of the tunnel he was running through. On a whim, he veered into one on the left, planted a hand in front to stop himself from crashing into the wall, and felt an explosion of pain as his wounded palm touched the cold bricks.

Behind him, his pursuer skidded to a halt past the passage Tyler had jumped into. It would be upon him in mere seconds, and that's why Tyler didn't stop. He sprinted through the curving passage, scratched the top of his head hard on the low ceiling, and continued through in a stooped position, all the while listening to the bestial panting of the chaser behind him.

If Tyler had to slow down, it did, too. Tyler was a pretty tall guy. At six foot two, he was at least at eye level with most of the people he interacted with. The deformed person in this basement that his phone had revealed, though, towered over him by at least a head, and had much broader shoulders.

Tyler had no idea where he was running. All he hoped for was for the corridor he was dashing through not to come to a dead end because, if it did...

Luckily, the passages branched here, too. He jumped into one on the right side, deemed it safe enough to straighten his back without bumping his head into the ceiling, and broke into a sprint across the unidentifiable room that extended into another tunnel on the other side.

By the time he turned into the fifth corridor, he no longer had any sense of orientation. For all he knew, he was running in circles. The beast that kept chasing him had fallen significantly behind, and that was all that mattered. He heard it slowing down, the breaths carried in the echoes of this place growing more labored with each passing second, the footsteps slower, heavier, and more ungainly.

Tyler couldn't keep up the pace, either, so when he finally found a desk in a cluttered room to duck behind, he gladly did so. He turned off the torch and controlled his breathing while listening. He could no longer hear the thing that had been chasing him.

With his breathing normalizing and adrenaline going dry, Tyler was finally able to think about the close call he'd had with death. The events of the last few minutes were too dream-like, too impossible to be real.

He kept poking his head above the desk to glance at the entrance. The basement had gone eerily quiet, a calm before the inevitable storm. When he could no longer take the overbearing darkness, he turned on the torch on his phone and shone it at the entrance.

He dreaded the idea of seeing the massive figure of his pursuer standing in the doorway, but luckily, the cone revealed nothing. Good. Good. But he was a sitting duck here. The longer he—

Tyler winced at the pain in his wounded hand. During the chase, it was mostly muffled, but with the moment of danger gone, it returned stronger than before. He looked at his hand to assess the damage. Either it was his imagination or the dirt that had accumulated on it, but it looked way worse now than it did earlier.

His side was killing him, too. When he noticed the blood reaching all the way down to his thigh, he knew he could no longer ignore it. He had to patch himself up before things became worse. He just needed to stay alive long enough to get out of this place, and then he could seek medical help.

Bandages. I need bandages.

He didn't think he'd find any in a place such as this one, and if he did, then they'd be soiled. He stood on wobbly legs, gritted his teeth through the pain, and staggered out of the room. He made sure to pay more attention to his surroundings this time.

How the fuck did a big creature like that even sneak up on him without him noticing?

That's what worried Tyler the most. If it was capable of being so stealthy despite its size, then what else was it capable of?

He couldn't tell how long he wandered before he ran into what looked like a storage room. The floor was cluttered with all sorts of ancient trash. Tyler approached the rotting desk in the corner of the room and rummaged through the items splayed on top. One in particular caught his attention.

Duct tape.

Perfect.

He placed his phone on the desk with the light facing up and clumsily took the tape between his injured palm and chest. With his other hand, he located the edge of the tape and pulled. It made an obnoxiously loud ripping noise as he unstuck it. He bit the tape to tear it from the rest of the roll and tasted adhesive on his tongue.

He stuck the tape on the edge of the desk and stared at his wounded hand, bracing himself for what he knew was going to be a bitch of a task. The first thing he did was dab the excess blood off his hand using his shirt. Every touch made his injuries burn hotter. When it was done, he took the tape that he'd stuck to the edge of the desk and wrapped his hand with it.

The scream-inducing pain he expected never came. Instead, his mind replayed his final moments before he lost consciousness and woke up down here. Just before he got pushed down into the shaft, the old man had shot him. It all happened so goddamn fast. He saw the fucker appearing behind Quinn, a twisted smile on his face. He saw him whacking Quinn, too fast to react. He saw him raising the gun, pointing it right at Tyler's face, and…

His wounded hand momentarily spasmed with pain when he remembered that exact scene.

One moment, his hand was in front of him defensively. Then came the loud bang, and the next thing he knew, he was missing one and a half fingers.

That motherfucker. He was going to pay for that. This entire fucking house was going to pay for what they did to him and his friends. Tyler didn't care if he had to burn the whole fucking place down and die along with it, but he was not going to let anything in here survive.

He finished sticking duct tape directly across the stump of his ring finger, and Quinn popped into his mind. Where was she now? Did she manage to escape from Rufus? Did he kill her?

No, he would have other plans for her. She would take Gretchen's place, a fate worse than death.

And what about Caleb? Where the hell was he? Tyler hadn't seen him since he'd entered the house. Maybe he was so scared out of his mind that he was holed up in a hiding spot and refusing to leave. Maybe—and this was just as likely—he was dead.

When Tyler was done patching himself up, he stared at his handiwork. It took him three strips to cover all the open wounds. Clumsily done but more than enough to do the job. There was no way the tape would be coming off any time soon.

He did the same with his side, applying multiple crisscrossing layers to make sure the wound didn't bleed through.

"Hoo, shit," he said to himself when he finished everything.

He was leaning on the desk with his good hand, flexing and extending the fingers of the injured one to make sure he still had a good range of motion.

His eyes fell on the half-open drawer of the desk. He could see something in there through the crack. His heart fluttered because he knew exactly what it was.

He tried to open the drawer, but it was stuck. He tugged harder, and after the fourth attempt, it popped open with a loud banging noise. Tyler shone the light at the drawer, and a smile stretched his lips.

Inside was a revolver and bullets.

Twenty-Eight

Basement Empty Office

Tyler hadn't appreciated how much work his dominant hand did until he could no longer use it. Holding the revolver in his left hand felt unnatural, like holding it with a limb that was half-numb from anesthesia.

He still had enough fingers on his right hand to use it as his shooting arm, but he didn't even need to test the grip to know something like that, let alone suffering the recoil from the shot, would cause immense pain.

Tyler had never fired from a revolver, but he played enough video games to know the cylinder had to be opened sideways for reloading. All the chambers in the gun were empty, but there were nine bullets in the drawer. The revolver itself could hold six. After loading the bullets and snapping the cylinder back into place, Tyler pointed the gun ahead of himself, testing its weight.

Goddamn, it was heavy. His hand was shaking a lot, too. How did people shoot anything if it was so difficult to hold the firearm steady? Not to mention that in a situation of high stress that tremble would grow tenfold. Tyler would need to get really close to the old man in order to make sure he didn't miss.

He lowered the pistol and inspected it from every angle. The small hammer indicated it was double-action, meaning he wouldn't need to cock it after every shot. Great when more bullets needed to be fired in rapid succession, terrible for an amateur like Tyler, who would probably be wasting bullets like candies in a tight spot.

Nine bullets.

That should be more than enough. He reckoned that either he or the old man would be dead long before all nine bullets were fired.

The crash in the distance reminded him that the old man wasn't the only threat. Tyler preferred not having to look over his shoulder while searching for a way out of there, so the creature needed to die.

He checked the battery on his phone. 41 percent. Perfect. He duct-taped the phone to the right side of his chest so that the torch was facing ahead of him. That way he had a hands-free light source—and he could use his injured hand in case the need arose.

He stuffed the remaining three bullets that didn't fit in the revolver into his left pocket. If he had to reload during combat, he would transfer the gun to his injured hand and dig the bullets out of his pocket with his uninjured hand.

With everything ready, he raised the hand holding the gun, bent at the elbow so that the barrel was facing the ceiling. A distant scream of frustration rolled through the basement.

"All right, motherfucker. Let's dance," Tyler said.

*****

The torch on Tyler's phone skewered the darkness, illuminating the path ahead of him. The corridors were too quiet. Did the thing residing down here somehow understand the danger Tyler would pose to it with a firearm? Had it simply retreated somewhere?

This place was way too big. Too many passages, too many rooms. What the fuck was Rufus keeping here?

You must never go into the basement, Gretchen had told Tyler.

He was glad he remembered her words now that he was armed, and not while being chased by the thing. An invisible magnet kept pulling his mind back to the figure his torch had illuminated in the darkness. Every time that happened, he diverted his thoughts to something else because he was sure that the monstrosity he saw had been a visage of panic distorting reality.

When Tyler heard the clang in the distance, he didn't shy away from it. He followed it. He walked through a crude tunnel tarnished with old smears of blood. Ahead, the passage expanded, and he saw something other than the stagnant darkness pressing him from all sides.

Some kind of a red light.

He hurried toward it, the gun still at the ready in case something jumped out in front of him. A few times already, he became aware that his forefinger had slid over the trigger without him being aware of it. He had to remind himself to follow the proper trigger discipline, which was to keep your finger away from it unless ready to shoot.

As he approached the illuminated room, shapes came into view. Large, metallic structures that Tyler recognized as shipping containers sat in the spacious room. The dim, red light was coming from a light bulb hanging overhead.

Tyler's foot kicked something that rattled. He looked down to see a fat chain ending in an open shackle. His eyes traced the links spooling across the floor. They led inside the open container, one flap of which lay open.

That's when a wave of cold washed over him because he finally understood. That was no shipping container. It was a cage.

Tyler's mind instantly went to the videos he used to see on the internet of wild animals being released into the wild. It was always a cage like this one. Bulky, sturdy, heavy enough to require machinery to be carried. It had to be designed that way to withstand the sheer strength of the animal.

What in God's name was it doing in the basement of a remote house?

He already knew, somewhere on a level that was too shallow to register. The human brain was simply too good at dismissing the unfamiliar it deemed impossible. The gun in his hand suddenly felt too insufficient.

Tyler approached the cage. His heart raced at the thought of what creature he would find inside.

Empty.

That didn't make him feel any better. He would have felt safer knowing the animal was chained down here, locked in the container where he could keep it in his sight. Like this...

He turned around because he was suddenly overcome by that familiar feeling of being watched. He pointed his gun in front of himself, and this time, he consciously moved his finger across the trigger.

No one in front of him.

He was jumpy. He needed to get a hold of himself.

Composing himself, he walked past the container, slightly gagging at the stench that permeated the air. It smelled like a gas station bathroom, the kind where someone left a huge, soft dookie inside the toilet and pissed all over the seat.

A staircase leading up stood in front of him. *Finally.* Tyler raced up the steps a little too eagerly. To his dismay, the door at the top was locked. Bashing it with his shoulder did nothing. He contemplated shooting the lock, but it looked too sturdy, and he didn't want to waste bullets on what might end up being a futile task when he needed them for defense.

Defeated but determined not to give up, he returned to the basement. There were still so many corridors to explore here, so many rooms to check. There had to be a way out of—

A small *pop* and *crackle* ahead of him interrupted his thoughts. He had only looked down for a second, but when he raised his head, the red light was gone. Then came the unmistakable sound of footsteps—circling him, not approaching.

The sound of a shark biding its time with its prey.

There was a small rattle, just like when he kicked the chain. Then the footsteps morphed from dull to metallic. Tyler pointed the gun at the other end of the container, which was also open. Every step caused an echo to resonate inside the cage, to grow louder as it drew closer and closer.

Until it stopped just shy of the flap.

Tyler's hand was shaking too violently, and he knew there was no way he'd be able to align a good shot like that, but he was too frozen with fear to focus on regaining control of his body.

Just come out already so I can pull the trigger.

But it didn't happen. Even after a long time of waiting, nothing came out, perhaps aware of the firearm.

Tyler had been so focused on the cage that he somehow completely missed something else important. His left side suddenly felt too exposed, too vulnerable, and the darkness there coalesced into something palpable, something... deadly.

He pointed the gun at the darkness, his body still stiffly stuck in the same position. That's when he heard it. The patter of footsteps racing at him from the blackness. It was already here. Flanking him.

Tyler squeezed the trigger hard. The gun kicked upward with a deafening bang, causing a massive reverb all the way to his shoulder. The flash that went off from the gunshot was more than enough to convince him that he really was stuck in a nightmarish reality. He absolutely freaking knew this couldn't possibly be real because there was no way on God's green earth that the monstrosity that came into view could exist.

The thing let out a shrill cry. Just before the darkness returned, he saw the creature retreating into the safety of the shadows. He had missed despite the thing having been at point-blank range.

Footsteps were running away from his location, and as he ran back to the tunnel he came from, all he could think was: *Quinn was right. She was fucking right.*

Not an animal. Not a human being. Something that shouldn't exist, but it did. He had referred to it as a 'monster' even before seeing it, which was more of a substitutional moniker. The word was used for all sorts of things, even for people, but it was so easy to forget what that term really meant. It was supposed to be reserved for terrifying entities lurking beneath children's beds and closets. For things that were so scary mankind didn't dare to name them. For things that only existed in fairytales.

In the instant when the flash of the gunshot had gone off, Tyler saw a dirty, balding scalp perched above a tall, protruding forehead. The porcine eyes retained a hint of intelligence, or so it seemed to Tyler. Lips had either curled back or didn't exist. The teeth suspended above the gums that seemed too tall were brown. Not canines typical for carnivorous animals but oddly human-like. One cheek was more sunken than the other, the chin oblong.

Tyler had caught sight of a veiny neck, muscular shoulders, and a hairy chest. He didn't see the rest of the creature, but he knew that the word 'monster' wasn't an exaggeration at all. Not for the thing living in the basement.

He stopped in the corridor, turned around, and pointed the gun at the darkness where the pattering footsteps were raging. The creature was running here and there, apparently either disoriented or searching for Tyler.

"Right here, you fucker!" Tyler taunted it.

He knew he shouldn't have done that, but he was too high on adrenaline and eager for payback.

The footsteps went silent, only for a moment. Then, enraged, they began running right in Tyler's direction.

"Come on!" Tyler egged the monster on.

He supported the revolver with the injured hand and waited, waited, finger on the trigger itching. He would only have two seconds tops to react before the monster collided with him. The light of his phone didn't reach far ahead enough to give him more time. He couldn't hesitate when it happened. He couldn't—

The moment he saw movement appearing in the light, he pressed the trigger hard, muscle tense in anticipation of the recoil that was about to follow.

Bang!

The enclosed space made Tyler's ears ring. His hand kicked upward. Shit, he missed again because the monster kept running at him. He saw it in its full glory.

It was completely naked. Uneven patches of matted hair covered the body that was so muscular it would put a gym bro on steroids to shame. The abdomen, despite bulging with fat, was threaded with underlying muscles. The arms and legs were too long compared to the short torso. Tyler caught sight of an incongruously small penis penduluming between its legs.

The face of the creature was contorted in what looked like a mixture of rage and hunger, and its lack of stopping made Tyler realize one thing in horror.

Nine bullets were not going to be enough.

He fired again. This time, the monster's shoulder flinched. But it didn't stop. Just before lunging at Tyler, it stretched its arms out in front of itself and opened its mouth in a caterwaul that was partly muffled by the ringing in Tyler's ears.

The sheer weight combined with the speed of the monster was a deadly combination. The moment it crashed into Tyler's gut, he was picked off his feet and flying backward. Time seemed to slow while he was in the air. Then, with a jolting crash that knocked the air out of his lungs, his back hit the floor.

The monster was screaming, spittle flying into Tyler's face and eyes. He saw a hand with jagged nails swipe the air just in front of his nose. He put his hands in front of himself for defense and felt something scratching his forearm.

Son of a bitch!

The gun wasn't in his hand anymore. He'd lost it in the fall.

The monster put one dirty hand on Tyler's face. It used the other to pin his shoulder to the ground. Tyler batted at the hands, but they were too strong. He bucked with his legs, managing to get a few kicks in, but it did nothing to weaken the monster's grip.

Looking down, his eyes fell on the creature's dick. Might as well go for the weak spot.

He reeled his foot back and brought it forward as hard as he could. He missed. Did it again. He felt the heel of his shoe connecting with the sagging ball sack. The monster still didn't let go.

Tyler kicked again. And again. Only then did the thing finally back away, holding its oversized hands over the penis. Tyler rolled over to his belly and noticed the gun on the ground a few feet ahead of him.

He threw himself forward and stretched his hand as far out as he could. His fingers grazed the pistol enough to make one end tilt, but not enough to take hold of it. Had he used his uninjured hand, he probably would have been able to snatch the gun with no issues, but his hurt hand was missing one whole finger and the tip of his index, and his brain was still automated toward using the dominant extremity.

That one second would cost him his life because, in the next moment, he felt the weight of the monster crashing on top of him, the fingers digging into his back through the shirt for purchase.

Tyler knew he could only focus on one thing—he could either go for the gun or fight the monster off. He didn't stand a chance in a fair fight against it. It was too big, too strong, and too fucking fast for someone its size.

The only logical thing to do was to go after the gun.

Tyler dug his toes and fingers into the ground for a grip to crawl forward, but the monster was too goddamn heavy. He threw his elbow back, connecting with something, but if the monster felt any pain, it didn't show it.

The next thing Tyler knew, a hand manacled around his wrist, and his arm was pulled back. He screamed in pain but refused to yield. With his wounded hand, he reached forward. The gun was close. So freaking close.

The tip of his middle finger touched the butt of the revolver. Then once more, just enough to shuffle it less than an inch closer—enough for Tyler to grab it. His fingers crawled over the gun, squeezing it tightly. Then he rolled to his side as much as the monster allowed him to, ignoring the ever-growing pain in his shoulder.

He didn't even try aiming. He just pointed in the general direction of the monster's head and pulled the trigger. The flash went off, and a red dot appeared in the creature's chest close to the clavicle. Instantly, the grip on Tyler's wrist faltered as the monster tottered backward. It tripped, fell on its rear, and collapsed on its back.

Tyler noticed that blood oozed out of a small hole in its gut. It seemed that he hadn't missed all shots after all.

Just as quickly as it fell, the monster scrambled to its feet and ran in the opposite direction. It was no longer screaming but letting out sounds of pained whimpers.

With the support of the wall, Tyler got up, the gun pointed in front of him at the hip. He shone the light at the droplets of blood leading out of the passage. He took a few steps forward where the trickle turned into a streak.

"Yeah! Fuck you!" he shouted.

He was feeling too triumphant, too powerful. Cracking open the cylinder, he loaded the three remaining bullets into the chambers. Five bullets remained in total.

He could chase the monster down, finish it off where it was, but there was no need. The retching sounds it made were a clear indication that it was dying. And it would die in agony, just as it deserved.

He turned around, and sure the monster wasn't going to keep following him, strode down the corridor in search of a way out of the basement. A few minutes later, he found it—a small staircase leading up to the first floor. Once there, he dropped to his knees and caught his breath. When he looked up, he saw a familiar corridor meandering around the corner. He was close to the foyer!

Emboldened by this knowledge, Tyler staggered up and followed the hallway. Sure enough, there it was. The entrance. Right in front of him.

The padlock and the chains no longer seemed intimidating. All he had to do was shoot the lock, and it would fall apart. Don't even bother getting to the Chevy. Just bust open the door and run for your life. It would be *that* easy.

He pointed the gun at it.

A muffled bang upstairs snapped his attention away. Quinn. It had to be. Tyler looked at the door again. The exit was right there. He was so close to getting out of this. So goddamn close.

But Quinn...

He couldn't save her. There was no way he would be able to do that, he kept telling himself. Rufus was a trained killer, and Tyler...

He lowered his gun.

No.

He wasn't going to run again. Not like he did with Gretchen. Quinn was his friend, and if saving her meant risking his own life, then that's what he was going to do because what else were friends for?

He spun around, pried his eyes away from the door, and went to look for the stairs.

Twenty-Nine

2F Bedroom

After the gunshot that ended the trucker's life, silence took over. Quinn was too afraid to look anywhere near the window, so she sat on the edge of the bed facing the door, heaving in quick and shallow breaths.

She hoped that, by the time she looked through the window again, it would all be gone. The truck. The dead body. The puddle of blood. That way, she could pretend it had never even existed in the first place. The truck never drove by, never stopped by the house. She never called out to him and got him killed.

God.

She didn't even know his name. What if he had a wife? What if he had a child, for Christ's sake? Quinn didn't know anything about the driver, and neither did Rufus, but that didn't stop him from killing him in cold blood. The old man would probably check the driver's pockets. Maybe he'd find a picture of his loved ones in his wallet. Maybe unused coupons or membership cards. Maybe just money.

Whatever he found, Quinn was sure Rufus would discard everything except the driver's license and the money. Everything else, including personal mementos, would be torched or thrown to oblivion.

When she did finally face the window, a sob choked in her throat. The thick grass swallowed the trail of blood leading from the puddle where the driver had been shot toward the house. Not the dead body, though. The height of the grass could do nothing to conceal the sight of Rufus dragging the limp corpse of the driver under the arms toward the house.

Halfway there, he dropped the trucker carelessly like he was a sack of potatoes, wiped his brow, and looked up at the window. That look of sadistic enmity was back on his face, directed at Quinn. It was a look that said, "Just wait till I'm done here. I'm coming to get you next."

He pulled the body out of sight. After that, Quinn heard the sound of something heavy being dragged across the floor downstairs with an occasional thud that might have been the driver's heels or head hitting door thresholds or stairs.

She couldn't tell how long this lasted, nor the silence that came after. When she saw the lights on the road turn on, she snapped at the truck that was easing toward the house. Rufus was going to add the truck to the scrapyard behind the house most likely.

After Rufus parked the vehicle out of sight, silence came again. When she heard the door downstairs slamming shut violently, she knew Rufus was on his way up to teach her a lesson in obedience.

She wanted to look for a weapon, but it was too late. Footsteps were already stampeding up the stairs. Looking for a defensive tool this late would be like cramming thirty minutes before a test and hoping for a miracle.

Instead, she remained seated on the edge of the bed, accepting her fate.

What would it be? Would he cut her legs off like he did to the woman in the room? Rape her? Beat her up so badly she wouldn't be able to stand?

The footsteps stopped in front of the door. Quinn gulped, steadied her breathing, and braced herself.

When the door barged open, Rufus looked about as furious as Quinn expected him to. She told herself she wouldn't flinch or sob, but she couldn't help it. The hungry look in Rufus's eyes broke her with fear.

"Please..." she said.

Rufus's shoulders relaxed, just a little. The features of his face went slack, but it didn't make Quinn feel any better. She knew Rufus was going to punish her no matter what. The question was—how? Was it going to be a violent beating, or was he going to put her through mental torture?

"See what you did to that driver?" Rufus asked.

Mental torture it is, then.

He was going to guilt-trip her, which wouldn't be a difficult thing to do. The environment Quinn was raised in gave her a crippling fear of letting people down and being a fuck-up. Rufus was going to try to break her so badly that the shattered fragments could never be glued back again the way they were—and Rufus would be the one to put her back together in his image.

The old man closed the door behind himself, meaning he planned on staying in the room for a while. He tapped the barrel of the gun on his knee. Quinn gulped. She hadn't realized until then what exactly it was that made her so utterly terrified of Rufus.

It wasn't just the gun, the violent temper, and the ability to kill without hesitation. It was the crazed look in his eyes. The merciless, unblinking stare that made Quinn feel like a mere object in front of him.

Rufus hiked his pants up. He was wearing a stained t-shirt, pajama pants, and boots, which Quinn hadn't noticed until then. He must have slid into the boots the moment he heard the commotion. They were probably right next to his bed along with the gun, exactly for this kind of scenario.

Rufus's eyes drifted to the dress, which was still on the bed. When he looked back at Quinn, she knew she was going to be in trouble.

"I told you to put the dress on," he said.

"Please…"

"Put it on. Now."

He said it calmly but sternly, his voice dancing on the edge of impatience. The rattle in his pocket caught Quinn's attention. A ring of keys was hanging out of his pocket, tantalizingly close. Those keys would open every important door in the house, she knew that. If she could somehow get the keys...

But it was no use. Even if she did manage to get them, there was no way she would be able to make it to the front entrance *and* locate the right key to unlock the door.

"Rufus, you don't have to do this," she said.

She thought that by using his name she might evoke some dormant humanity inside him. To soften him up. It was a mistake. Rufus's eyes went wide; then he frowned as if Quinn knowing his name was an intrusion of privacy he didn't appreciate.

"If I have to ask you again, I'm taking your clothes off for you, and believe me, that's not going to be pretty," he said.

Quinn stood from the bed. There was no use begging Rufus. He wanted what he wanted, and he was going to get what he wanted—one way or another. Rufus didn't move out of Quinn's way when she walked around the bed to take the dress. She had to sidle between him and the bed while that objectifying gaze lingered on her.

From here, she could see that the color of the dress had faded slightly. She looked at Rufus as if waiting for his guidance or permission. She knew what she had to do, but hearing him say it made another sob escape from her mouth.

"Take your clothes off," he said.

"I saw in the basement what you did," she said. She didn't know what the endgame for that was. Maybe just to reestablish a fragment of control over her life. Maybe just to rile Rufus up. "The newspaper clippings. The driver's licenses. I saw it all. I know what you did at Riverpoint."

Rufus smiled. "You're a smart girl. But you don't know the full story."

"Then what is the full story?"

If nothing else, she was stalling.

"Riverpoint offered special treatment for couples trying to conceive. They said the success rate is high. But they didn't inform us of the side effects, and Margaret and I were too eager to have a baby to question them. We'd tried everything through traditional and non-traditional means. No dice. So, Riverpoint's highly secretive treatment was the only choice left.

"It worked. Margaret was pregnant. We were over the moon. But something was wrong. She was experiencing frequent pains. The doctors wouldn't let us see the ultrasound. And with the NDA we signed, we couldn't tell Riverpoint to fuck themselves and go to another hospital. So, we had to go through the pregnancy to the end. Except there were increasingly more complications.

"And then Margaret's water broke, and I rushed her to Riverpoint. And she died during childbirth. But the baby survived. The hideous thing you saw in the basement…"

"It's your child," Quinn said.

"They wanted to kill it. Said that, with all its deformations, it would never have a normal life. And again, the NDA stated they had a right for euthanasia in case they deemed the baby too sick. But it's my son, and I couldn't let them kill him."

"So you burned down Riverpoint and got the baby out," Quinn said. "People got killed in the fire. Other babies. Have you ever considered what your wife would have wanted?"

"Margaret and I wanted children more than anything. She would understand why I did what I did."

This man was lost beyond redemption. Not only did he commit murder to save his deformed child, but he'd been keeping it in the basement and killing innocent passersby over the years. Quinn could mention that to Rufus, but she was sure he would find a rationalization for that. In his own eyes, he was just a father doing his duty toward his child.

"Strip," he commanded.

No more delaying.

"Please," Quinn said.

Rufus turned around and placed the rifle on the vanity stand.

"Okay, okay. I'm doing it," Quinn quickly said in the hopes of dismantling Rufus's anger.

She took her shoes off first then pulled her shirt over her head and dropped it to the floor. She watched as Rufus's eyes softened with each piece of clothing she took off. By the time she was in her bra and underwear, the old man's mouth hung slightly open in a look that Quinn knew all too well.

Sure enough, his hand slid to his crotch, and he began rubbing his penis slowly. Quinn took the dress into her hands before Rufus interrupted her.

"No," he said. She looked at him, his hand still on the now-visible bulge. "Take it all off."

Quinn was shivering. The temperature in the room suddenly dropped by forty degrees. She was about to ask him to turn around, but the horny look on his face told her it would be a futile attempt.

She unclasped her bra and let it fall to the floor. Rufus's mouth opened just a little wider, and he stroked his penis through his pants a little faster. Quinn felt so violated with her breasts exposed to this old pervert.

"Keep going," he said breathlessly.

Quinn took her panties off. She knew what the old man was about to do to her. She knew how men functioned. Rufus was not going to stop stroking himself and leave the room once she put the dress on. To him, she was a fuck doll to help empty his balls.

There was something soothing in the acceptance of such a tragic fate. The moment Quinn embraced it, she stopped fearing Rufus.

"You're not going to get away with this, you know," she said as she took the dress.

"Oh yeah?" Rufus looked surprised by the comment, but that quickly turned into an amused smile. "How do you think this is going to play out, sweetheart?"

"Trucks are outfitted with GPS," Quinn said.

In truth, she didn't know if that was really the case. A friend of hers used to drive trucks for a while, and he said his boss once reduced his pay for speeding in a certain area. He had lied to the boss that the tracking thingy was not working properly and that it was incorrectly measuring the speed.

The question was—did it only measure speed, or could it also track the location of the trucker? Quinn assumed—*hoped*—for the latter because it made more sense. If that were the case, it would only be a matter of time before the truck was discovered.

"You know what GPS is? It tracks the location of the truck," Quinn said.

The reaction of shock she expected Rufus to display never came, which could only mean one thing.

"I wouldn't count on that, sweetheart. This location is pretty remote. GPS stops functioning long before a truck passes my house," Rufus said. "Did you see the road outside? Trucks aren't even allowed here. That dumb driver was probably late on a gig and was taking a shortcut through here."

"You're... you're lying," Quinn said in an attempt to reestablish that one small dot of control, but it wasn't working.

Rufus's words had managed to shake her belief that rescue was coming. Logic kept convincing her the police would arrive sooner or later, but Rufus was easily overpowering that logic.

"Sweetie, this isn't my first rodeo." He chuckled. "Now, why don't you shut your slut mouth and put that dress on?"

Out of ammo for any comebacks, Quinn was forced to do as he said. She unfurled the dress and poked her head through the neckline. It didn't smell musty like she expected it to. Pretty soft as well, indicating it was washed recently.

She didn't like the way the dress felt, though. Too much draft on the lower part of her body. Too short, as well, revealing a large portion of her legs, no matter how much she tugged down at the hem.

Rufus's face softened again. He approached her, and it was all Quinn could do to not recoil as he placed a hand on her cheek. He smelled so badly Quinn had to suppress a gag. It was a cocktail of sweat, blood, and old people.

He leaned into her neck and sniffed her deeply. "Oh, Margaret. You're so beautiful."

His hand slid down her clavicle, over her breast and nipple, and went lower, lower...

Quinn pressed her lips and eyes shut and prayed for this all to be over as fast as possible.

Rufus's hand went under her skirt, and a coarse finger touched her private part. Quinn let out a whimper, but she kept her eyes firmly closed and tried to imagine she was in a happier place while Rufus's hands glided over and squeezed her ass and caressed her folds, pressing harder and harder.

Think of something else. Anything else. This will all be over soon.

But she couldn't think of anything else. Rufus's touch was too painfully real for her to detach herself from this nightmare.

She was craning her head as far away from him as she could. Rufus might have seen that as a sign of submission because he kept kissing her there. Quinn's eyes fell on the rifle on the vanity stand. So close and yet so far. If she could reach the weapon...

But how would she do it? She needed to lull Rufus into a sense of safety, to make him believe the fight in her was gone. And when she was close enough to the weapon—

He grabbed her by the chin and pulled her head toward him. From this close, she could see just how blemished his face was. A constellation of moles and age spots dotted his face. Ridges were carved across ridges. The thin lines that served as lips were dry and tucked inward. The thick nose glistened with grease.

When he opened his mouth to kiss her, tears flooded her eyes at the sight of his dentures and the smell of dead cats wafting from his mouth. It didn't matter that she kept her mouth stiffly closed. His tongue probed her lips while his finger slipped inside of her, causing a jolt of pain.

The things Rufus was doing to her were supposed to be reserved for someone special, a partner Quinn would trust enough to willingly let her do these things to her, to enjoy the experience.

"Please, let me go." She cried.

She couldn't do it. She couldn't pretend she was okay with this even if it meant getting the weapon and saving her life. She just couldn't.

"Open your fucking mouth," Rufus said.

She did as he asked. He grabbed the back of her head and pulled her onto his lips. He stuck his tongue into her mouth, wiggling it around like it was a wet frog. This time, she was unable to suppress the gag. The area around her mouth was covered in Rufus's spit.

"Get on the bed," he said.

Something defiant inside Quinn awoke, the last line of defense before the inevitable happened.

She shook her head.

"Get. On the bed," Rufus repeated.

"No. I won't," Quinn said.

She tried to push herself away from him, but he held her by the arm too firmly. "Do as I say."

The fear, perhaps temporarily gone, gave way to anger. In that moment, Quinn didn't care about the consequences of her insubordination. If he was going to take her virginity, then she was going to give him hell for it.

Quinn spat in Rufus's face. The old man flinched and closed his eyes. He wiped his face, and for a second, Quinn thought that he liked her defiance, that it was a sick kink he had or something. Then his face contorted in rage, and he slapped her. Hard.

Quinn collapsed onto the bed. She felt strong hands grabbing her by the hips and throwing her in the middle of the bed. Her attempt to run was quickly interrupted by Rufus's hand pressing the nape of her neck, pinning her into the mattress.

"No!" she screamed.

She felt her dress getting yanked violently above her waist and a rough hand grabbing the inside of her thigh, spreading her legs.

"No! No!" Quinn bucked like her life depended on it, but it was no use.

Rufus was too strong.

"You can forget about me being gentle, sweetheart," Rufus said.

She couldn't see him from here, but she imagined him using one free hand to pull his fully erect penis out. How much would it hurt? How long would it last? If she stayed still, would he finish sooner?

Her head was turned in a way that she could see the rifle on the vanity stand, frustratingly close to her, still out of reach. She felt the tip of the old man's penis rubbing against her vagina. She tried to buck her hips, but it did nothing to slow Rufus down.

Quinn closed her eyes, bracing herself for the pain that would come.

Before it could happen, a deafening bang filled the room. The next thing she knew, Rufus was no longer on top of her, and she just faintly heard him moaning in pain in the corner of the room. Quinn opened her eyes and saw the old man holding his shoulder, blood trickling between his fingers.

When she looked in the direction Rufus's eyes were locked onto, she thought for a split second she was dreaming. Tyler stood at the doorway, pointing a pistol ahead of him, a plume of smoke billowing from the barrel.

"Payback, motherfucker," he said.

Thirty

2F Bedroom

Quinn looked different, Tyler noticed. Firstly, her lower lip was bleeding, but that was only a minor difference compared to whatever else it was that changed about her in the last few hours. It took him a moment to understand it was the yellow dress she was wearing. Jesus, how did he miss such a glaring change? Fear and panic must have been doing a number on him.

On the other side of the bed was Rufus, holding a hand over his bleeding shoulder and panting. It gave Tyler immense pleasure to see the fucker in pain. And Tyler was just getting started. The old man was going to pay for everything he did.

"Tyler!" Quinn shouted as she quickly scrambled to the opposite side of the bed of where Rufus was, pulling the dress down to conceal her bare rear.

The figure slumped in the corner next to Rufus caught Tyler's attention.

Oh no.

Gretchen. The look of terror on her face…

She was dead. Rufus had killed her. That fucking son of a bitch. And Tyler had left her to die. He had a chance to save her, and he had been too afraid for his own life to do it. And now it was too late. She would never get to leave this place.

She had said she wanted death, but the expression frozen on her face contradicted that. No one wanted to die. Not really. When they felt life draining out of them, any suicidal ideations disappeared.

"You killed her," Tyler said. "You fucking monster!"

"Tyler. We have to go. Now." Quinn tugged at his free hand.

"No. Not yet," Tyler said. "Grab that rifle."

Quinn stared at Tyler, looking like she didn't understand what he was saying; then she swiveled around until she located the rifle. She took it clumsily, the stock not pressed fully against her shoulder. If she had to shoot, the kick was going to be insane.

Rufus stood, looked at his bloody hand, and produced a raspy laugh. "You shot me."

"Yeah. And I'll fucking do it again," Tyler said.

Rufus's eyes grew wide. "No." He took a step around the bed, intent on approaching Tyler, but the way Tyler firmly pointed the barrel of the revolver at the old man's head made him freeze.

"Where's Caleb?" Tyler asked.

Rufus didn't answer.

Tyler white-knuckled the revolver. He was tempted to fire a warning shot, but he needed the bullets—*four left*—plus he wasn't sure if he would hit Rufus or not. "I'm not fucking around, old man! What did you do to our friend?!"

"You people broke into my house," Rufus said.

"Where is he?!"

"Tyler," Quinn called out again softly. "Let's just go."

But there was no leaving. Not while Rufus was alive. He at least needed to be bound before they went to look for a way out—and he needed to be bound really tight because something told Tyler the old fuck was slippery.

"You're going to come with us. We are going to the police. And you're gonna go to prison," Tyler said.

"Or what?" Rufus mocked.

In his periphery, Tyler saw Quinn aiming the double rifle at Rufus, but she was shaking too much, and her aim was low. Letting her handle such a powerful firearm was a mistake. She had never even fired from a BB gun, let alone something with as much recoil as a double barrel. Panic, closed spaces, and an amateur with a firearm all combined into a potential disaster.

He couldn't take the gun from Quinn right now, though. Rufus was too close for an exchange, but not close enough for Tyler to have a guaranteed shot.

Tyler got lucky with the shot to Rufus's shoulder. Too lucky. When he entered the room and saw the old man forcing himself on Quinn, he pointed and shot, but only now was it dawning on him that he easily could have hit Quinn instead. Aiming seemed so much easier in video games. In real life, even a slight deviation in the crosshairs could cause the bullet to stray.

But Rufus didn't know that, and as long as he believed Tyler could shoot him, he wouldn't do anything stupid.

"Or I'm going to kill you," Tyler said.

The words that came out of his mouth sounded timid and unconvincing. Rufus sensed this because he chortled.

"Really? You're going to kill me?"

He took a small step forward, just to show he could.

"Stay the fuck back," Tyler said.

"Come on, let's not fuck around. You're not going to shoot me. You don't have it in you."

"Oh yeah? I already shot that ugly fucking thing you've been keeping in your basement."

Rufus's eyes went wide with shock. He wasn't expecting that. Good. Let him feel a fraction of what the people he tortured and killed felt.

"No," the old man said.

"Oh, I did. Three fucking times. It ran away squealing and bleeding before it died," Tyler replied with a complacent smile on his face. "

Rufus ran at Tyler with a deep cry. Tyler pulled the trigger, but the old man had swayed to the left just before the gunshot went off. Rufus was too fast for his age.

The next thing Tyler knew, his back had hit the vanity stand, and he was fighting for control of the revolver with the old man, and Quinn was screaming somewhere in the background.

"You killed my son?!" Rufus hissed.

Yeah, and I'm going to kill you, too, Tyler wanted to say, but he was too busy wrestling.

Another shot went off. Plaster rained down from the ceiling. Tyler was trying to point the gun at Rufus's head, but the barrel swayed to each side too violently. One more shot went off, the vibration muffled by the multitude of hands on the pistol.

In the end, Rufus was stronger than Tyler. He'd been doing physical labor for years, and his hands were uninjured, unlike Tyler's. One punch to Tyler's face was enough to disorient him. The second one made him lose the grip on the pistol and fall to the floor.

Tyler's nose was on fire all the way to eye level where the sinuses extended. He blinked and saw the figure of Rufus standing above him, the barrel of the revolver pointed at him. This was it. This was how Tyler was going to die.

He put his hands in front of him, turned his head to the side, and squeezed his eyes shut, praying for a quick death.

The shot that ripped through the air was much louder and of a deeper tone.

Quinn.

She'd pulled the trigger and managed to shoot Rufus in the hamstring. The old man yelped as his knee buckled under him. He didn't even have time to turn before the stock of the rifle connected with his teeth.

Rufus collapsed like a drunk person. He wiped his mouth, looked at the blood on his fingers, and then he snarled at Quinn, revealing rows of red teeth. Meanwhile, Tyler caught sight of the revolver on the ground. He jumped to retrieve it before the old man could. Rufus didn't even try going for it. Not with the rifle pointed at his face.

Tyler was on his feet, the revolver trained at Rufus's forehead. He felt something warm and wet trickling out of his nose. He wiped with the back of his hand, and it came off red. His sinuses burned. He wondered if his nose was broken.

"Okay. Okay. You won." Rufus raised his hands defensively.

Neither Quinn nor Tyler lowered the firearms this time. Rufus was a snake, and Tyler wouldn't be surprised if the old man had more tricks up his sleeve—a final hail Mary to turn the tables.

Quinn approached Rufus close enough so that the barrel of the rifle was merely inches from his face. Too close because Rufus was fast, and he could snatch the gun away from her if he so wished it.

As if that very thought had occurred to him, the old man looked at Tyler, perhaps gauging whether he could take the rifle away from Quinn before her friend intervened.

"Quinn…" Tyler warned her.

But Quinn wasn't listening. She was rage-crying.

"You sick fucking fuck," she said through clenched teeth.

"Quinn." Tyler put a hand on her shoulder.

"Don't fucking touch me!" she recoiled and screamed so loudly Tyler's hand pulled away as if he'd been burned.

"Okay. Jesus, okay," Tyler said.

"Where's Caleb?" Quinn asked, her attention diverted to the old man again. "Where the fuck is he?!"

Perhaps realizing Quinn meant business, Rufus pointed to his right. "D—down the hall. Iron door. He—he's in there."

Quinn sniffled. "You were gonna rape me. You were actually going to do it."

Rufus didn't try denying it. One would think that a gun to the head would make a person concoct any sort of lie just to save his life. Not Rufus, though. Rufus was too proud for that. Even now, he was scheming. Tyler could see it in the look of indignation on his face that said he wanted to tear both Quinn and Tyler apart with his bare hands.

"Quinn, come on," Tyler said. "We need to find Caleb."

Quinn wasn't taking her eyes off Rufus. "We can't let him live."

"We can't kill him. We don't want to become murderers because of him."

"I'm not letting this fucker live."

Quinn wasn't going to leave until Rufus paid for what he did. It wasn't about their own safety anymore. It was about payback, and when Tyler looked at that remorseless face of the old man, he completely understood. People like Rufus didn't learn from slaps on the wrist. They just became better at not getting caught.

Tyler wanted payback, too. For his mutilated hand. For Gretchen. For all the other people Rufus had killed.

But was killing him really the answer? It was like throwing acid at someone using bare hands. Why cause damage to oneself just to hurt someone else?

"What do you want to do about him?" Tyler asked because it was easier to leave that decision in Quinn's hands. Because a selfish part of him that wanted Rufus dead didn't want to be the one dealing with the emotional fallout that would follow once this was all over.

Quinn cocked her head slightly. Rufus's hands were still up, eyes flittering from Quinn to Tyler.

Quinn lowered the barrel of the rifle at the floor. No, not at the floor. Tyler knew what was coming even before the explosive gunshot caused Quinn's shoulder to kick back violently.

Where Rufus's crotch was stood a mangled mess of flesh spurting blood onto the splintered floor. Rufus didn't scream. Not right away. He didn't even flinch. He stared down at what was once his penis. Then understanding set in. Tyler could see his chest inflating, and what started as a series of shocked moans quickly built up to an effeminate crescendo louder than all combined gunshots so far.

Rufus put his hands between his legs, screamed continuously, and writhed right and left while a fast-growing puddle of blood expanded beneath him.

Tyler's own crotch pulsated painfully at the sight. He was tempted to put a bullet in Rufus's head to end his suffering, but then his screaming started to wind down to whimpering.

Satisfied with the results, Quinn threw the rifle at Rufus's feet. Maybe she wanted Rufus to see his own weapon was his undoing. Maybe she just found no use for the firearm anymore.

With his spasming dying down, Quinn approached him, stepping over the puddle of blood. Rufus looked up at her with unfocused eyes. Maybe he was hoping Quinn would offer help to him. She kicked him in the leg to turn him over, which caused a loud but clipped yelp from him. She bent down, searched his pocket, and pulled something out that jangled.

Keys for the main door, Tyler assumed.

While Rufus was still dying, Quinn turned around and started toward the door.

When she noticed Tyler's inability to take his eyes off Rufus, she said, "He'll be dead within minutes. Let's find Caleb and get out of here."

Thirty-One

Torture Room

Quinn heard the moan long before they entered the room. A moan was good, she told herself. It meant it wasn't a threat. It could only mean…

Caleb!

In her haste, she brushed past Tyler and swung the door open. She and Tyler were going to find Caleb tied in a chair or something, she was sure. Beaten up badly, perhaps. Maybe he'd have trouble walking. Tyler and Quinn would help him. They'd get out of this place. They'd call the police. The three of them would be quiet on the ride back to civilization. Just the sound of Tyler's Chevy blasting down the road.

And what would happen after?

Those thoughts vanished from Quinn's mind when the door fully opened and she realized the scenario she'd created in her mind was nothing more than a childish fantasy. She thought she had overestimated Rufus's cruelty because that made it easier to deal with the reality of his evil. The truth was—and this is what she realized when she saw Caleb—she had vastly underestimated just how far Rufus's malevolence stretched.

"Oh. Oh my God." Quinn put her hands over her mouth and nose.

Tyler peeked over her shoulder, and he whispered, "Oh fuck."

Quinn blinked, waiting for the horror to disappear because this had to be a conjuration of her own mind, because there had to be a limit to the depravity in this world.

Caleb raised his head and produced a small moan. It was difficult to see everything that had been done to him, but Quinn's eyes swept over the details nonetheless.

Caleb's face was a roadmap of deep, crisscrossing scars. Only one eye stared at Quinn. The other was a socket with a soupy mess that trickled down his cheek. His lower lip had been sliced off in a crescent, revealing gums with crooked and missing teeth.

The thumb and forefinger on his hand ended in short, messy stumps. The other three were a bumpy, broken mass with nails jutting upward from the beds. Skin peeled off his shoulder like a banana all the way down to his elbow. He had cuts all over his body. A dark, concave circle covered one nipple. A foot lay forlornly in the corner of the room, detached from Caleb's ankle, the stump of which was blackened and smoking.

At the sight of that, Quinn smelled the distinct stench of burned meat. She turned away from the sight and cried silently. She wiped her tears, took a few breaths as deeply as her tightened lungs allowed her to, and turned toward Caleb again because, no matter how difficult this was, he needed their help now more than ever.

"Caleb. We're gonna get you out of here, okay?" she said. Shallow words of comfort that would do nothing to blunt Caleb's suffering.

Caleb raised his head again and said something. It sounded like "ease" or "these." He had to say it a few times for the terrible truth to set in. The little pink morsel on the floor in front of Caleb's face confirmed that, and Quinn had to physically stop herself from screaming.

"Phease." *Please.*

But he couldn't say the word properly because his tongue had been cut out.

Oh God. Why. Why.

Tools were scattered all over the floor, stained with blood, letting Quinn imagine what had been done to Caleb more vividly than she ever asked for.

It was impossible to tell how long they had been standing there, staring at the remains of their friend. It was Tyler who made the first move, and Quinn was glad he did because she didn't know if she ever would have been able to budge.

"Hey. Caleb." Tyler got down on one knee in front of Caleb. "We're here. We came to get you out. We..."

Caleb whimpered. It was the sound of a badly wounded animal.

"I know. I know," Tyler said, his voice strained despite his attempt to stay calm. "You're going to be okay. We're going to..."

He didn't finish that sentence because, like Quinn, he knew any dispensed words would be an empty promise. There was no going back from this. Not for Caleb.

"Phease... Kih ee. Kih ee."

He kept saying those two words over and over. When Quinn finally understood what he had been saying, she broke down with an uncontrolled sobbing fit.

Kill me.

"Tyler." Quinn put a hand on his shoulder, suppressing a choking sob. "Tyler."

He turned around. His eyes were red-rimmed and glistening with tears. He stood, wiped them, and turned away from Caleb.

"What are we gonna do?" he asked.

"We... we have to..." she started but couldn't bring herself to finish the sentence. "We have to..."

Tyler's features went taut, but then he nodded.

Thank God.

They looked down at the pistol in his hand. He opened the barrel-looking thing in the middle and revealed a bullet nestled inside one of the six holes.

"This... this is the last one," Tyler said.

His voice was shaky. Quinn had never heard him like this, so vulnerable and defeated.

She nodded. "Okay. Okay. It'll be quick for him, right?"

"Kih ee. Phease," Caleb kept saying, his voice tenuous.

Tyler looked over his shoulder at Caleb then back at Quinn. "Are we really doing this?"

Are we? Are we really killing our friend? Quinn asked herself because she herself couldn't come to terms with it, especially now that it was becoming so real.

"It's what he wants," Quinn said.

"But is that what's really best for him?" Tyler asked.

"Look at him, Tyler. He…" Quinn pressed her hand against her lips. "He's dying. He's suffering. The least we can do is… is make it easier for him. We owe him that much. For…"

For getting him in this situation.

Tyler nodded. "Okay. You're right. You're right."

He popped the rotating thing back into the gun. His hand was badly shaking.

"You don't have to watch this," he said.

But Quinn had to. In his final moments, she wanted to be there for Caleb, for him to see a comforting and familiar face. For him to not die alone.

"I'm staying," she said.

Tyler didn't argue with that. He slowly turned to face Caleb. "Caleb? Buddy, it's gonna be all right. It'll be over soon. Okay?"

Caleb's eye was closed. He was making pained noises that sounded oddly similar to what Quinn heard heavily drunk people mumbling in the streets. Tyler pointed the gun at Caleb's face. Caleb's eye opened, and it seemed as though his suffering left no room for fear. If anything, Quinn would have assumed he was eager for it all to be over.

"I'm sorry, buddy," Tyler said, shuddering. "I'm so sorry."

He closed his eyes and looked away. Quinn had been determined to keep looking, in case Caleb searched for her face, but she couldn't do it. She put her hands over her ears and looked away.

When the echo of the gunshot receded and the moaning went mute, Quinn knew the act was irreversibly over.

Boris Bacic

Thirty-Two

2F Hallway

They cried for a long time outside that torture room. Then they sat in silence with seemingly no urgency of leaving.

"A trucker stopped here earlier," Quinn said after what felt like hours. Her voice was hoarse and quiet. "I tried to call to him, to get him to help me, and..." She squeezed her eyes and lips. After a shuddering gasp, she said, "Rufus killed him. Because of me."

She couldn't stop crying after that. Tyler stroked her back, but he didn't say anything. He didn't know what to tell her except maybe offer hollow words of comfort.

When she finally calmed down sufficiently, he said, "Rufus killed Gretchen because of me. I had a chance to save her, but I ran because I was scared. If only I had..."

He felt tears returning, so he shook his head. Silence stretched between them a moment longer.

"What are we going to do with Caleb?" Quinn asked.

"What *can* we do?" Tyler asked.

"We can't just leave him here."

But that's exactly what Tyler thought they should do. The person in the room behind them wasn't Caleb anymore. It was a dead body. The more they focused on it, the more that image of Caleb would etch itself in their minds, and he wouldn't have wanted to be remembered as that defiled carcass.

"We'll come back for him," Tyler lied because he had no intention of ever returning to this place. Once they call the police, they would take care of the dead bodies. Caleb's, Gretchen's, and anyone else's.

"I... I can't stay here any longer. I'm going crazy," Quinn said.

"Yeah. Yeah." Tyler nodded. "Are the keys on you?"

She raised the ring of keys for Tyler to see.

"Then let's go." Tyler stood and helped Quinn to her feet.

She was still in the yellow dress. The distant thought of cracking a joke about how she looked in it died well before it sprouted into a bud because nothing about this place or situation was humor-worthy.

"You wanna get your clothes?" he asked.

"I just want to get out of here," Quinn said. "Please."

"Okay. Yeah."

They sauntered down the stairs like a pair of zombies. It took them about ten minutes and a few times getting lost to find the main entrance. Quinn bounced the keys in her palm.

"What are we going to tell the police?" she asked.

"What do you mean? We'll tell them the truth." Tyler shrugged.

"Think they'll believe us? A crazy story like this?"

"They'll have to verify it. When they enter this place…" He nodded to himself. "They'll know."

Quinn raised her head and massaged her shoulder. She picked a key from the chain, inched it to the lock, and—

A cough escaped down the hallway to their left, too real to be ignored. Tyler and Quinn exchanged a quizzical look. Then, their eyes shifted to the source of the noise. Quinn gasped.

A figure stood in the corridor to the left of the foyer. Tyler was sure he was hallucinating. He had to be.

It was Rufus.

His crotch and the inside of his thighs were drenched in blood, but he was *standing*. And moreover, the hauntingly sadistic look was back on his face as if he had been just warming up.

For the longest time, they stood there, locked in a staring contest. Then, Quinn threw the keys on the floor. Tyler could tell what she was about to do because of the way her shoulders tensed up and her hands balled into fists.

"Quinn, don't," Tyler said. "Just leave him be. The police will get him."

But that's not what Tyler feared. What scared him was Rufus's cunning—the way he just stood there, taunting them to come closer, the corner of his lip curved into an effervescent smile. A trap, no doubt.

"Quinn..." Tyler said.

"You fucker!" Quinn jackknifed into a stride at the old man.

"Quinn!" Tyler grabbed her by the shoulder, but his hand slid off, and Quinn continued ambling at Rufus.

"He's dead! You fucking killed him!" she cried out.

Tyler ran after her, pleading with her to turn back, but Quinn wasn't hearing him. She was a speeding train, and the brakes were not working.

Rufus wasn't budging. The smile on his face grew wider. What the fuck was he planning?

By the time he noticed the shadow slinking toward Quinn from the side and the heavy footsteps stamping closer and closer, Tyler was too far to pull her out of danger's way.

"You murderous fucking—"

Her words came to an abrupt stop when a massive figure crashed into her. Her shoulder smashed into the wall, making her slide to the floor, and causing a framed picture to crash down. Shards of glass spilled on the floor. A satisfied titter erupted from Rufus's mouth.

The figure that barreled into Quinn now stood directly below the ceiling light in all its glory.

It was even more intimidating now than it had been in the basement. It seemed unbothered by the bullet holes Tyler had inflicted it with. From this view, it was clear that it wasn't a monster at all. It was merely a feral, disfigured human being, made this way by Rufus.

When their eyes met, Tyler thought he detected the faintest glimmer of intelligence and rational thinking, something that would allow them to resolve this diplomatically, not using violence. But any traces of humanity that might have existed there were wiped out by Rufus when he shoved the creature down into the basement and raised it like an animal.

There was no capacity there for existential crises or dilemmas. Only an insatiable rage toward living things appalled by its grotesque appearance. It was Rufus incarnate, his child in the true sense of the word.

With Quinn's head lolling as she was close to fading out of consciousness, all attention of the creature was focused on Tyler. He bent his knees and got ready to run. He wished he still had the revolver with him, even if it was empty. Maybe pointing it at the creature would remind it of the pain it caused to it, therefore causing it to retreat.

Quinn blinked a few times, regained her focus, and when she looked up at the monstrosity standing above her, she screamed and pushed her back harder into the wall.

That caught the creature's attention. Its head snapped at her; its upper lip rose in annoyance and what looked like disgust. It roared, raised its hands to its ears, then grabbed Quinn by the neck. Her screams trailed to a choke as the monster raised her to her feet, squeezing her throat.

Tyler sprinted at it. Crashing into it felt like crashing into a wall of flesh. The creature barely even budged. It let out a huff and swatted at Tyler with one hand, but Tyler put its neck into an armlock.

Years ago, Tyler's cousin who was serving overseas in the Marines taught him how to do an arm and head lock. Using the proper technique, even someone with little physical strength would be able to cause the opponent to tap out.

Not this creature, though. Its neck was too thick, too muscular. It felt like strangling a log. Tyler tried in earnest to wrestle the thing to the floor, but even that couldn't make it budge.

The creature had raised Quinn above its head. Her back was pressed against the wall, face red and neck squeezed so hard veins bulged on her forehead. She was batting at the monster's arms, kicking her feet, but it was doing nothing to weaken its grip. Her mouth was making strained sounds similar to rope being stretched taut. Her flailing had weakened significantly. Her eyes had rolled into the back of her head.

Tyler released the headlock. He found the bullet hole in the creature's shoulder and pressed his thumb into it as deeply and as hard as he could. The thing bellowed. That finally got its attention, but only for a second.

The massive hand that slapped Tyler caused him to not only collapse on the floor but also whack the back of his head hard enough for the room to start spinning.

He blinked the vertigo away and propped himself on his elbows. Quinn's limbs dangled lifelessly. Her mouth and eyes hung open, and even then, the monster kept crushing her throat, squeezing harder with each huff that caused spit to fly out of its mouth.

There was a moment of vacuum where Tyler braced himself for the inevitable catastrophe that was about to follow. A miniscule moment of safety that did its best to protect the brain from immense trauma.

The creature let go of Quinn. She collapsed to the floor, and for a moment, Tyler was hopeful that she was going to gasp for air, get up, and the two of them would run for their lives. But she just lay there, eyes open and bloodshot, staring vacantly at Tyler.

No longer there, just like Caleb.

"Quinn... Quinn..." he said through tears, crawling over to her.

He didn't even see the monster towering over him anymore.

"Quinn. Wake up." He shook her.

He convinced himself he could reverse this. He could somehow fix the situation, bring Quinn back. He just needed those few seconds back. Just a few seconds. *Please God.* If he could just turn back time for those few seconds, he could do something. He could…

Rufus cackled. He'd been standing in the corridor the entire time.

"Atta boy," he said.

The monster approached. Tyler was still cradling Quinn in his arms. He looked up to see the abomination staring down at him.

It bent down and grabbed Tyler by the neck with its massive hands. Immediately, his airways stopped working. Tyler was next. The same fate awaited him. He almost didn't care. A part of him wanted to allow the monster to finish him off.

But then his gaze flitted over the monster's shoulder. It was the grin down the hallway that caused his thoughts to veer, his survival instinct to kick in. That triumphant smile of the old man that said, "I win. I always win."

No. It can't end like this. Not like this.

Tyler's eyes fell on a shard of glass from the broken picture. He swept his hand across the floor, and once he took hold of a shard, he squeezed it hard in his hand. He ignored the burning caused by the glass cutting into his palm.

Raising it, he stabbed the sharp end into the monster's forearm. Immediately, the hand holding his throat retracted as the monster let out an infantile whimper. Tyler collapsed onto all fours, heaving in breaths of air, his throat scratchy from having been choked.

He looked up at the monster, and he was far from finished. In that moment, he had become vengeance itself.

He brought the sharp tip of the glass down on the monster's foot. It easily pierced through the thick, dirty skin and caused blood to ooze out. The monster cried out louder, an ineffable scream of pain. In the background, Rufus shouted something. No longer a victorious cry but one of trepidation.

Tyler wiggled the glass in the monster's foot, causing blood to violently trickle out. He pulled the glass out, stabbed it sideways into its calf, then dragged the shard down, splitting open the skin and flesh. The knee buckled, a shoulder bumping into Tyler's forehead.

In the background, he saw Rufus's face contorting into various painful expressions. Good. Tyler was far from done.

The creature's hand grabbed Tyler by the face. A stubby finger was digging into his eye, harder and harder, the pressure immense. He yanked the glass out of the creature's calf. His hand was screaming in pain. Slashing the back of the monster's hand made it let go immediately.

Instantly, the pressure on his eye abated. Tyler tottered back, hand over his eye. When he blinked, the vision in that eye was blurry.

The monster was cradling its heavily bleeding hand, letting out yelps of pain. Tyler clambered to his feet. It was time to end this. He approached the monster. Now he was the one dwarfing it.

The thing looked up at him, and for a second, those eyes almost looked like a little boy's because wasn't it exactly that? A child stuck in a monster's body?

But in the end, child or not, it was a murderer.

"No! Stop!" Rufus shouted. "You're hurting him!"

Good! That's what I'm hoping for!

Tyler reeled the shard of glass back, and roaring at the top of his lungs, he thrust the glass forward. The tip embedded itself into the side of the monster's neck. The creature went silent—whether in surprise or because Tyler hit a vital artery there, he couldn't tell. In the background, Rufus screamed something.

When Tyler pulled the makeshift knife out, blood spurted violently out of the perforation. The monster's hand compulsively went over the fresh wound, its mouth working like a drowning fish.

When Tyler brought the shard forward the next time, he stabbed the monster directly in the jugular. Its eyes grew wide. Perhaps its underdeveloped brain understood its end was nearing. Perhaps now, at the end of things, its dormant human instincts were becoming active to fight for its life.

The monster's hands closed around Tyler's forearms, but its strength seemed to be drained because its grip was feeble, nothing like the Herculean squeeze it gave Tyler earlier.

Their eyes were locked. There was something behind the monster's pupils. Something that suggested that it indeed wasn't just a ravenous brute. The pitiful gleam in those eyes almost made Tyler feel sorry for it. *Almost*. But then he saw Quinn's lifeless body slumped behind it, remembering her last moments, and his resolve grew more intense.

His face inched closer to the monster's. He wanted him to be the last thing the creature would see. To know fear just as its victims did. His grip was loosening. He would not be able to hold the glass much longer.

I just need a few more seconds.

Tyler turned and pulled the glass sideways. The monster produced a gurgle that sounded like thick things passing through sewage pipes. Its throat tore open, and blood oozed out so abundantly the monster's torso was covered in red, the hairs matted against the chest.

Tyler didn't manage to make the gash long enough before the monster slumped forward, the glass still stuck in its throat. It rolled over on its back, clawed at its neck, choking, coughing up blood, spitting it upward like a fountain.

"No!" Rufus pushed Tyler out of the way and dropped to his knees. "No! Not my son! Not my baby boy!"

He put a hand behind the monster's head, the other on its chest, and his cries trailed to whimpering.

"My boy. No. Please don't die," Rufus said. "Don't leave me. Don't—"

He threw his head back and let out a wail that caused his voice to crack.

If someone were to hear Rufus's desperation without having any other context, their hearts would have broken at the sight of an old man losing his only child. But Tyler knew who and what Rufus was, and the pity could simply not manifest itself.

The monster's spastic motions were dying down. Its eyes were darting here and there before ultimately settling on Tyler. It was looking at him, not with fear or contempt but with some kind of reverence.

It had been stuck in the basement all its life. Rufus had kept it alive, but he had cocooned it in that darkness, offering sustenance and nothing more. Tyler, on the other hand, had opened its eyes, shown it pain, and maybe that's what it needed to know what it meant to be alive.

Or perhaps, it was simply grateful for its release from this travesty of a life.

Its jolts and coughs became less frequent, and then, with eyes still fixated on Tyler and the corner of its lip oddly curved into a twisted smile, the creature stopped moving altogether.

"No, no, no! No!" Rufus rocked back and forth, cradling his son's body. "No! Dominic! Please! Please don't leave me! I'm begging you!"

While the old man was crying, Tyler tore a loose plank from the floor because Rufus's death would need to be stretched-out and painful. The old man's screams had wound down to pathetic sobbing and snuffling. The monster's head was in his lap, and he was caressing its head.

Rufus looked up at Tyler, tear-stricken. It was so otherworldly seeing this murderous lunatic so broken and weak.

"You killed my child," Rufus said.

"You killed my friends," Tyler said.

Rufus's eyes fell on the plank, which Tyler was grasping hard.

"Go on, then. Finish the job," the old man said.

Tyler laughed. "You think I'm going to show you pity? After what you did?"

"I don't care what you do. You destroyed my family." Rufus looked at the monster's face and let out another sob. "Dominic…"

"Quinn was right," Tyler said. "We shouldn't have left you alive. I won't make the same mistake a second time. You're never going to hurt another person."

He raised the plank above his head. Rufus looked at the weapon. If he felt any fear, then he was too broken by pain to show it. Any empathy that Tyler would have felt otherwise; any hesitation over crossing this threshold… they were long gone. Snuffed out by Rufus.

A part of him had hoped Rufus would beg for his life, plead with Tyler not to kill him. It would have made things so much more satisfying. Oh well.

Tyler let out a fierce cry as he brought the edge of the plank down on the old man's head.

THIRTY-THREE

FOYER

With everything finished, the pain that had been held at bay the entire time crashed over Tyler, sapping his energy. Exhaustion was taking its toll, too. He could hardly stand on his feet. Blood dripped from the plank in his hand. A morsel of meat was still clinging to it.

On the floor in front of him was the ruined mess of Rufus's corpse. The body had sustained minor injuries. As for the head, though…

The neck sprouted into an amalgamation of a broken lower jaw and dentures jutting at odd angles. In the grotesque mess that glistened under the light, an eyeball could be seen, still intact and judgmentally focused on Tyler. A piece of Rufus's skull was still attached to the neck, and inside of it as if it was a bowl of soup, sat blood and brains and chipped bones.

The shredded crotch was the icing on the cake of the beautiful sight. The old man looked so defiled, so desecrated. Exactly how he should have been. Justice for Tyler's friends and all the other victims of this fucking house.

Tyler tossed the plank into the blood puddle of Rufus's head. He was supposed to feel better. Instead, emptiness hijacked his every nerve. Emptiness and that overwhelming exhaustion that dug its claws deeper and deeper into his skin.

He approached Quinn, got down on his knees, and looked at her face. Her eyes and mouth were still open in horror. When loved ones died, the ones affected by their deaths sought comfort in little things. In the knowledge that the deceased person died painlessly, that they simply slipped into oblivion without even feeling it, that it had to be this way.

Those were the threads they held onto because they helped them cling to their sanity, to make the agony of loss more bearable.

There was nothing peaceful about Quinn's expression. Nothing about her death was natural or fateful. She didn't want to die. She didn't *deserve* to die. None of the people in this house did. And now, a life-long friendship had ended, just like that. All because some psycho…

Tyler felt like he should cry, but there was not an ounce of strength left in him for that action. He closed Quinn's eyes and mouth. The skirt of her dress had bunched up above her waist, so he pulled it down to conceal her private parts. If he tried really hard, he could convince himself she was at peace. Maybe even that she was sleeping.

"I'm… I'm so sorry, Quinn," he said.

But Quinn couldn't hear him. She would never hear him. Never open her eyes. Never tease him or Caleb. Never go on drives with them. Never get high with them. Never make that little snort when she laughed at something. Never give them fun facts about random things.

Standing up, Tyler gave her one final look. He contemplated loading her and Caleb into the Chevy, but just the thought of driving his friends… two dead bodies that were formerly his friends, made a rope of fire unspool inside of him.

Dead.

The word didn't fit. Not with Caleb and Quinn. It wasn't supposed to be a topic they would open in many years. Maybe ever. Definitely not this early. Not when their lives were only just beginning.

The irreversibility of their deaths blindsided Tyler so suddenly that he felt his legs trembling under the weight of his body. In that moment, the unraveling of regret began, and Tyler found himself with his friends leaning on the car, smoking weed, and playing truth or dare. The house was across the road, a noncommittal sight worth no more than an aloof glance. He could see Caleb's worried face as he agreed to a dare. He could see himself and Quinn stifling their laughter.

Then, he saw himself running across the road to stop Caleb, to tell him he was right, that the idea was bad. If Quinn protested, then Tyler protested harder. He even threatened to leave them stranded if they went inside the house.

Eventually, they tossed the cans of beer in the grass, finished smoking, got in the car, and drove off.

Off to whatever else the world had to offer.

Then, he was back in the house. Standing in front of a dead Quinn. Behind him, Rufus's corpse. Upstairs, Caleb. No way to fix this. Once someone was dead, they were *dead*.

Jesus fuck, how did it come to this? How? How?

Even then, Tyler's eyes were dry, but the pain kept crushing him. He had to get out of this house before the remainder of his sanity betrayed him.

He gave up on the idea of bringing Quinn and Caleb with him. There was no way he would be able to get them to the car anyway. Not in his current state. He wasn't sure if he himself would make it before he collapsed and, if he did, whether he would pass out at the wheel.

"I'll come back. For both you and Caleb. I promise," Tyler said to Quinn.

He lingered there a moment, unsure what for. Maybe a miraculous response from Quinn. Maybe he just wanted to remember her face as best he could before the rot claimed her.

Turning his head away was the hardest part. Leaving the corridor was not. He made sure to squish Rufus's eyeball under his shoe on the way out because that fucker's corpse couldn't be violated enough.

In front of the entrance, he picked up the keys from the floor. They were right where Quinn left them. Through the glass above the door, he could see sunlight peering in. It was morning.

Tyler picked out a random key from the ring and inserted it into the padlock. It didn't work, so he tried the next one. The fourth one turned in the keyhole, releasing its grip on the heavy chains. Tyler tossed the padlock over his shoulder, and the chains slid off without so much as being touched by him.

He hesitated in front of the door. It felt like he was about to cross a threshold there was no coming back from. As if he didn't deserve to leave this house. Not when his friends were dead.

In the end, he knew Caleb and Quinn wouldn't judge him for surviving. They would want him to get out of here just as he would want them to do the same.

He reached for the doorknob. Suddenly, the vast, open world outside the house seemed so much more intimidating. The house was easy, he finally realized. All he had to do was survive. Out there, though... He was already thinking about what was to come.

After the drive back, he would go to the police. There would be millions of questions. He would be put into an interrogation room with a stern-faced detective whose job it would be to get a confession out of him. They would be skeptical of Tyler's story. They'd think he was the bad guy. He wouldn't be allowed to sleep until they checked the house out.

Then there would be even more questions. The press would be involved. The story would be fueled by lots of false rumors that would make Tyler the hero, the victim, and the perpetrator—depending on who was asked.

That didn't worry him, though. He could deal with the backlash and the gawking from friends and family members. It was his time alone that scared him shitless. The vacuum that begged for contemplation. That's when Quinn and Caleb would occupy his mind the most. That's when he would run through the millions of scenarios of whether he could have done something differently, and he would hate himself and punish himself for it, over and over, a purgatory from which he would never escape for as long as he lived.

Why he hadn't acted faster or said something different or found a better weapon or drove down a different road or…

He knew what was coming, but he was indifferent to all of it right now because that relentless fatigue was enveloping him from head to toe.

Tyler twisted the knob and pulled the door open. The bright daylight made his eyes smart so badly that he had to raise a hand to shield them.

He leaned forward to take a step outside when a sound behind made him freeze. A familiar guttural groan belonging to the monster from the basement.

But…

No. It was too reedy, like… like…

Tyler turned around. At first, he saw nothing. Then, movement in the darkness of the corridor. A hand grasping the edge of the credenza retreated from the foyer. A pair of eyes—no, *multiple* pairs of eyes—blinked at Tyler from the corridors surrounding the foyer.

Then, Gretchen's voice boomed inside Tyler's head with a crushing revelation.

I gave birth to two of his babies.
He always takes them away.
I never see them again.
I'm pretty sure they die.

The sentences undulated on repeat over and over, the terrible understanding dawning on Tyler.

I never see them again. I'm pretty sure they die.

Except, how could Gretchen possibly know that? The answer was: She couldn't. She only knew what Rufus had allowed her to know.

From the threshold of darkness, a small figure emerged and curiously stared at Tyler. Disheveled hair that hadn't been cut perhaps in years, front teeth that bit over the lower lip, the skeletal structure of both the head and the body somehow... wrong.

When those big eyes gazed up at Tyler, he thought for a moment that maybe he could rescue them. That they weren't too far gone. They were cavemen in contact with another living human for the first time in life and needed careful approach. But then he *really* looked into their eyes, and he knew he'd underestimated the influence of the throes Rufus had subjected these children to.

Even at such a young age, those eyes harbored the same primitivism as the monster from the basement. The same feral hunger that irrevocably erased any traces of their humanity.

The house itself seemed to produce shuffling sounds, each drawing closer to the entrance than it had been—and with them, the eyes grew bigger and more numerous. Tyler took a step back, slowly. His eyes were trained on the child in front of him.

When something brushed against his ankle, he looked down and saw a little girl of similar deformities gingerly touching his pant leg. On instinct, Tyler pulled his foot back with a gasp, and he knew that was a mistake the moment he did it.

The little girl, at first startled, looked up at him and took a deep breath through snarling, stained teeth. Tyler knew what was coming. It was like falling off a building and waiting for the moment when the body would finally hit the floor.

When the little girl screamed, the entire house seemed to scream—a litany of voices conjoining in an orchestra of horror.

Tyler screamed as well as the little figures piled on top of him.

Soon, his screams were drowned out until it was only the children's voices that dominated the house.

THE END

House of Decay

Final Notes

Thank you so much for reading *House of Decay*. This book wouldn't have been possible without my ARC team, my editor, cover designer, and of course, the most important asset—you, the reader. It's still incredible to think I'm able to put books out for the whole world to read.

If you enjoyed this book, I'd appreciate it if you left your honest review on the Amazon product page. Your review matters, and it helps the author. Also, if you'd like to stay in touch, subscribe to my mailing list. As a token of appreciation, you will get my free book, *The Grayson Legacy*.

You can do that by opening the link below. I promise it's not a virus.

www.dl.bookfunnel.com/63a17lay5z

MORE FROM THE AUTHOR

- Radio Tower
- Retown
- Suicide Town
- They Came From the Ocean
- They Came From the Mall
- It Lives in the Woods
- The Town the World Forgot
- The Keeper
- Apartment 401
- Maria
- The Fertility Project
- The Gathering
- Her Home
- Sinister Melody
- Camp Firwood
- The Door

… and many more. Check out the entire catalog on Amazon.